THE RESURRECTIONIST

THE RESURRECTIONIST

PAUL T. SCHEURING

Printed in the United States of America
First Printing, 2022

One Light Road, Inc.
Mill Valley, CA

Edited by The Artful Editor, www.artfuleditor.com
Cover design by James T. Egan
Interior design by Phillip Gessert

ISBN 0-9984502-2-3

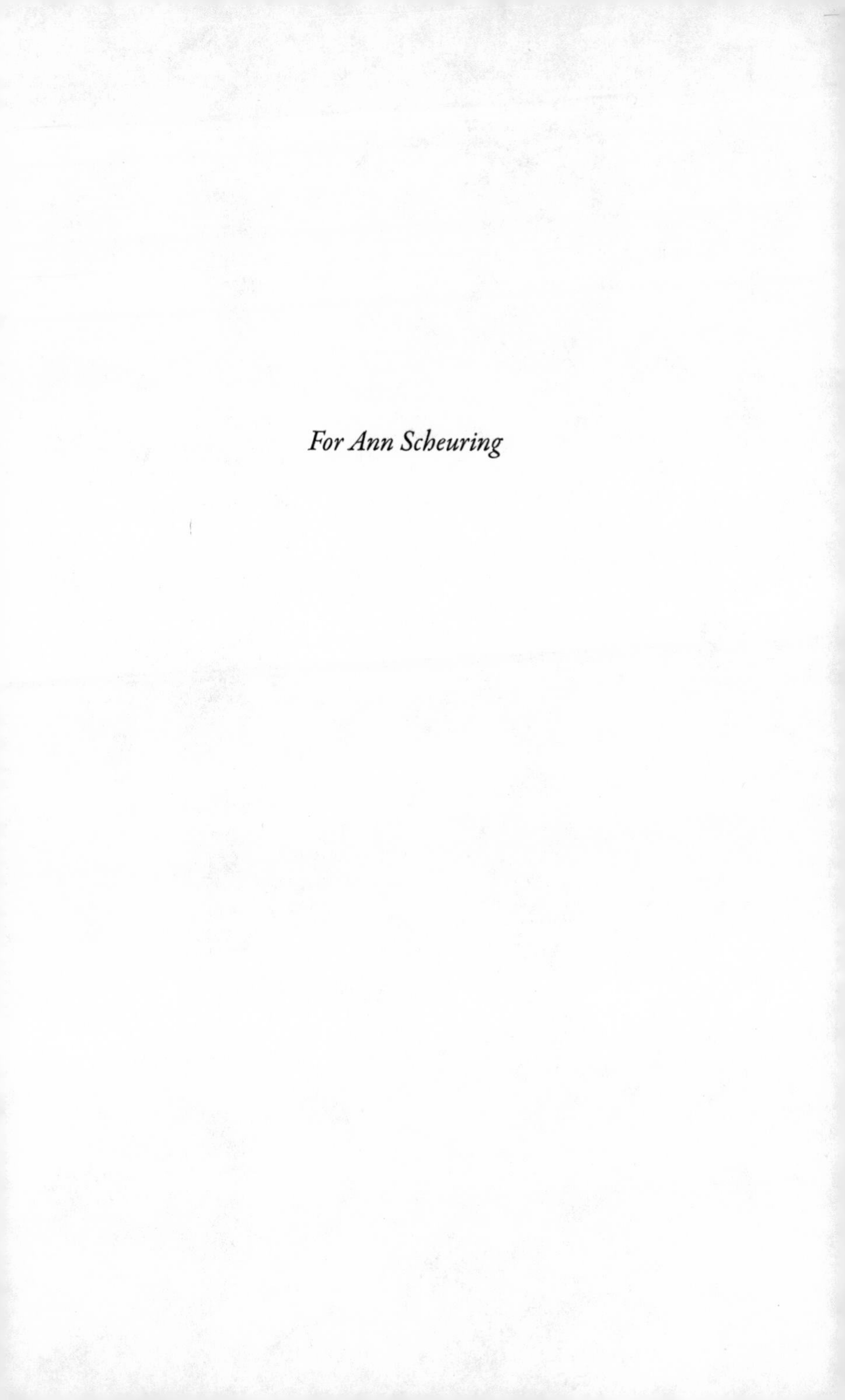

For Ann Scheuring

AUTHOR'S NOTE

CAN YOU PUNISH a man after he's dead?

In this world and not the next?

Allowing that whatever afterlife there may or may not be and its workings are the province of God, mysterious and unobservable, what can we ask about the limits of punishment in this world, once you have already executed a man and his body now sways, lifeless, from the gallows?

There's not much more that can be done, one would assume, right?

Our species, however, has shown an endless capacity over the centuries to see otherwise, usually with impressive wickedness and creativity.

Take England in 1752. After a rash of particularly grisly homicides had rocked London, the notoriously breathless London press became even more so, threatening to hyperventilate: England is descending into moral chaos! Will the Crown do nothing about the layabout war veterans, the gin epidemic that renders so much of the country insolent, licentious, violent? The Crown, sensing this was no ordinary panic but one that threatened to have legs, quickly had their barristers up at Whitehall pass the Act for Better Preventing the Horrid Crime of Murder, more commonly known as the Murder Act of 1752 (though I prefer the extra flourish in the official title—meant, I assume, to clear up any confusion about whether homicide was indeed, qualitatively, abhorrent). Buried within the act was a proviso that those convicted of the crime of murder experience "some further terror and peculiar mark of infamy to be added to the punishment of death." Forever hushing the offending cull was no longer enough; now, upon execution, the criminal would be either dissected or gibbeted, a practice wherein their corpse was hung in chains some thirty feet above the city and often left there to slowly decay for decades.

In the end, of course, I suspect no one up at Whitehall believed the dead man in any way *experienced* being dissected by anatomists (part of our story to come) or picked apart by carrion birds high over the street. That man's sentient mind had long since shut down. His soul, if he had one, had already migrated to new realms within which all sorts of greater untold punishments potentially awaited. No, the horror to be experienced by the prescribed further terror and mark of infamy was not meant for the dead man but the man in the street (or the woman, if I may foretell our story a bit) who might have the misguided urge to commit a similar crime. It was meant as deterrence, in the most ghastly and public fashion imaginable.

Did it work? History does not show an appreciable change in the murder rate in England subsequent to the act. More important, in the intervening sixty-odd years leading up to our story, most capital punishment ended at the gallows; juries seemed hesitant to mete out "further terror" to any but the most extreme cases. Many outlying communities, such as Thundridge in Chapter One, simply ignored the new law, finding it the overwrought busywork of the bewigged swells up in London courthouses, with whom they had little to nothing in common. Better to trust the moral authority of their own clergymen, keep the punishment simple as God intended, put the man in the ground as quickly as possible, and be done with it. It was there that real justice would be effected, anyhow.

This was not good news for the aforementioned anatomists. The study of anatomy was booming in England at this time, and with it, the need for cadavers so that professors and students might better explore and understand the human body, ushering in much-needed medical advances in the process. Schools were popping up everywhere, the appetite for bodies insatiable. Predictably, with so much demand and so little official supply, other, blacker markets developed.

If one could not harvest corpses from the gallows, there were other places they could be found with ease and in abundance: cemeteries. It took very little to go out into the night and steal something no one in their wildest flights of imagination would imagine being stolen. Until that point, people protected their dead as much as they did their rubbish—that is, not at all. A small but very lucrative trade developed, involving those that were willing to dig and those that were willing to pay.

This is where my interest was piqued. What did that overlap look like, between the ostensible world of light that is medicine, with its noble aspirations to cure the world, and the dark, shadowy world that traded in, of all things, dead bodies? A more antithetical set of bedfellows I cannot imagine, especially in England, with its rigid class structures: the university-educated doctor of high station conspiring with the brutish, illiterate criminal of such compromised moral standing that he would breach hallowed convention, steal from the Lord's own soil, and traffic in the sludge and decay of rotting corpses.

Who were such men? What sequence of events, justifications, and mistakes had led them to engage in what seemed to me the darkest vocation imaginable? Were they monsters? Or, like the rest of us, occasionally cornered by fate and forced by circumstance to make ends meet by whatever means possible, carving whatever small dignity they could from their broken life in the process?

I researched and wrote this book to find the answer.

RESURRECTIONIST

noun

1. a person who brings something to life or view again.
2. a believer in resurrection.
3. also called resurrection man. A person who exhumes and steals dead bodies, especially for dissection; body snatcher.

ONE

THUNDRIDGE, ENGLAND, 1820

There is a seven-foot-tall man buried in Thundridge churchyard.

The locals say he was foul in the head. That as a blacksmith's son, he'd spent his youth, even before his frame took on its terrifying dimension, proving an inner monstrosity. By four he was catching field mice, and while his father was engaged elsewhere, the dear boy would furtively plop the poor, squirming creatures in the old man's forge to watch them incinerate. All to see, with glee and fascination, how quickly the living could become the dead.

By his teens he had long since left school and home and developed a reputation on the wharves of Falmouth as a drunk of epic renown, a world-class loafer by day, an inveterate porch-climber at night. Few were the women in Falmouth who did not encounter him in their residences at one time or another, drunken, sweaty, gargantuan, looking either to pilfer valuables and liquor or, as was more often the case, to fulfill his dark yearnings.

He was, in short, a terrible man who spent many a moon in Falmouth Gaol cursing both his captors and the universe at large for his plight. Some years into his reign of terror, the good people of Falmouth, spearheaded by a vigilante group of seamen, managed to convince him to leave their fine city and never come back. They broke his jaw and six of his fingers before he finally consented.

His return to Thundridge, unsurprisingly, did little to change his ways. Now it was the womenfolk of Thundridge that had to suffer; it is said that he raped no less than a dozen across the county in the two years he was back. Add to that the number of men he beat senseless to get to said women, in a couple of cases to the point of killing them, and it's little surprise that sometime shortly thereafter, he found himself standing atop the gallows, a noose around his neck, his head sheathed in a black burlap sack.

When the trapdoor was finally released beneath him, it's said the weight of his hulking form nearly brought the whole structure down with him. The scaffold groaned, flexed, but ultimately held, and soon the people of Thundridge were looking upon the lifeless, swinging form of their homegrown monster with a mixture of incredulity and relief. Then, apparently, applause broke out, followed by singing, and after that, drinking, which lasted for the better part of two days.

Then came the question of where to bury such an unholy cretin. For burying a man of this sort in the local churchyard would only, at least in some ways, memorialize him. It was suggested that he be tossed in the sea, gibbeted, dissected, or left in the wilderness to the animals so that the whole of him would be dispersed and the land would never again know his stain. In the end, however, the local minister prevailed, saying that all men, no matter how great their transgression, deserved a chance at redemption, even in death. To bury him, or anyone, anywhere beyond sacred church ground was to consign them to eternal hellfire. Which was a destination most of the townsfolk thought the man deserved. Nevertheless, the minister, with God in his corner, won out.

So it was that the seven-footer was buried among the noble, God-fearing souls interred in Thundridge churchyard.

More than a few of the townsfolk say the soil there turned black in the days that followed. That beneath the lush grass that carpets the graveyard, the earth itself has steadily been decaying, the worms and other subterranean life dying off en masse. That the trees are dropping leaves, though it is nowhere near autumn yet, that birds steer clear of the place, where before they found a pleasing respite and silence.

Cager has heard all of this. He has spent an undue amount of time learning everything he can about Thundridge churchyard, about this seven-foot man.

Cager, you see, is going to dig him up.

He rows across the river to get to the churchyard. The sun is long gone, and the world is asleep. The ten-foot walls that surround the churchyard are imposing in the moonlight; from this vantage, it seems almost a fortress. Such are the times that graveyards are built like this. All across England, bodies are disappearing, and townsfolk are taking greater precautions to protect the decaying remains of their loved ones.

They fear corrupt souls wander the land, demons intent on despoiling all that is holy, the bodies they disinter perhaps used in dark ritual or worship of the devil. What else would you think, were you to come out one morning and see that the grave of your wife or father had been unceremoniously torn open and their decayed body nowhere to be seen? Who takes *bodies*?

Cager does, for one. Or intends to.

He is an entering apprentice at St. Bartholomew's College of Anatomy in London, an institution he's chosen because it is one of the few in England to have adopted the Paris manner of anatomy instruction. No more leaning over a professor's shoulders or watching from high in the rafters as a lecturer slices into a pickled, rubbery subject. In the Paris manner, each student would put his scalpel to flesh—*fresh* flesh—with no limit as to how many subjects one could dissect, with one large caveat. The explosion of interest in anatomy in the last few years—and especially given the growing popularity of the Paris manner as a teaching method—meant that corpses were now in high demand. And supply—official supply—was at the moment proving decidedly low in England. A student with a very strong stomach and a willingness to bypass the middleman could set himself up to dissect all day, every day, as long as he was willing to "get his hands dirty."

The school turned the requisite blind eye, and the phenomenon of grave robbing was still so nascent that the authorities had yet to put together a universal legal response to the issue. Some regions would impulsively jail you if you were found in possession of a corpse. Authorities in others, finding no statutes in their law books concerning the possession of dead bodies—for such a thing, until now, had largely been inconceivable—simply threw their arms up in exasperation. It was a mixed bag—one never knew what to expect if discovered. What was certain, however—legal concerns aside—was how such an incident would affect one's reputation. Most professors and people that had a name of any renown, a name they traded on and employed as a seal of their business and integrity, knew better than to be caught with the deceased in their possession.

Cager, thankfully, is not saddled with the problem of a name. For the most part, no one outside of his hometown even knows of his existence. Here, far from that hometown, he is just an anonymous shadow in the night, if one filled with the ambition to become the greatest surgeon England has ever known. He is eighteen, charged with the promise of becoming, of discovery. The feathery prospect of the unknown has brought him to this godforsaken churchyard some fifty miles from London. What's on the other side of what I don't know, on the other side of what I haven't yet experienced? What does that world look like? What does it feel like?

His reach has always exceeded his grasp—that's why he is the first in his family to leave the coal shafts in Lancashire and attend university. Everything is possible. The unknown can become known if you but persist. Say yes to the world, and she will say yes to you, unveil her secrets.

And what greater secret is there than death? What does death, beheld face-to-face, actually look like?

He pulls the rowboat up into the shallows, beaches it on the muddy bank. The river is black as oil behind him, the night ahead split through with silence. His footsteps on the muddy shoreline are like impositions, as if this side of the river is somehow aware of his intentions and unwelcoming.

Up toward the churchyard he moves, mattock and shovel in hand.

The ground squeams beneath his boots with every step, the soil sodden from the unseasonably wet summer. The earth yields all its pungencies, the smells of life and death and decay, surface things wed to it—such as moss and tree stumps and scrub—the aromas of things beneath, unseen, in the soggy tangle of loam that stretches interminably downward.

He pauses. Up ahead there is movement, barely discernible. Shadows rearranging themselves.

Cager instinctively grips the mattock tighter as his eyes adjust and the shadows incorporate into a form crouched at the base of the churchyard wall.

A man. Rising at the sight of him. Gnarled, knotty, a study in decrepitude.

He steps into the moonlight. He is older in silhouette than in practice—from afar he is a seventy-year-old, not too short of the grave himself. Up close there is still vitality in him. Cager guesses he is perhaps only fifty years old, in the accelerated way that peasants are fifty years old. He wears a dirty singlet, burlap trousers, and mismatched boots. Though his back is stooped, his arms and shoulders are spiderwebbed with thick veins forced to the surface by decades of manual labor. A body both tempered and broken by incessant toil.

He nods to Cager with impassive eyes.

Cager nods back.

The man before him is the first resurrectionist he has ever laid eyes upon. It is a silly word, resurrectionist, for no life ever comes of their dark work, only money. Or perhaps, in Cager's case, knowledge.

Little is said as they prepare to scale the wall. They must stay far from the front gate and watchhouse, where the faint warmth of a candle within suggests the unseen presence of a sexton.

The resurrectionist's name is Job. The *o* in it is flat; so, rather than evoking the Old Testament stalwart, it instead suggests, as every inch of the man's sinewy body does, that this is a person that has been brought onto this Earth for toil, and toil only.

He is a workhorse for the medical schools, a man who has

apparently dug up dozens, if not hundreds, of bodies. Cager found him through the whisper mill of students and staff at St. Bartholomew's. *Job*. The name came up again and again. His prices were reasonable, his work sterling, his discretion top-notch. All said he would be the perfect guide in Cager's first attempt at lifting a body.

In this case, the body is not for Cager's studies. School's yet to begin, the inaugural lectures not for two weeks yet. Cager's after the purse the corpse will fetch. St. Bartholomew's, at a guinea a week, does not come cheap. Not for a boy from Lancashire. So Cager has decided to kill two birds with one stone: he will get a head start in the ways of the anatomy student and, at the same time, make money for a tuition that he could not otherwise afford.

There is the added incentive of being the first new apprentice to get his hands dirty, the one that has already done the daunting deed before the others even show up to the first lecture. The old hand. The bold one.

It's no coincidence they're after the seven-foot man. One of the first things Cager has gleaned from St. Bartholomew's is the value of rare subjects. Children with birth defects. Siamese twins. The monstrously corpulent. Poor souls warped with elephantiasis. Those who were shunned by society in life, hidden away in shame behind closed doors, became something different when buried beneath six feet of dirt. In a matter of hours, they went from loathsome things worth less than a boot nail to highly coveted commodities, the procurement of which could net a resurrection man the equivalent of a year's salary. But the window to cash in was small—a body was considered viable for dissection only in the first two weeks after death. Thereafter, decay rendered the corpse medically useless and, to the resurrection men, worthless. So, upon learning of the giant's death in the papers and realizing the windfall it represented, Cager immediately took it upon himself to find a resurrection man and hurry to Thundridge as quickly as possible before anyone else got there and unearthed his glorious, malformed diamond before him.

He has made good time. The giant has been in the ground scarcely four days. If he disinters the body tonight and conveys it overnight to London, Cager sees no reason why the cadaver can't be on an anatomist's table tomorrow, for the most part still fresh and worth the price of fifteen guineas he's arranged in advance with his buyer. That buyer? His future lecturer, the esteemed if very idiosyncratic Dr. Percival Quinn—one of the most learned anatomists in all of London, instructor at St. Bart's, and collector of medical oddities. Fifteen guineas—even when half is carved off for the resurrectionist—would be enough to pay tuition through Easter.

In short, an auspicious moment, this. Cager chuckles inwardly. They are about to scale a wall like common footpads, all in the hopes of pulling a murderous wretch out of the ground. Funny the things you will do for the esteem of people you have not even met.

The resurrectionist pulls on a jacket—though Cager thinks it's far too warm a night for it—then stirrups his hands in an indication that Cager should use them to climb the wall. He steps up into the man's grip and hoists himself atop the wall, where he sits for a moment surveying the dark churchyard.

The resurrectionist passes up his gear—a weathered old spade, a peasant's shovel. Both sawed off to a length that will fit in his satchel, both blades constructed of pauper's wood.

Cager nods to his own mattock and shovel at the resurrectionist's feet, whispers that they are new, they are better, that their iron heads will make short work of the graveyard's loamy soil.

"Metal carries," the resurrectionist says. "Your blade there finds a rock, the top of a casket, it'll ring in the night like nothing in the natural world. Now pull me up."

After a moment, Cager relents, grips the older man's hand. The resurrectionist strains, grunts, pulls himself up, mounts the wall alongside him.

He eyes the watchhouse across the yard, catching his breath, then drops the full ten feet to the churchyard below. Cager follows a moment later.

They hurry together through the headstones, the moon above choosing that moment to retreat behind a row of clouds. The graveyard, deprived of that silver-blue light, is a collection of blacks and semi-blacks, shadows and dimensions flattened into an inky soup. It is reduced to a simple void of silence and headstones, the two men's movements in stark relief against it. They are the sole living things here.

In short order, they find their aim: a newly dug grave, as of yet without stone.

Cager reaches a hand to Job in the darkness. *Give me a shovel.*

"Could be others were buried this week too," Job says stoically. He holds up a hand—*wait*—and without another word, moves deeper into the graveyard in search of more freshly turned soil.

For a moment, Cager is alone. The resurrectionist moves so deftly that his footfalls are lost to Cager's ears before the man's taken ten steps. By that time, the darkness has consumed him.

Cager listens. Wills his eyes to adjust to the void around

him. Yes, he can make out the mound at his feet and the crouching forms of headstones around him, but beyond that, he is a blind man. Relegated to other senses. His ears. His nose.

There is nothing to hear. No birds. No wind. No resurrectionist.

What assails his nose is only displeasing. The pervasive smell of death and the work of death. Turned soil. Carved stone. Rusting fences and gates. A deep, musty decay—an odor generations old but perpetual here—the residual smell of the dead being put to earth, one after another, week after week for decades on end, decomposing, feeding the soil, saturating this acre of land with a foul insistence that only grows with each corpse that comes apart beneath its grass.

As if the earth here inhales life and exhales death.

You are standing atop a thousand dead bodies, Cager. All lying on their backs. Looking up at you. Anticipating with those gooey and empty sockets what you are about to do. Judging you with the dark wisdom of the dead.

You dare carve into our world, sinner?

You should have stayed in Lancashire.

Yes, Cager, we are the dead. We *know*.

You should have become a coal miner, dug the right kind of things from the earth.

But you saw the hanging, didn't you?

All of the people in your town were so titillated by the public spectacle of it all, weren't they? A murderer being dispatched right there in your own town square. Some responded as anyone with proper conscience would, releasing white doves, imploring God to grant the man salvation, but you, you were drawn to the singularity of it, a body yielding its life in such sudden and dramatic fashion. And when they opted thereafter to add that "further terror and mark of infamy" required by law—in this case, public dissection—you, like the rest of the townsfolk, bought a ticket! How thick the crowds were in the Shire Hall that day! How shrewd those ticket sellers, turning the event into a days-long travesty, subdividing each hour into five-minute blocks within which one might catch a fleeting glimpse of the disgraced before being ushered onward.

You all came: man, woman, child. The body lay in state there, much as we do here, though without the dignity of clothes, the cocooning privacy of earth. No, that man lay bare both inside and out, his innards available for all to see, thanks to the anatomization of the night before. But the crowds were so thick, weren't they? You couldn't truly see the corpse between all the people. You saw flashes of pale skin drained of blood. Viscera, pink and already drying, like a shank of ham a day after the slaughter. What is that thing? you thought. What is this other being we become when we die? But you could not get a proper glimpse, could you?

The first day was all you were allowed, not being landed. Tickets to the second day were sold only to the educated elite, the professionals and gentry of Lancashire. You heard the whispers of what they saw—without the distraction of crowds, they might get a truly intimate experience with the corpse as it was further anatomized: the dissection of the eye, the removal of the tongue. They were admitted to the innermost sanctums of the body, and you were not.

The seed was set then, wasn't it? You would be an anatomist. How you pined to know!

Well, now you will.

Most surely you will.

The resurrectionist returns. Cager finds himself grateful

the man is back. Job nods to the grave. "We've got the right one." He presses the old peasant's shovel into Cager's hand. "Dig."

Cager, faintly dizzy, complies. Begins putting shovel to earth.

"Not at the foot. The head. We haven't time for both."

He spreads a canvas sack flat on the grass beside the grave, and a moment later sets into the earth with the wooden blade of his peasant shovel. "We leave no mark. Soil goes atop the sack, gets returned when we're done. Grave is to look as if it was never disturbed."

All the while, the two men's tools whisper, turning soil in the night. "Good people of the parish won't be looking for grave robbers if they don't think a grave has been robbed."

Soon the hole is three feet deep—halfway to six—and equally wide. Too narrow, Cager thinks. What does the resurrectionist intend? For his part, Job says little, other than whispering, "Speed. *Speed.*"

The hole becomes too deep for the men to work side by side any longer. Cager finds himself at the bottom of the growing shaft, passing soil up to Job above. The exposed earth is surprisingly warm around him, alive with worms and the seepage of recent rains. Job seems to be sizing him up. Cager looks up to see the man eyeing the crown of his head. Which is at this moment just a few inches below the grass line. "You're about five foot six?" Job asks.

"Five feet, seven inches," Cager returns proudly.

"Get out," Job says.

Cager complies, and in short order, the resurrectionist trades places with him, deftly dropping down into the hole. In an impressive feat of contortion, he folds his body inside the narrow shaft in such a manner that he is soon carving at the base of the shaft with his bare hands.

A moment later, his fingers find the head of the casket.

The dizziness returns to Cager at the sight of that pinewood box. A thing meant to be undisturbed for eternity. And yet here they are.

He looks back at the watchhouse. As ever, the window hovers there in the darkness, circumscribed by the candlelight within. If there is anyone in there, they seem none the wiser.

Job reaches out of the hole, pulls a pry bar from his satchel. "It's time."

Cager wonders how this can be so, given that their shaft is scarcely three feet wide and the lid of the coffin is more than twice that in length. Most of it is still tucked away in the worm-ridden soil.

The resurrectionist deftly slips out of his jacket—that jacket Cager found so unseasonal—and quickly spreads it across the exposed top of the casket, doubling it over as if to insulate the massive box. He quietly wedges pry bar between casket and lid. "The watchhouse," he says up to Cager.

Cager again looks to the watchhouse. Still nothing. He is, for a moment, confused. It is a seven-foot man they're trying to pull from the earth, and yet the hole they've dug wouldn't allow for the lifting of the lid of a child's casket, much less a giant's. "We need to widen the hole, don't we?" he finds himself whispering.

"Speed," is all the resurrectionist says in return.

He stiffens against the pry bar, fulcrumming it into maximum tension, then shoves hard all at once. There is a split-second, intense crack as the lid of the coffin snaps in half at the shoulder. Cager understands now the purpose of the jacket—it, along with the walls of the hole, is meant to absorb the sound.

Still, this is too quiet a place, this place of death. The sounds of life, the sounds of activity, announce themselves too readily. That muted crack caroms up from the earth, past Cager, escapes into the night air.

Job emerges from the hole right behind it. Both men look to the watchhouse.

Nothing. Just that constant, oblivious, dull glow.

Satisfied, Job drops back into the hole, pulls away the jacket, beneath which is revealed the broken lid of the casket, still in place despite the jagged fracture that bisects it. Its contents are still concealed underneath.

"Stand back," the resurrectionist says. "So the gases can escape."

The words turn Cager's stomach. He instinctively steps back as Job lifts the lid, revealing the giant. Both men cover their mouths and noses against the stench that swirls up past them. But it is soon gone, and all Cager can feel is relief. The dead giant is not the horrid sight he's anticipated. Instead, the man seems . . . at rest. Pale with sleep. No signs of decay anywhere. No hint in those calm features of the atrocities he committed in life.

Cager nevertheless wants to get out of this place as quickly as possible and cannot see how they're going to get the supine man out of his coffin and up through their narrow shaft.

The resurrectionist produces a length of rope from his satchel, quickly slides it into the coffin, loops it under the corpse's armpits. He nods to Cager in an indication he's to grab one end of the rope while Job holds the other. "We slide him up and out. Stand him up. Pull him out of the hole."

Ah. It comes clear to Cager then. Why pull a body out

lengthwise when it takes half the time to do so vertically? *Speed.* Just as the resurrectionist said.

"One, two, three . . . " Job whispers.

They pull.

But they're not met with the sort of weighty resistance Cager anticipates, the sort a seven-foot corpse would invoke.

The rope jumps in their hands instead, comes up slack. For a moment, Cager thinks it's the rope that's given.

Instead, he realizes what has given is the body.

The rope has come up through it, torn it in half.

Job curses under his breath. Quickly climbs down into the hole.

He unceremoniously reaches deeper below the lid of the coffin, his hand disappearing from view as he probes around the giant's unseen chest. He sets his jaw, displeased.

"Jellified. Rains and heat must've turned him into a soup down here at the gut."

Cager cannot help but look at the vile slop of viscera that hangs on the rope. The dark sludge on the resurrectionist's hand.

His stomach roils anew with nausea.

"Get me the sack. Now," the resurrectionist says.

"For . . . *what*?" Cager asks incredulously. His mouth is coppery, everything in his body tensing. It's not a matter of if he will vomit but when.

"Plenty here still to salvage," the resurrectionist says, scrambling up, grabbing the sack himself.

In a matter of moments, he is relieving the decaying giant of his limbs. Pulling first one arm loose, then the other.

Cager steps away, gasps.

"Give me a hand, goddammit," the resurrectionist hisses.

Cager cannot. Cannot even bring himself to look back at

the grave. Instead, he focuses on that dim window far across the churchyard, trying to suppress the bile churning in his gut.

Behind him, the resurrectionist climbs out of the hole. He grabs Cager. Nods to the mound of soil on the grass. It's time to cover their tracks.

Cager summons whatever reserves he has left, begins quickly shoveling the soil back into the grave. This, this, he can do. Yes, if only because with each shovelful he might start to cover up this whole horrid affair, forget it ever happened. Put the earth rightly back where it belongs, seal up this casket that no sane man would have unsealed in the first place.

The resurrectionist pushes the soil so quickly and silently back into the hole that within a matter of minutes, the grave site appears once again the unspoiled mound of dirt it was before their arrival. Cager is dumbfounded by Job's grim efficiency. They've truly left no mark. The man is as advertised—a true professional.

If only Cager were too.

As they quickly bag up their tools, Cager's eyes cannot help but drift to that burlap sack Job's pulled up from the hole. It is the last thing he wants to look at, but as such, it is therefore the first thing he looks at. He can't *not* look at it.

That sack: the opening not yet cinched, the contents visible within. Body parts, yes, but one in particular that Cager had not seen the resurrectionist liberate from the casket. The giant's head. With the black, ropy innards of the torn neck trailing beneath.

Cager throws up.

It comes out part squeal, part scream. Everything he's eaten that day splashes out onto the grass half digested. The act violent, insuppressible, driving him to his knees.

Even in that moment, he knows.

The resurrectionist knows.

The horrible retching sound has split the night and even now echoes back at them off the high walls of the churchyard.

Both men's eyes go to that dim window across the way.

There is now a form in it.

The watchman. His dark silhouette looking out at the yard.

A second later, he is gone from view.

"*Move*," hisses the resurrectionist.

He yanks Cager by the collar with surprising strength. Together they run for the far wall, their feet skipping and stumbling over the dark, uneven ground, their unholy cargo jouncing wildly on their shoulders.

They are atop the wall before they know it. Somewhere in the darkness behind them, a gun is discharged into the night. Impossible to tell whether it's a warning shot or something more intentional. With it, all nuance is lost. The resurrectionist unceremoniously heaves the bag of body parts outside the wall, launches himself after it. Cager is not a second behind. Their bodies thud to the ground outside the wall in much the same manner as the bag moments before, bones and muscle thickly complaining that a body was not meant to be so treated, living or dead.

The men gather themselves. There is groaning and wincing and swearing. But mostly there is burgeoning panic, and so they collect their cargo, scrambling down the bank toward the rowboat.

Far upriver, the corner of the churchyard comes into relief against the night. A lantern. The watchman, emerged from the far gates and rounding into view. The telltale silhouette of a rifle in his hand.

It is all so foreign to Cager it seems a dream state—the taste of vomit in his mouth, the ragged hot gasps that escape his lungs as he runs, the mortal fear that consumes his entire being as if he is prey, a well-placed shot away from being killed. How has life suddenly become *this*? That mortal fear expanding, widening, into an immortal fear, as if what pursues him is not just a watchman but propriety itself, society and God and all their expectations and judgments. His parents! If he should die here, collapsed by the riverbank with a bullet in his back, the shredded, decaying remnants of a human body in his possession—Lord, what would they think?

They would say the devil got to him. That something dark had entered into him, a motivation beyond human comprehension and morality.

Could he disagree? This had all come about because of his initiative. His initiative alone.

They are already into the boat, Job knifing it out into the flow of the river, those strong, old arms grinding the oars in their locks as Cager looks on from the stern, shocked, his weight as equally dead to the effort as that of what's left of the giant at his feet.

Job never looks up for the pursuer that has no doubt reached the bank by now. Instead, he focuses with singular intensity on the floor of the boat as he rows, teeth gritted into a determined snarl.

Despite himself, Cager finds himself slipping lower against the gunwale. Seeking cover as he peers back.

The watchman is visible back there on the shoreline, lantern on the ground at his feet, attempting the laborious process of reloading the rifle. Already the inky night is starting to envelop him, render him ever more indistinct.

Each deft stroke by the resurrectionist hastens the process. And once they catch the main current of the river, the man is lost completely to the blackness.

The resurrectionist idles the oars, and there is only silence. The river carrying them. The night indifferent.

"No doubt they're going to be raising a mob," Job says. "Not good they know we're out here. Hopefully, we make Hertford before they do."

We. It evokes something for Cager, though not what Job probably intends. He becomes aware again that there is a third person—parts of a third person—in the boat. He has the strange sensation, solely because it is a body, that it has a point of view, like it's listening, a participant. Bodies are not yet to him what they seem to be to Job. Meat.

The resurrectionist, as if reading his thoughts, reaches for the sack, places it in his lap. He pulls the giant's head out a moment later.

Maybe it's because Cager's already voided his stomach, his body awash with post-vomit relief, that he's able to look upon the macabre spectacle before him. The resurrectionist inspects the severed head as one might a watermelon at a market. Prodding at it subtly with his thumbs. Turning it over, looking into the dark pulp of the neck with consternation, as if he'd just found a rotten section in the fruit.

"There's sawdust and salt in the satchel," he says. "Salt the limbs to soak up the fluid. Pack them back in the sack with the dust, snug as you can, so they don't move around. Last thing we want is the coach driver hearing body parts rolling around behind him."

Cager smiles wanly, tries to defer. "Sounds like you've got a better handle on it."

The resurrectionist ignores him, setting upon the giant's teeth with a pair of pliers.

"Brain of a giant would've gotten us quite the stake," he says between grimaces, "but it's putrid. Set of teeth, though—get you a guinea for sure."

Cager watches with a combination of fascination and revulsion as the man systematically removes the teeth, the sickening sound of the roots snapping in the decaying gums apparently lost on him.

How do you become so feral a creature? Cager wonders.

How does pride abandon you to the point that you traffic in the dead? That you let their rotting decay cover your hands, their jellied guts stain your clothes?

What has quit in you?

TWO

JOB

THE BOY IS soft.

But all boys are soft these days.

They have not fought.

They have not been bled dry by this country.

It is all right.

We are all born into different times.

Complaining does nothing.

Blaming does nothing.

There is only action.

What a man does or doesn't do to move forward.

How he confronts circumstance.

The past cannot be respun.

The world cannot be rectified.

Only your path can.

Keep your head down, focus on the thing before you, and do it with diligence.

Only then will the Light be known.

These are his thoughts as he pulls the teeth from the skull, slides them into his pocket.

As he guides the boat downriver toward Hertford.

He feels for the boy, in that he has witnessed the death of the youngster's innocence tonight.

Yes, look at him as he sits there in the stern of the boat, trying valiantly to be stolid, erect.

But his eyes don't lie.

The resurrectionist has seen those eyes before—not just in cemeteries but in surgeons' theaters, ships of the line, battlefields.

Boys in that liminal state of becoming men.

Pretending to be men, but still boys.

Wanting to be men, but still boys.

That fear is beautiful.

Keep it, the resurrectionist thinks as he watches the boy.

It hurts, but keep it.

It is your innocence.

Keep it forever.

Hertford is a clutch of dark, silent buildings when they arrive.

They tie off at the docks, make sure that anything offensive in their cargo is secured away from sight, its odor neutralized.

The resurrectionist has brought along a dozen heads of garlic, a few onions to help in this effort.

He seals them inside the sack with the giant's limbs and sawdust, cinches the sack so tightly that there is no give anywhere. It is fragrant in the right way, tight as a drum.

A moment later, the men are up into the cobbled lanes of the town.

Ahead there is commotion. People coming together, a dozen, perhaps.

The boy stiffens for fear the mob has arrived in Hertford before them.

A horn splits the night, which unsettles the boy all the more.

But the resurrectionist finds solace in it.

For he knows the sound.

It signifies not a mob but rather the local coaching inn.

Royal Mail coaches come and go, even at this late hour, their drivers taking refreshment inside while hostlers refit their vehicles with fresh horses.

Blacksmiths and wheelwrights toil in the stables nearby.

All of the forms rendered in warm chiaroscuro by lanterns everywhere.

The light of the world.

The light of life.

Job and the boy approach, move through the cobbled courtyard past the booking clerks, step into the coffee room.

The resurrectionist considers the half dozen drivers and servers inside, huddled over soup, tea, coffee.

The housekeeper appears before them, nods in welcome. "Put down the wares, have a seat."

She is young, though years of long nights have doubled the age of her skin.

The resurrectionist knows better than to sit. It's only a matter of time before the mob from Thundridge appears.

"We need a coach," he says, "for London."

"Public int running till sunup."

"Private."

"Oh, but private costs, specially east of two in the morning. All the private coachmen are safe at rug upstairs, sleeping off their guzzle."

The resurrectionist nods, unfazed. "Guinea now, guinea on arrival. Find me a driver."

The keeper surveys him briefly, then the ashen-faced kid next to him. "Have an emergency on your hands, do you?"

"No emergency, just a desire to get home."

She gives them both another brief once-over—these two strangers that have entered her inn in the wee hours of the morning, their clothes wet and splashed with mud—then nods and heads upstairs.

Once she's gone, the boy turns to the resurrectionist and in a fitful whisper hisses, "We've got an incomplete subject now. Give them two guineas, we'll make nothing on this one."

The resurrectionist nods knowingly.

"But we'll make it home," he says, casting a glance out at the dark streets outside.

It is only a matter of time before those streets are filled with the thunder of hooves, of men shouting, emboldened by drink, waving hatchets and guns.

These men will beat them first.

Beat them as they urinate and spit on them.

All the while cursing them in God's name.

They will use the guns to scare them into submission; they will use the stocks to deepen the beating.

But they will not shoot them.

For that is too merciful a death, too quick.

Instead, once the grave robbers are softened up and can no longer offer resistance, the mob will use hatchets.

They will take them apart incrementally.

Job has seen this.

Partners, lost to the mob.

But it will not be him, not tonight.

He has too much yet undone.

The housekeeper returns, descending the stairs with a coachman in tow.

He is a haggard, drunken thing with jaundiced eyes.

The very image of him causes the boy to tense up all the more.

Everything in the man suggests criminal.

(Even more criminal than themselves!)

For a long time, he hovers before them, eyes going from Job to Cager, then back to Job.

Finally a corner of his mouth curls up into an amused smile.

Tobacco-stained teeth hint from within.

"Ah, Jayzus, this one don't gotta gin up, not for me," he grumbles at the keeper, nodding to Job.

The other side of his mouth joins in on the smile as he thrusts a dirty hand forth to the resurrectionist.

"How are ye, Job?"

THREE
CAGER

THE COACHMAN IS an Irishman named, as best Cager can tell, Fife. Something thereabouts comes out of his mouth during introductions, but drink, fatigue, and an Irish brogue have turned the man's voice into a slurry that is hard for Cager's late-night brain to tease apart.

They are already underway. Fife's coach—a decrepit growler pulled by a pair of failing horses—jounces over the dark roads leading back to London. The weak carriage lamps do little to light their way; mostly they just illuminate the haunches of the horse team before them, their tails frayed by mites, the shadows they cast on the road ahead weak, flickering ghosts. Beyond that, a blackness perpetually hastened into.

Cager sits in the carriage beside the resurrectionist and what remains of the giant. The windows have long since been removed, the vehicle a far cry from the grande dame she must have been a few decades before when she was new and the elites that rode in her enjoyed new leather upholstery and insulation from the elements. Now the night air comes in unchecked, and everywhere is noise—the snorts of the team, the tired squeals and lurching crunches of the carriage and axletree as they meet each new pothole, the buffeting winds swirling, quavering, whistling in and out of every available crack.

Fife calls down from the driver's seat, voice raised against the wind. "They was cutty-eyeing you pretty good, the lushingtons back there at the coach house."

Cager whispers to the resurrectionist, "How do you know this bloke?"

"We soldiered together," the resurrectionist says, then turns, calls up to Fife. "Think you'd be good enough to stop at Earl's Court on the way in?"

"For you, my liege, the world," Fife calls down sardonically. Then, with a knowing nod back toward the canvas sack in the carriage, "Just tell me you don't got a squeaker in there."

The resurrectionist looks down at the sack, its reduced size.

"No. No child. Just parts," he clarifies flatly.

Cager registers this. My God, then the man knows Job's business.

Fife shakes his head, casts a glance skyward. "Parts. Grand."

By the time they reach the sleepy village of Earl's Court, the clouds have parted enough to allow the moonlight to again give dimension to the land. Farmhouses and cob walls and cart sheds suggest themselves in the darkness. Cager feels like he has reentered the world, awakened from a dark, cumbrous dream. He cannot remember ever being so spent, mentally or physically. His back aches, more from the traumatic carriage ride than his earlier toil in the cemetery. But he is glad to be here, away from the hinterlands and the dark deeds they have apparently left behind there. Back to the oblivious normalcy of civilization.

Earl's Court is where Professor Quinn keeps a country home.

The resurrectionist climbs out of the growler once Fife pulls up at the gate, and in short order raps the handle of his abbreviated shovel against the ironwork.

For a moment, they are left to the silence of the night, standing in the dark lane, waiting for a sign from within the walled grounds.

What issues forth from that dark place is not what Cager anticipated: guttural sounds, hissing, feral growls. Beasts somewhere within, stirring, displeased.

Then a man appears on the other side of the gate. A footman, lucid and energized, though, by Cager's watch, it is nearly four in the morning. He unlocks the gate without a word and admits them with a cursory nod to Job—everybody seemingly knows the man—and soon they are moving through the shadowy grounds of Percival Quinn's estate, the likes of which Cager would never have expected in so somnambulant a village, or anywhere else in the world.

All manner of creatures wander through the half-light: geese, rabbits, pigs, and hedgehogs among the manicured topiaries, apparently free to roam as they wish. Still, Cager feels his skin stippling with goose bumps. What he heard outside the walls was not a rabbit or a pig.

He looks to Job beside him, who remains silent, inscrutable. Then to the footman, who has been walking beside the slow-moving growler through the grounds, then, in turn, to Fife, who considers everything from high in the driver's seat. None seem, at least outwardly, to share Cager's unease, save for the horses, which begin to bristle, slowly at first, then with increasing agitation as they get deeper into the compound. They whinny, test the reins in Fife's hands. There *is* something here.

Then, as they approach the clutch of dark foliage surrounding the manor house, it comes—an extraordinary crash of branches, a horrid, echoing snarl. Something materializes from the darkness of the trees, launching itself at the carriage.

Before Cager can react, he is face-to-face with a leopard, its eyes rendered iridescent by the glow of the carriage lamps, its teeth suspended in a glistening snarl inches away, the creature's assault somehow arrested just outside the paneless window of the carriage.

For a moment everything lapses into strange, surreal stasis. Nothing moves. Not Cager, who is too mortified, or the leopard, who Cager can now see is bound at the neck by a chain fastened to a nearby tree. The chain is stretched perfectly taut, freezing the cat in its unnatural bipedal stance outside the carriage, a foot short of its prey. Neither do the horses or carriage move, as Fife has instinctively reined the team to a sudden and expert halt, his grip so tight that they can scarcely lift their heads.

Job shifts beside Cager, breaking the brief stillness of the tableau.

He nods to the footman. "Tell your lord he ought to consider tying up his cat somewhere farther from the road."

They pull up into the courtyard before the manor house a few moments later.

Here there is more exotic fauna: a jackal, zebra, ostrich,

buffalo. They sleepily consider the new arrivals but, unlike the leopard, do not seem to take any lasting interest.

Fife opts to remain outside with his growler and a rest with his pipe as the footman ushers Cager and Job inside the house. Before entering, Cager's eyes fall across one last, heretofore unseen, member of Quinn's menagerie—an eagle, chained to a rock in the center of the courtyard.

It opens its eyes, displeased to have been awakened, and watches their approach with a black and unsympathetic gaze.

So this is how the upper class lives, Cager thinks as the footman guides them through the foyer and into the drawing room. Floor to ceiling, there are framed engravings and oil paintings—windows to a vaster world Cager has only heard of but until now has never beheld with his own eyes. Africa, with its strange foliage and animals. The Orient, with its otherworldly topography, people, vehicles.

The plasterwork molding that frames the walls and ceiling around these images is similarly a living thing, suggesting that broader, unknown world. Nymphs and satyrs and classic figures of myth drawn from the four corners of the world watch from on high as the three men move through the space below them.

But what strikes Cager most is the cleanliness of the light. Chandeliers he has seen before, but the paraffin candles within Quinn's residence emit none of the stink or smoke of tallow. There is no subtle haze here, no olfactory price to pay for the ability to see at night. There is just light. Pure, unadulterated light.

So this is how the rich live.

Even so, something else, more insidious than any odor, begins to assert itself beneath the pristine, genteel affects of the place.

It scarcely differentiates itself from their echoing footfalls on the marble floor at first but slowly becomes more present, insistent, as they move through the drawing room and into the back rooms of the manse.

A wail. A wail most primal and unsettling.

Somewhere ahead, unseen, is a creature in the throes of a pain scarcely imaginable by the sound of it.

The other men seem to take it in stride. The dread that had dogged Cager earlier in the evening reasserts itself as they step into an ill-lit hallway and move toward a door at the far end, from beneath which spills a thin sheen of light.

Within that room, no doubt, are the creature and its pain.

The footman opens the door, motions for them to enter, then closes the door behind them once they are inside.

Professor Quinn doesn't look up at their arrival. He's clad in a blood-stiffened frock coat, circling a work bench upon which lies the unfortunate creature they've been hearing: a pig, tied down with rope, its entrails exposed and pulsating even as it squeals and vainly tries to escape its fate.

"Come," he says to the men, encouraging them to get a better view. As they step forward, he instructs an assistant to again take a scalpel to the pig's innards. They've apparently been working their way inward through the creature's copious layers of fat, its network of blood vessels, with a thoughtful diligence that is lost to their subject. "We tried to give her whiskey to numb the pain, but unlike their countrymen, pigs don't have a taste for the stuff. So we proceed without anesthesia."

The pig's cries intensify as the assistant makes a deeper, delicate incision in her gut.

A moment later, something most astounding comes into view: the sow's womb, stretched to capacity by a sizable litter within. By the paraffin light, Cager and the others can just catch sight of the piglets through the translucent walls of the uterus. For a moment the squeals are forgotten, and all Cager can behold is the majesty of life—the secret processes that go on away from the light of the world, the unknown spaces of creation.

All four men in the room are rendered briefly silent by the sight, a collective reverence in them. Yes, life. A seed seen in perfect, secret becoming before it splits the surface of existence.

Finally it is Quinn who speaks. His eyes never leave the pale, oblivious forms that undulate within the writhing mother. "The first time, as far as I know, we've beheld a baby within the womb. Without destroying the mother in the process."

He begins to remove his frock coat. Looks to his assistant. "Seal her up. She is to me holy as Mary in this moment. I shall be both heartbroken and furious if she dies."

They have repaired to his den. Quinn is distributing drinks to the men. Scotch, pristine, he assures them—not the whiskey that the sow snouted but ultimately rejected. Around him are shelves of glass jars containing pickled organs, both human and animal.

"What do you have for me?" he finally asks, with a nod to the burlap sack.

"The giant," Job says.

Which elicits a wry curl in Quinn's lips. For it's clear to everyone in the room the sack is a wee bit small to accommodate a giant.

"Parts of him, anyhow," Job clarifies. "He went putrid. Hotter and wetter this summer."

Quinn nods as if it makes sense. "A challenging year, isn't it?" He puts down his snifter, crosses to the sack, opens it. Unceremoniously removes the parts of the giant.

They are indeed gargantuan, even if they are piecemeal. The pale hands are enormous. The feet and ankle bones extraordinary. He places them on his desk, sits back down, studying them, absently drinking his scotch again.

"Well done, Micajah," he says, using Cager's proper first name, the one submitted on the application all those weeks ago.

There is something in his presence that is comforting to Cager. These pieces of the giant, in his calm, clinical hands, suddenly become not the stuff of sin, of the macabre, but instead subjects. Objets de science.

"How was your first night as a sack-em-up man?" he asks, using the street term for a resurrectionist. He does this with a knowing nod, a half-wink to Job.

"All in the name of science," Cager says, surprising himself with the impossibly wry tone he somehow affects. As if he is suddenly an old hand like Job, like Fife, inured to the whole sordid business.

"All in the name of science," Quinn repeats. There is nothing wry in his refrain.

Job produces the sack full of teeth from the giant. "Full set."

"No skull? Skull of a giant would've been quite the subject."

"Left it there. Brain was black. Stunk to the point it would've outed us on the road. Smelled from a hundred feet."

Quinn nods. Fair. He numbs his gums with scotch, looks to the subjects they've brought to him, then to Job. "What's a fair price?"

Job quietly deliberates, then nods. "I know the number was fifteen, but that's the premium only a full skeleton fetches. Parts, like we brought you—what do you think? Two guineas?"

Quinn smiles. "You undersell yourself." He stands, digs into his pocket. Produces a handful of coins. "Four. Two each."

He eyes Cager as he dispenses the coins to each man. "You may not care about money, but the boy will need it." Job pockets his share of the money in silence, moves over to the professor's bookshelves.

Cager considers the coins in his hand, moves to return them to Quinn. "I'll just be paying you for instruction. You might as well take them back now."

Quinn eyes him appreciatively. Something sad in this man, Cager decides, even when he smiles. "No," Quinn says, taking one coin but returning the other. "Go live a bit. Life is too precious to be too responsible too soon."

Cager looks up to see Job returning to them, having taken a book from the shelves. It's an incongruous sight, Cager thinks—the shiny, patrician leather tome in those cracked, grimy hands—but one to which Quinn himself seems well accustomed. "Your pound of flesh," Quinn says.

Job tucks the book under his arm, offers a small smile. "My

pound of flesh." He nods warmly to Quinn, pats the boy on the shoulder, and exits.

Outside, Job divides his coins, slips half his allotment to Fife. Cager attempts the same, but Job waves him off. "Don't overpay him. It'll just end up in the cesspool. Take the shape of a half dozen pints first, but it'll end up in the cesspool all the same."

"Just keeping the anatomists away," Fife counters proudly. "Won't be no interest in this one. Liver's already putrid!" He cackles, engages the team, and in short order, the growler exits the grounds of Quinn's estate.

They are scarcely out onto the lane—the sky now warming slightly, differentiating itself from the land—when Fife's forced to bring the horses to a halt. Before them, in the middle of the road, a man and a woman on a gig so decrepit it makes Fife's growler look like the king's business in comparison. They take up the whole of the road, making no effort to move.

"Move it, Jobber," the man snarls. Though he is young, his mouth is a study in decay, the likes of which Cager has only seen in old men. Blackened teeth. Failing gums. His hair is black and indifferent, his eyes of a blue so shocking and pure they are hard to look into. The woman beside him is also young, prematurely aged, her clothes threadbare, her blond hair ragged and inexact, as if it has been shorn with a knife. There's a great heaviness in them, a coiled fury. And they, too, seem to know Job.

The resurrectionist eyes them. "Get wide, Fife," he says. It is the first time Cager has seen the man discomfited, tense.

As Fife coaxes the team around the gig, the couple watches, scrutinizes the growler and its occupants. Their eyes fall across Cager, catalogue him. Never has he seen a pair like this—so still, so dark.

"Still sellin' Quinn yer weak wares, are ye, Jobber?" calls the man.

It's then that Cager notices the pair also have cargo in the back of their gig: two burlap sacks, the telltale contours of bodies within. More sack-em-up men bound for Quinn's estate.

"Who's the lad?" the woman taunts. "Make a fine subject, right there. Top price for young muscle."

"Climb back in your hole, Gray," Job says sternly.

For a moment the carriages are parallel, dark looks going back and forth, then the spell is broken when the man snaps his reins and guides his gig onto Quinn's property.

Fife shakes his head. "Dicked in the nob, those two."

A moment later, he's got his team engaged, and the growler is headed east for London.

Job looks to Cager. "You bump into them—anytime, anywhere—you run, understand?"

"Yes, sir," Cager responds, sensing that no other answer will suffice Job right now. "Why's that?"

"We all deal in death. But we don't *make* death. Those two . . . leave it everywhere they go."

FOUR

JOB

THE RISING SUN is no match for the sickly yellow fog of London.

It remains an indistinct thing on the horizon, rendered hazy and subordinate by the exhaust of the city: the effluvia of tanyards, of breweries, sugar bakers, and soap-boilers.

All of them belching smoke and gas and unknown chemistries into the air in hopes of progress.

Of lifting the masses.

Even at this early hour, it is like breathing through hot wool.

The boy and Fife are gone—the boy back to his boarding-house, Fife back home, a guinea in hand, the promise of a bed and those half dozen pints to inaugurate the following day.

The resurrectionist hurries, dodging livestock, sedan chairs and their porters, the cess in the street, the cess dumped from windows above.

He is bound for the hell of St. Giles.

That squalid rookery of narrow lanes and cholera, of whorehouses and gin shops.

Thirty thousand souls are crammed here in the few short blocks that link the gambling dens of Covent Garden to the alchemists and astrologers of Seven Dials.

His Irish neighbors call it the Holy Land because they must call it something.

Must find hope or humor in the fact that they have fled

the rural poverty of their own country for an even more crushing poverty here.

Scattered among them are African faces, French, Ceylonese.

The flotsam of the world that have ended up on English shores because of persecution, their own crimes, or the naive belief that the greatest empire in the world might offer them opportunity they would not know in their homelands.

They have been shuffled from neighborhood to neighborhood in London, serially rejected.

Culled as if through a series of sieves, falling through each until there is no further to fall. And so they are here.

They live twenty and thirty to a cellar, with no windows to suggest the wheel of night and day, no walls to allow privacy of thought, emotion, or body.

Job is headed home.

Even as he crosses Great Russell Street, he can hear the din.

The drunks and the fights and the catcalls of the prostitutes.

The world doesn't know it, but the greatest luxury a man can have is silence.

That is why the resurrectionist does not fear the graveyard.

For something is forged in those places of the dead, burnished and perfected by the fear that drives all others away.

Peace.

An immaculate silence.

He shutters his mind to the early-morning bombast, the muck and filth.

By most measures the night was not a success.

His pay came in at a fraction of what he'd anticipated.

The boy'd nearly gotten them caught.

And they'd crossed with Beauchamp and Gray outside Quinn's estate.

They would be a problem at some point.

Their souls more rancid than anything in that giant's corpse, anything in the abandoned cesspits of this place.

But there was one thing, as always, that redeemed the night.

The reason he hurries, as he does now, on aching, aging legs.

The book tucked under his arm.

He ducks down into the dark, cool interior of the cellar.

The dirt floors are so pounded by foot traffic that they are like pavement, though dank and dark with moisture, as all soil is below street level in the city.

Even in summer, London wears her winter beneath the surface.

There is a single window here, small, broken, patched.

Huddled within the claustrophobic space—no more than a man's wingspan twice over in both directions—is a rudimentary table, a bathing barrel, two chairs, and two chaff-filled mattresses.

He has fought for this place, sometimes with fists.

Neighboring families put as many as eight people in similar cellars.

But he shares his with only one person.

She is still asleep on one of the mattresses.

She is Ivy, his daughter, all of seventeen.

A burgeoning world of possibility in that sleeping form, though she does not know it.

A future illimitable, unconstrained, if she would but believe it.

He looks at the book in his hand.

The words on the cover are a hopeless jumble for him.

They are the province of the gifted, the ones that can read, like his daughter.

He will not wake her, not yet.

He quietly places the book beside her so it will be the first thing she sees upon awakening.

He hefts a couple of jugs and makes his way over to the standpipe in Covent Garden, where he will wait his turn among the ever-present crowds to get his fill.

Then he will return and fill the barrel and repeat the trip twice more.

First she will bathe, then he will.

And for a moment, they will feel clean.

FIVE
QUINN

THE FIRST STUDENT vomits within moments. Percival has scarcely pulled back the sheet covering the corpse on the dissection table, and already the boy has turned away and fails to suppress the upsurge of nausea in his throat.

Every year the same, Percival thinks. The weeding out begins.

He nods solicitously to the boy, who does his best to clean up his mess before politely pardoning himself—with great relief—from the operating theater a few moments later.

Percival looks to the six remaining boys, their faces alternately a study of indifference, cocksurety, and poorly concealed dread. Every year the same.

The boy from the other night is here. Micajah. A good sign. Even if his studied expression of nonchalance is as affected as the rest. He is well turned out this morning, his blond hair shiny with pomade, his clothes, unmistakably working class, nevertheless crisp and without wrinkle. There is promise in his bearing, a sweetness to his face. He has, if nothing else, the look of a physician—a thing Quinn is coming ever more to understand is no small part of the equation. Quickly fading are the days when patients were comfortable in the presence of a wild-haired, blood-freckled barber-surgeon. No, now they expect their physicians to be clean as a priest. And this boy, when he is not dredging up corpses, has that mien. He has a chance.

Percival motions to the cadaver before them. A corpulent woman, perhaps forty, excessive flesh and breasts hanging distally so that she has the appearance of being nearly as wide as she is tall. She is a good subject in that in the two days since her death, the rigor mortis has slackened, but the more overt signs of decomposition have not yet asserted themselves. The perfect time to get into a body.

"Beautiful, isn't she?" he asks. It's a thought that issues forth unbidden. Something meant for inward consumption. His head, he already knows, is not in the right place for instruction. But instruction is what is expected of him. The boys have paid for it. So he proceeds, doing what he's never done in all his years of instruction: teach by rote, intoning a sort of mechanical, soulless script that will at least edify the boys, if not himself. It is contrary to all that he believes about teaching—that both teacher and pupil should learn equally from it, and in the process, above all else, anatomy will advance.

"We know little about her. Not her age, nor her name, her heritage, how she lived, nor what she ate. Death has sealed her mouth, and for that, she is a mystery. But is that correct?"

He eyes the students, most of whom are perfectly willing to keep his gaze the whole time rather than look upon the corpse before them.

"We cut a tree," Percival says, "and the rings tell us something, don't they? The age of the tree. If summers were wet or winters too cold. Perhaps, then, it is the same with the human body. Through it we may be able to look into the past, see what it was that struck this person down, and from it we may learn so that the next may not die the same death."

The next. It is a turn of phrase he has used in a hundred

previous lectures. But it runs roughshod through him this time.

"Let's get to work, shall we?"

The boys look to him, for the most part mortified. He motions to the implements laid out on the tray beside the cadaver—the various blades, saws, and scrapers. "Everyone's to take up an instrument, everyone's to participate."

The looks on their faces! How he used to revel in their shock when they realized they had to participate in dissection, on the first day! But again, the whole of him is not here. His words are well-honed affect, nothing more.

He produces his favorite scalpel from his frock coat. "Every moment counts when it comes to dissection. When a body dies, it goes into a process call autolysis. Self-digestion. It begins to consume itself for lack of oxygen. Even now as I blabber and you dither, she is coming apart inside. The liver and brain are the first to go putrid. If you wish to study those particular organs, you are going to need the freshest body you can get your hands on. Especially in summer. Were it winter, we would have ten days to investigate her, but given it is summer, and a hot one at that, we will be lucky to have even half that time." He says this as he deftly and unceremoniously slices her abdomen from sternum to pubis, revealing first the gelatinous, yellow-brown layer of fat under her skin, then the gray-blue jumble of viscera further beneath.

The boys predictably cover their mouths and noses as the acrid odor issues forth. Percival makes a second, perpendicular incision across the abdomen, adroitly folds back flaps of skin and fat so that the cadaver's intestines are in full view. "If you don't like the smell now, wait till the heat of the day," he says. "Ours is a race to stay ahead of the decomposition.

Because the abdomen is the first to putrefy, we start there. I need a volunteer."

Further mortified looks.

Finally it's Micajah who dutifully raises his hand.

Yes, Percival thinks, he will be the one to differentiate himself. He is as scared as the rest, but that adolescent need to prove himself burns more brightly in him than the others. He will go where the others won't. Do what they won't. You are a fool, boy. But because of it, you have a chance.

He hands the boy his scalpel. "Find out what's wrong."

The boy considers the scalpel, the cadaver's exposed abdomen. "I don't know what I'm looking for."

"You're looking for what killed her. Trust your intuition. Learn what a body feels like. It is a remarkable thing, a holy machine. In harmony, its components will feel like they are all of one idea, one design, one consistency. You are looking for what doesn't fit. A tumor. An abscess. A thing too hard or a thing too soft. A thing that does not fit."

The boy, predictably, is belaboring the intestines, if only because they are the first thing revealed to him. He kneads them in his hand, unduly puzzling over them, unable to find anything anomalous to his layman's feel.

"Anything?" Percival asks.

"Not that I can tell."

"Then take them out. She doesn't need them anymore."

Another hallmark moment: the first violation. When a student must take blade to a body and cut away what heretofore had been critical to life and dispose of it as if it were nothing more than table scraps. When the body goes from the virgin, inviolable province of the human soul to a work-thing of science, an assembly of disparate, inanimate, investigative possibilities.

In this disassembly the romance of identity is lost. The proper names and narrative biographies, of such existential import in life, come apart, and only the impersonal constituent pieces remain. Puzzle pieces where before there was a person, beauty.

We are all just parts.

Or so Percival has always thought. He had been disabused of sentimentality by his studies. He had been through the looking glass, seen the true substrate of life. There is only death beneath. Death waiting to make itself manifest. Parts waiting to decay.

God plays no role. We are configurations of cells convincing ourselves otherwise. Arising, dividing, mutating, withering, dying, according to the ever more discernible rules of science. The romance is lost. And yet . . .

And yet.

As he looks upon this boy, rooting around now in the stomach, the spleen, gallbladder, pancreas, naive fingers searching for an answer in this thing that only days ago walked the streets of London.

There must be more.

It can't be this impersonal.

He knows it's not this impersonal. Now.

For a thing decays in him too. A thing probing hands in any autopsy would not grasp. A thing irreducible and immune to discovery in an anatomy theater.

It is the mundane contentment that he half experiences at best most days—the blessing of stability. A life where one has the luxury of mistaking small problems for large. A life unknowingly fragile until it is properly dimensionalized by the onset of tragedy.

Death is coming to Percival Quinn, in the most personal manner imaginable.

A death not his own.

He keeps a pied-à-terre nearer to London and St. Bartholomew's, a house at No. 21 Leicester Square, though much has changed since he purchased it two decades before. He would scarcely have called it a pied-à-terre then—rather, it was one of a number of country houses created by the division of Leicester House, the royal residence that had occupied the area previously. As a young arriviste at the time, he'd counted a who's who of fellow surgeons, ambassadors, artists, and baronets as his neighbors. London had not yet encroached. The traffic that regularly locked up the north side of the square, as it does now as he makes his way home, was nowhere to be seen. The city then was far away, the summer nights filled with birdsong rather than the bray of horses and the rasp of steel-rimmed wheels against the paving stones. Nowhere was the yell of the monger or the invective of the drunk.

Then it was its own little enclave, a bohemian Eden of ideas separate from the world. There was wine and conversation, and everything was possible. French orientalists mingled with Swedish painters, architects with earls. It was everything the young idealist in him wanted. The Napoleonic wars were yet to show a downside, England was ascendant, all things were possible. Over bottles of claret, he and his neighbors were redreaming the world.

But dreams are hard to contain, aren't they?

This question that is not a question has often assailed him

as he looks on the growing crowds that transit the square. That frequent the shops that slowly but inexorably replace the houses his fellow dreamers have systematically abandoned as they sought out a newer version of that displaced peace, further afield, away from these masses that their own dreams have conjured.

We dream of a more perfect future, but we can never control it, can we?

The dream, as all dreams do, overruns its banks. And the dream has its way rather than the dreamer.

That is why Quinn, following the cue of his fellow idealists, has bought the estate out in Earl's Court. To hear the birds again. To reduce the scope of his dreams and know peace.

It was a plan that was coming together quite nicely. He'd found a good woman and married her. She was fifteen years his junior, innocent to ambition, naive enough to believe in God. In short, his antithesis. In his youth, he would have found her simplicity insufferable. Now he found it redemptive, a lodestar. For in her presence, her unknowing ease, he had found a model, a path forward—a way to unwind all the vanities and ambitions whose pursuit had led him, by middle age, to contemplate, for the first time in his life, suicide.

Genevieve. *Neva*. The reason he still keeps this place in Leicester Square. The reason he even now steps over drunks, dodges liveries with aging legs to get back to her.

It is required she be here, you see. On the cusp of the city. Near St. Bartholomew's. For it is she who is dying.

When Quinn enters sometime after ten that evening, he's

surprised to find Brewer, the young lady's maid, still moving about the house.

"Brewer, what're you doing awake?"

Brewer, a rumpled chemise in her hand, nods upstairs. "I don't sleep until my mistress does." This is said with her characteristic stoicism, a servant—like so many—trained from an early age not to editorialize. Quinn and Neva have tried for years to liberate her from such self-abnegation, though to little avail.

Quinn looks up the stairs. "How is she?"

Brewer holds up the chemise. There is an apple-sized circle of blood on it.

"Has she slept at all?"

Brewer shakes her head, begins filling a basin so that she might rinse the blood from the nightdress. "She wants to take a bath."

"Would you draw her one, Brewer?"

Brewer nods. And Quinn is away up the stairs.

Despite being pale and weak, she is restless. Upon seeing him, Neva wants news of the outside world—how his lectures went, what the newspapers say, what the people in the streets are wearing given the unusual heat.

It is understandable. She has been in this bed for the better part of two weeks.

Mostly she just wants him to talk and through it be part of the pageant of life—if only vicariously—which she can otherwise only hear at a remove through the window across the room. She has not been on her feet in four days. Has not crossed to that window. Has not laid eyes on the world. Her world is now this room. The intricacies of its ceiling molding, its wallpaper, the subtle shapes in the wood veneer of the nightstand. And the stories he brings.

He tells her of all the mundane things of his day, feeling the unnatural heat of her flesh with the back of his hand as he does. She is indeed burning up. Each day hotter than the last. The baby inside her stands no chance.

The child is nearly full-term, so near birth now that the full scope of the oncoming tragedy can no longer be denied.

Neither mother nor child will survive delivery. They are twinned in an accelerating dance of death. Inexorably, each new day sees the miraculous transfer of life-giving nourishment via umbilical from mother to fetus, one body feeding another that is at once of it and separate, shaping it, building it, readying it for the world. And yet that very gift holds in it a larger promise of oblivion. For as the baby grows, the cage around it does not.

There are deformities in Neva's ilia.

Like so many in England at the turn of the century, she suffered a bout of rickets in her youth, though compared to most, she managed to emerge from it without any apparent long-term debilities. She thanked the Lord for this. (Quinn, upon first hearing of her case and treatment, thanked the regimen of cod liver oil and sun exposure that had been prescribed her.)

It was not until after they conceived the child did they realize that rickets had indeed left its mark upon her. A hidden curse, deep beneath the surface. It had subtly warped the contours of her hip bones. And as a result, the birth canal was constrained to the point that delivery was impossible.

They met this realization with distinctly different approaches. Neva stoically, if not always joyfully, recognized whatever was to come as God's will. Quinn secretly raged against such humble surrender.

He has tirelessly sought a solution the only way he knows how—with his knife. He has cut into dozens of living, gestating animals, teased apart the tendons and hips of human cadavers, probed dead wombs in search of answers. There must be a way to take a child from a mother. Early. In a way in which neither dies. This means, as far as he knows, one of two things: widening the ilia or circumventing them altogether. The latter has been done. He has heard it has been done.

Word came out of Africa that the first surgeon in the empire had successfully cut directly through the abdomen into the womb of a living mother, with both child and mother surviving the surgery. That the surgeon was a woman—Miranda Stuart Barry, having to masquerade as a man in order to perform the life-saving surgery—lent the story an unfortunate complication. The British army, under whose auspices the procedure occurred, had been understandably shocked to learn that soldier-surgeon John Stuart Barry was, in fact, a Miranda and, for the moment, was keeping details of the event a bit vague until it could better publicly frame how it had been so grandly duped, to say nothing of the fact that a woman had accomplished what no man in the history of this great empire had until now. As such, official case studies of the procedure were yet to be circulated in London. Even so, word had made its way through the medical community, radiating outward from Bart's across the land. Caesarean section was possible. Even if the method, the specifics of the procedure, were still sequestered two continents away with Mrs. Barry.

Heartened, if still operating largely in the dark, Percival

has by now cut numerous fetuses from pigs, dogs, rats, always with limited success. Yes, occasionally the offspring survived, but invariably either the trauma of surgery or, more commonly, the blood loss killed the mother. The vascularity of the uterus means that too many veins are cut, their networks too complex to bind. All the mother's blood—that miraculous transference of nourishment focused with such determination on the child—unfailingly spills out on his table, and he is helpless to stop its flow. All that is left at that stage is to watch as the delicate spark of life slowly dims in the mother's confused eyes until there is nothing left in them but a grayness worse than black—eternal and cold.

His kingdom for Mrs. Barry.

It is one thing to practice on pigs, another thing entirely to put knife to human flesh in this regard—a thing he has not done. He is left only with the hope—an unsteady one—that when the time comes and he applies what he's gleaned from his work with the animals, he might save the child with some deft scalpel work, though at the terrible expense of Neva. This is not something he's even willing to contemplate. The child is yet a nameless thing to him, unknown, but she is the living, breathing thing before him right now. *Neva*. The one that set him free of himself. Their bond by marriage is just a certificate in a church. But the accident of them, their symbiotic imperfection, it is the only holy thing he knows in the universe. How else to explain the impossibility of one person reaching another, affecting them, calling forth from each a selflessness neither knew they had? There is nowhere he could get to in a body with his knife that would explain that.

Besides, he promised her early, shortly after they realized their predicament, that he could fix this. He could save them both. And each day he had not. And each day the fetus grew.

Until that horrible day when it reached such a size that it could no longer be aborted. That day, he knew, was the day his promise had consigned her to death.

"I'd like to name the baby Oliver," she says.

They sit by the window together. At her request he has assisted her, with great difficulty, to a chair where she can look out and down at the square. Her body is wracked with pain, but her eyes absorb the goings-on below with surprising reverence. It is well past midnight now, but the promenade in the once-genteel quadrangle continues unceasingly—men and women in consort, if more raffish in both character and behavior than what is seen here during daylight hours. Drunks and women of ill repute. Touts banging drums, handing out leaflets for the late-night amusements of bull-baiting, pugilism, cockfighting.

"Why there is not a permanent night watchman in Leicester Square, I do not understand," Quinn says.

Neva smiles. "It's beautiful. They're only after joy."

"The square has changed."

"What in history hasn't?"

He considers her as she considers the square. *She* has changed. Gone is the conservative child of gentry he'd first courted, for whom class distinctions and propriety were as inviolable concepts as any found in her Bible. The seriousness of her predicament, the newfound palpability of death that now suffuses her existence—though she steadfastly believes there will be a positive outcome—has liberalized her.

She looks upon the night urchins below. "We'll go down there one of these nights. When we're free of this. Brewer will look after Oliver. You and I, we'll dress up, but not so much. Because I want to take one of those leaflets." She turns, looks at him with amused embarrassment. "You know I've always wanted to take one of those leaflets."

He shakes his head. The notion makes him smile.

"We'd take it and follow them back up to Clerkenwell. Go into their taverns and pay our five pence and sit down in front of the bull. A bull! In a tavern! We'd have to be drunk."

"You wouldn't bait the bull, would you?" he asks wryly.

"Goodness, no. I'm a woman. I don't have that masculine need to prove myself. But the point for me would be just to be there, on the wrong side of midnight, the disreputable side, drinking gin or whatever it is they'd serve, in a tangle of the sweaty, stinky action, anonymous, no one caring whether I wore a cornette, whether the curls over my temples were elaborate enough."

"Oh, but a woman like you attracts quite a bit of attention in that kind of environment. And not necessarily the sort you'd like."

"You'd be there. With your scalpel in your pocket."

"You think I carry it around as a matter of course, do you?"

She smiles. It does not entirely conceal her pain. "Allow me my flights of fancy."

They look back out at the square together. For a long time, nothing is said.

Then, without looking at him, she says quietly, "When the time comes, and you can only save one of us, I want you to make that choice. I want you to save Oliver."

She lies in the following day. It is the first time he's seen her sleep without evident fitfulness, and so he opts not to disturb her. Better that painless oblivion, if only for a few sweet hours, than the excruciating alternative.

He busies himself by going up to Bart's. The wards. Moving among the poor and their afflictions. There are boils for him to lance. Cases of milk sickness. A child with cancrum otis, the insidious ulcer of which has already half consumed the unfortunate girl's cheeks, lips, and tongue. He will be able to arrest it, he thinks, but she will be scarred—the beauty of the flesh henceforth unable to hide the starker truth of the skeletal system beneath. There is the unsettling din of delirium that rings out from the typhus ward, though the victims there, half mad, scratching at the red eruptions that blister their skin, would call it Irish fever. There are those disfigured by the king's evil, that unsightly globular mass in the neck that can only be cured, according to their superstitions, by the king's touch. Quinn is pretty certain this is not the cure, and even more certain that His Majesty will not be making an appearance in the foul air of the wards anytime soon.

Mostly it is a losing proposition. The list of what can go wrong with the human body is long, the list of solutions short. Invariably his fellow surgeons fall back on the panacea of rebalancing the humors. Blood, black bile, yellow bile, and phlegm. Let some blood—a quart—and surely the body will find equilibrium again. The sheer amount of blood in the wards never ceases to amaze Quinn—errant jars, trays, bedpans everywhere, under beds, on tables, in the halls. A sea of blood spilled every day in this place. If that doesn't work, there is the second catchall remedy—prayer. A mind finely attuned to God is perhaps the finest tonic of all, it is said.

Every day the living are carted into this place, and the dead are carted out.

These are his dark thoughts as he moves up the hall, absently following an apprentice as he rolls a young corpse toward the morgue.

Quinn stops as he passes the morgue. Inside, the dead are being disrobed and cleaned, as always. A dozen to a slab, lined up neatly as an attendant applies a solution of chleruret of lime to their pallid flesh. Readying them for the dead house and burial.

Quinn has seen so many corpses he scarcely notices them anymore.

And yet.

There is one. Among the others. Not shaped like the others.

A gravid one.

Despite himself, he enters the morgue. Waits as the attendants leave. He approaches the corpse, considers it. A young woman, late-stage pregnancy. Ripe even in death. Her naked belly almost perfectly hemispheric, tight as a drum. For a long time, he considers her, how stately she is, laid out as she is in perfect symmetry, her pale skin so flawless it's as if someone in ancient Rome carved her from a block of Carrara marble and placed her here to serve as the perfect example of the female form.

The cause of death is unclear. There is nothing to suggest complications from pregnancy. No signs of hemorrhage or the work of forceps. By all appearances what killed so hale and perfect a form was something else. But what?

In the echoing silence of the morgue, with only a legion of indifferent corpses as company, Quinn slowly moves along the course of her, fingertips subtly probing her pearlescent flesh, seeking out that thing that does not fit, the pathological anomaly, however small, that might signal what felled her.

When he circles around to the other side of her, he finds discoloration in the neck. Subtle. Accompanied by swelling.

"She fell," comes a voice.

Quinn, despite himself, catches his breath. Looks up to see a gentleman framed by the door. The man, striking—as somber as the corpses, as immaculate. He is perhaps the cleanest thing Quinn has ever laid eyes upon. The leather riding breeches, a Garrick coat despite the heat, the entire tailored attempt at natural elegance that is now so much the rave, the hair shorn close à la Brutus. If the pregnant woman is a Carrara marble, this man is a Gainsborough with the brushwork polished out.

He approaches Quinn. "It was a riding accident. I should not have let her ride. But she insisted."

He stops on the other side of the body so the two men frame the dead woman. Quinn knows instantly that this is a proud man, one made uneasy by his wife's nudity in the presence of another man. Quinn tactfully, if subtly, steps back.

"I was away with work," the man says. "The people who found her didn't know who she was. I would never have had her brought here. We would have had her tended to with the family physician, at home, as it should be."

Quinn nods with deference. "The physicians at Bart's are some of the best in England."

"So good that both she and the child are now dead." The man's voice is measured, studiously so, but Quinn can nevertheless see fulminations within him. The proud wear pain as anger.

A moment later, in a fit of pique, the man casts his voluminous overcoat over his wife's form. "Where are her clothes? I didn't request that she be cleaned."

"Some of the apprentices take it upon themselves to sanitize the newly deceased. Prepare them for burial. I'm sorry for your loss."

"Her clothes, please. I'd like to take her home."

Quinn nods to the far wall, where the garments of the dead are hung. "Again, I'm sorry for your loss."

As the man sets about retrieving his wife's clothes and Quinn moves to leave him in peace, something overcomes him. Out in the hall. A sort of dizzy, burning imperative. He finds himself stepping back into the morgue after a minute.

"Would you be willing to lend her body to science?" he finds himself asking.

The man, in the process of dressing his wife, looks at him darkly.

Quinn, operating on two levels, finds his mind racing to keep up with the words that issue forth from his mouth. "You would be compensated."

The man doesn't respond, instead calmly finishes buttoning the riding habit around his wife's throat. Pulls her back into her skirt without saying a word. All of it very methodical, contemplative. Finally, he regards her in her clothes for a moment, as if she is once again whole. "You're sick," he says quietly to Quinn behind him.

Despite himself, Quinn presses. "People could benefit."

The man approaches, comes so near Quinn that the latter can smell the bergamot cologne on him. The fragrance—which Quinn in more tranquil moments associates with the fine escape of tea—is here strangely unadulterated by the visible sheen of perspiration on the man's skin. As if he's freshened up somewhere along the way, between the accident and the hospital.

"Your sort should not be working in this hospital," the man says flatly. His eyes are sharpened to points by fury. His voice is too studied, too proud to rise into the shrill register of anger. The words do that for him.

"And soon you will not be."

And then the man is gone. And Quinn is left alone in the echoing silence of the dead.

He learns who the man is soon thereafter when one of the governors of the hospital, evidently having been upbraided, finds Quinn as he finishes his rounds and prepares to return home to Neva. Quinn, it seems, has managed to offend one Marcus Selby Beddoe, hair merchant by trade, but more ominously, for Quinn's purposes, one of the prime benefactors of St. Bartholomew's.

"I've only narrowly managed to save your position, you know," says John Brown, a man as milquetoast as his name.

Quinn, properly contrite, invokes his domestic situation, though he would rather not. "It was desperation speaking. The subject was unique and would have been invaluable to the situation with Neva."

"Good Lord, I hope you didn't refer to Ella Beddoe as a 'subject.'"

"I did not. Still, as you can appreciate, it is not often one finds the corpse of a pregnant woman so near birth where the cause of death was not related to the pregnancy. For investigative purposes, she is a gold mine—a perfect, intact womb and fully formed child in vivo."

Brown considers Quinn briefly. "You haven't any ideas caroming around your head, have you?"

"How so?"

"You yourself called it desperation. Perhaps in hopes that a dissection of Mrs. Beddoe's body might providentially solve your wife's unfortunate case, you're already starting to think you might engage some of your compatriots to do their night work once she's in the ground?"

Brown half swallows these last words for fear someone might overhear, might realize he's privy to his preeminent surgeon's more unsavory methods of inquiry.

Quinn does not respond immediately, and Brown bristles. "You are not to dig that woman up."

"I never said I would. Or that I even entertained the idea."

Brown pulls him near. "The whispers, Percival. People know what you do. How you get your bodies."

"I am one of many. Don't play the fool. There is a shortage of cadavers in this city and an insatiable thirst for knowledge in the medical schools. If Bart's doesn't have enough bodies, the students will go elsewhere. To the private practices and lecture halls, which have no problem working with the resurrectionists. And thus medicine will be set back by a curriculum determined by unsanctioned knifemen and charlatans. So do what you want with me, but don't insult my intelligence by acting as if you don't know exactly how you benefit from my methods."

Brown nods after a moment. "I only ask that you do not insult our benefactors again."

"It was a moment of indiscretion." Quinn collects his things and moves to hail one of the sedan chairs in the street outside.

Brown follows. "Marcus Beddoe, so you know, is one of

the most consequential men in London. One not averse to harsh measures should someone cross him. Despite that, he is also a devout man. One that positively adored his wife. And one that wholeheartedly believes a body must be buried whole, in consecrated ground, so that it might be ready to rise on Judgment Day."

"I'm aware of the ethos," Quinn says as he motions a sedan chair over. "A body is to be put in the ground and only summoned thenceforth by the Lord, not some whiskey-breathed thief in the night."

"I could not have put it better," Brown says. He fashions a smile, nods good evening to Quinn, and disappears back into Bart's.

Quinn gives the sedan men his address at Leicester Square. The stout duo heft the poles, and soon the covered chair is weaving through the thronging streets of Smithfield. Quinn still prefers the dying mode of conveyance to the carriages and growlers that appear in ever larger number in the streets, if only because the sedan chair allows a deftness of movement that the horse-drawn vehicles do not. With good sedan men like these, every shortcut is available—stairs, footpaths, alleys too narrow for a carriage. Moreover, and perhaps it is a justification, but they are good for the environment of London. Many of the well-heeled look down on the foul-mouthed workingmen that often bear sedan chairs. Not Quinn. Unlike horses, they do not shit in the streets.

Percival Quinn has never done well with uncertainty. He has mapped out his future since his youth. Tomorrow follows today in an orderly fashion, the events of tomorrow willed into being by the works of today. Things, properly attended to, could be controlled.

That all seems quaint now, naive. How humbling the world! How unpredictable! The agency he'd thought he had was instead merely the hubris of youth.

He is helpless. He realizes this as he returns home to Leicester Square, moves up the stairs, sees more blood in the washbasin, hears the quiet, pained moans of his beloved wife in the room above. At once he is relieved beyond measure that she is alive, but at the same time horrified by the fugitive nature of it all. He really hasn't a clue when she—and their child—will simultaneously die. All his life, he has believed in himself, taken on the mantle of the knowing when pressed by patients and their loved ones. He has been the answer, certitude.

But now there is only a vast capriciousness, intangible and unknowable in every respect. It reduces him to a child, to that state of supreme vulnerability that requires solace rather than strength.

But what solaces this?

These are his thoughts as he finally lays eyes upon Neva. She coughs up blood, but she does not instinctively catch it with her hand or cover her mouth as one would expect. Rather, both hands are occupied, laid with surpassing tenderness on her ripe belly. As if assuaging the unseen child within. Calming it. Those hands like gods. Unseen to the child but present. Certain, even if the storms out here are colossal.

No, Percival Quinn thinks.

No, there is one thing he knows, if nothing else in the universe, in this moment.

He fully intends to dig up Ella Beddoe.

SIX
IVY

THIS BOOK HER father has left on her nightstand—*A Catalogue of One Thousand New Nebulae and Clusters of Stars*, by Sir William Herschel—is impossibly technical and complex, the last book one would wish upon a seventeen-year-old girl, and most certainly the only one of its sort amid the destitute squalor of St. Giles. And yet for Ivy Mowatt, sitting beside her father in the morning light of the courtyard, the book open in her lap, it is a skeleton key to a hundred doors in her head she didn't know she possessed.

"By the engravings, it looked like something you'd like," he says.

She flips through the plates, at the renderings of far-off heavenly bodies. "A thousand more," she says with fascination. "A hundred years ago, they thought there were *six*."

"Who was it again—the first bloke that found the six?" Job asks. He is testing her, knows full well she has the answer. But paternal pride wants to hear proof from her lips anyhow, wants to hear the confidence and ease with which she delivers it.

"Edmond Halley," she says, without looking up. "And if they've increased the known number of clusters and nebulae to six thousand, in just a century, you know what that implies."

"What does that imply?" He is training her—to have

answers, but even more so, to have the courage to give voice to such answers.

As a woman, it is her only way out of St. Giles—her ceiling in life otherwise is the position of chambermaid. More likely she will suffer the fate of the other women here—the all-too-familiar spiral of abuse and disease, pregnancy and pestilence. Surrounded on all sides by dung heaps, cesspools, and the foul sludge of the open sewers, they become jug-bitten whores or are beaten so badly into submission by the layabouts of this quarter that their eyes are dead even if their bodies are not, and they are reduced to waiting for the inevitable bout of cholera or pox to mercifully finish them off. Under less merciful circumstances, they are found dead in the low-tide flats of the Thames after a handful of six-bottle men have had their way with them. Women do not die happy grandmothers in St. Giles.

Ivy closes her eyes. Lifts her chin so that the warmth of the sun bathes her face. "Our sun is one star. And it gives off so much heat we can feel it from even this far away. Beyond are a thousand more just like it. And now, with these nebulae, these star clusters even farther out, there are suns everywhere. Imagine the sheer amount of heat. The sheer amount of heat in the universe. The sheer amount of light."

Job regards her. She seems to him in this moment to be wearing all that heat and light on her face. Embodying it. The few freckles on her cheeks dance in the sunlight, ecstatic in their tiny silence.

She opens up her eyes, her reverie shifting. "I wonder what they look like. The star clusters."

Job nods to the engravings in the book as if it's obvious.

"No, I mean up close, as we see our sun. Would it be a sky full of suns?"

He looks up, sees only the yellow haze that forever crushes London. His daughter is young, sees more with her imagination than with her eyes and so can pierce that haze, envision firmaments that his eyes, shuttered by wisdom and the truth of experience, no longer can. How perfect a creature, a youth with hope not yet shattered. That is what he has tried to sustain in her, that sweet credulity, the bittersweet illusion. Better that she should swim in the enchanting promise of a lie, even if it is certain to be shattered in the end. Better to have lived briefly in naive possibility than die knowing the illusion from the outset. Better to know, even in passing, the impossible beauty of youth, though she yet understands it only peripherally, without the vanity that comes with complete comprehension of one's charm and its attendant power.

For those reasons she wears this checkered, empire-line dress that he's bought with the proceeds of a decaying young boy out in Rosyth. Her elaborate ivory muslin neckerchief—which affords her an air of decency and chastity in the whore-tangle of St. Giles—was procured with money from an old woman's body up in Banchory-Devenick. That her feet might never touch the human waste that overruns the streets of the rookery during summer rains, she wears nankeen half boots paid for by the body of a well-respected businessman up in Bunhill Row. He has made something, however radiant and fleeting, out of his dark aptitude.

And yet, as he looks at her and she closes her eyes again, feeling the sun on her face, something is broken.

She is a porcelain thing, perfect, a lotus rising from the muck of St. Giles.

But there are bruises on her. On the inside of her arm,

revealed to him as the sleeves of her dress slip back when she pulls her arms up to cradle the back of her head.

They are dark. Separate. Round.

Fingers.

Someone has put hands to her in a very intense way. Squeezed in such a fashion that blood vessels have been broken.

He is an imperturbable man. The last twenty years have saddled him with so much misfortune, casting him into pits both figurative and literal, that reaction has long since been beaten out of him. The world goes on. You persevere. Nothing will break you if you keep moving.

But now there is an unfamiliar fire in him. Fury.

He slowly takes her wrist. She opens her eyes. He lightly rolls open her arm so that both can see the bruises.

"Were you out last night?"

Instantly she is defensive. "*You* were out last night," she says.

"It is not the same thing. I have to earn money."

"I went to the river," she says.

Job says nothing. He knows she will talk now.

She subtly pulls her hand away, lowers her sleeve over the bruises. "The river is the only place you can see the stars, what with the lights of the city and the smoke."

A thing he has said a hundred times to her before. "You are not to leave the house at night."

"How am I to see the stars, then?"

He wants to say to her there is more to the world than stars—such as the four- and five- and six-bottle men that wander the streets, the killers and kidnappers—but he knows the division this will cause, the dark realities of the world he has long tried to insulate her from.

"Tell me who did that to you," he demands.

She looks at him like it's a matter of little concern. "A couple of mudlarks cut up my peace. I drew their cork, don't worry." Yes, she is most certainly defensive—she only drops into the parlance of the street when emotions have gotten the better of her and she's posturing strength.

Job asks the question he doesn't want to ask. "Did they do anything to you?"

Knowing the meaning, she shakes her head, meets his gaze in a way that arrests him.

"You've raised me strong, Father."

For the last three years, he has been sending her to Thomas Cranfield's ragged school up on Kent Street. It sits at the base of London Bridge and is pure noblesse oblige—a token attempt by the otherwise unseen rich to educate the great unwashed. There is, of course, a ceiling to that education, Ivy knows, as the poor mustn't come into possession of too much knowledge. The boys are taught shoemaking and cabinetmaking, the girls how to knit, cook, wash, iron. If they just work hard enough, they might rise as high in position as valet or governess, where they would have the great fortune of attending upon the rich with impeccable care.

Thanks to the constant stream of books her father has brought her over the years, she is the most educated person at the ragged school, pupils and teachers alike. She goes only to honor her father and his unceasing sacrifice. He is as noble as they come, but he is uneducated, which is not to be unexpected given his line of work. When she was lucid enough to understand such things, he told her of his unseemly vocation, the thing that keeps him away at night, that causes him, more often than not, to come home the bearer of earth-shaking stink. It is heartbreaking to her that he is a night soil man, one of the accursed rips that clean out the privies and cesspits in the dead of night. He has invited her on occasion, with some pride, to come along and see what he does. But to witness one's father wallow in shit for a living is more than she is willing to bear, and she has never chosen to accompany him on his nocturnal shifts.

Whatever the case, he does not understand how remedial the ragged school's curriculum is, how debasing. It only serves to remind her how impossible her situation is. It is one thing to read books about distant nebulae, about ornithology, botany, and geology, another to effect that knowledge while brushing the snarls out of your ape-drunk lady's locks. Better, young lady, to have a good and unselfish nature, to remain cheerful in the face of adversity, so that you would be a good wife and mother. If a woman is so unfortunate as to possess higher learning, she should at least have the wisdom to know it is considered unrefined to display it in public.

So yes, there is anger in Ivy. She has tried over the years to bear it with her father's stoicism. But she is not him. She needs catharsis.

She is four blocks from the school. This is the favorite part of the walk for her. Especially when the tide in the Thames is low, as it is now. For out there in the flats, the toshers are wading through the muck with their velveteen coats, their ten-foot poles prodding for treasures left by the tide, the mudlarks following behind, grabbing the errant bits the toshers leave behind—sodden lumps of coal, spent candles, rotten scraps of clothing, misshapen globs of pitch—

anything that can be converted into a few dibs and a bite to eat.

She scans them surreptitiously, hopefully, for him.

He is there, as he always is. The tallest of the mudlarks. The oldest and most unmistakable. Shirtless and raw in the burgeoning heat.

He pauses at the sight of her. He is a primal thing, she thinks, hair uncombed, body smeared in filth, unapologetic. He fills the river with his indifference—the rest around him are lost shades, faceless things consigned to a permanent background in his presence.

He lifts his chin subtly to her. He is ridiculous. Too cocksure.

The marks on her arm are his. Left when he kissed her the night before. There is too much anger in him, too much ardor, too much defiance. He has foolish, uneducated ideas about overthrowing the upper classes, but he will never be more than a mudlark. He thinks violence is the only way forward, and given that the working class vastly outnumbers the elite, it's merely a matter of taking up arms and taking control of the country. He is all body and no mind—what must be done can only be done with the fist. She knows with near certainty that he will end up a four- or five-bottle man like his father, dead on the floor of a tavern because he's overestimated the abilities of his fists. He has no future. And she knows better than to have such a dizzy yearning for this bottom-feeder, to let him put his hands on her, kiss her with an aggressive fervor that borders on frightful.

The problem is that he's beautiful.

SEVEN

JOB

IT WAS A different man that ran the Yorkshire mill.

True, the name was Job Mowatt.

But it meant something different then.

It had a heft, he supposes, in the way that it meant something in his absence.

Funny how a name can presuppose a man, outweigh him.

Not now—all that has been pared away.

His name is no more than part of the anonymous noise of the city, a background irritant on someone else's lips—if at all—and even then just a bit of breath that wouldn't evoke feelings one way or another in anyone who might by chance have made out the specifics.

Probably better to be shorn down to nothing.

To be rid of the enterprising mind.

He who would lord it over all those workers at their spindles: twenty-nine hundred at its zenith!

The mill was to add another floor, another waterwheel!

How fortune had shone upon him.

It was not that he was moneyed then, not initially, though for his industry, he would soon find himself to be.

He would become not just the field hand he had been since youth but instead a landowner.

Four years of forced sobriety will do that for you, when not a single pence goes to the publican, though a few pints of ale at the end of the day would be a welcome reprieve from the otherwise moiling crush of your daily existence.

Four years of backbreaking labor, of going without, of eating a single meal a day, your body growing thin in hopes that your purse might grow fat.

By then he had enough money to buy a tiny plot of land in the West Riding with a sickly building situated on a crucial bit of stream frontage.

Four more years of this, of single-handedly turning that building into a mill, of single-handedly constructing from scratch the waterwheel that would power it, of procuring older spinning mules cast off by owners of larger mills as they relentlessly modernized their own operations, jettisoning workers in favor of machines.

Those richer millowners, all too willing to sell him their old wares, all too willing to watch as he powered his spindles with water and animals, much as they had done in generations past but eschewed them now in favor of steam, that great boon of the Lancashire coalfields.

He was a curio, this solitary man out there waging naive war against the laws of business and the natural world, laws they knew through experience to be inviolable: the laws of the cotton business, which required economies of scale, achievable only through mechanization; the laws of the human body, which was, in comparison to the machines now spreading across the land, a gross, inexact, and unreliable tool, one that could only be goaded and denied so much before it broke; and most of all, the laws of class, the distinctions of the world.

The quality were quality for a reason.

They were a different breed, privy to the larger truths of society, the arcs of history, the rise and fall of civilizations.

They knew the structures that were required to maintain civilization, and they were those structures.

England was an empire precisely for people like them.

People that respected the past and built toward the future, with great libraries that informed their decisions with the wisdom of the great thinkers of antiquity.

People that *read*.

An illiterate field hand was not much more than a Malabar or an African or a dog, no matter his determination.

Capable of service but not leadership.

Job had been born into a house without book or pamphlet, into a community without teacher, school, or library.

Mostly he was born without time.

The luxury of years in youth to tease apart words and unspool the alphabet.

The mandate of the earth swallowed all other aspirations beyond growing what needed to be grown and getting it to market.

But a person does something long enough, he gets good at it.

He carded by hand a hundred thousand seeds—a million—from the bolls, spun them and boiled them to set the twist, observing with great satisfaction, as a machine does not, the color deepening throughout the process, the organism maturing into a whole new thing that seemed nothing like a plant but instead an instrument of civilization. His instrument, his contribution.

Those fibers would become textiles down the line, and after that clothes on people's backs.

The middlemen recognized the quality of his homespun cotton and paid a premium for it.

They wanted more.

He took on more workers and paid them well because he knew the great price they paid with their hands and their bodies and their minds.

The mill-owning gentry around him took notice.

He was still that uneducated curio, but one whose operation, while still meager, had to be considered legitimate competition.

This name, Mowatt, was not on any registry anywhere—surely he was of peasant stock.

Still, to that name now were being ascribed words like "mettle," "humility," "self-determinism," "artisanship," "sovereignty of mind and intent."

Things the gentry, who had never tilled their own land or turned their own spindles, had never cultivated in themselves.

Every season his output and workforce grew.

He took on a wife of country stock like him, Mary, and soon they had a child.

He allowed himself a drink every now and again.

And often, on the tail end of that drink, he would contemplate with some satisfaction the fact that he had somehow broken the sacrosanct shackles of English class, gone from gallied peon to one the community around him was calling a "mushroom," as if he had sprung to prominence and fortune overnight.

Yes, if that night was thirty years long and had begun with his birth and ended on this evening, with this drink, after all those decades of unrelenting toil.

Oh, the illusion that it was his doing, his industry, that had delivered him to such a place!

How vain we are in success!

The larger world is, in fact, only spinning as it has always done, and we are swept along.

Swept along by the changing fortunes of England, he is one day a newly minted entrepreneur, the next a man struggling against high taxes and skyrocketing food prices.

For it is Napoleon's world, not his—King George's world, not his.

They are squared off across the Channel, and war comes to the land.

A dozen years of war with ever-tighter trade restrictions.

Belts are tightened each and every year, the ledger nipped and tucked wherever it could be.

Where before he was that noble, beloved, and self-made millowner who paid his workers well—who was of their stock, one of them—now things evolve.

He cannot keep them all on the payroll, cannot compete with the other millowners with their tight ledgers and deep pockets.

Old money is old money for a reason.

It is deep and strong as a great anchor in open sea, able to withstand the storms of history as they come and go.

There is no longer need for homespun—what is needed now is quantity, speed.

A soldier's clothes, like the man in them, are not meant to last.

It is not long before Job goes to the other millowners, asks for a loan. They claim without much anxiety that they are stretched to breaking too and, as such, cannot help.

They say they fear their remaining workers, who have grown restive as a result of wage cuts.

The ones that term themselves Luddites and call for the rejection of the machines that have taken their jobs.

Job would be a Luddite too, he thinks, if he could afford it.

Better a life of the hands, even if it be slower, than a sped-up world that cannibalizes itself for profit.

Job knows the millowners are playing the longer game, as they always have—there is opportunity here in war.

In this case, to flush their less capitalized competitors from the market.

To improve their margins by pruning their workforce.

Without access to money—the strange, conceptual form of money that keeps the elite going—the loans, the bonds, the stocks, the sundry financial instruments that only they understand—Job is ruined.

His workers, the ones he's let go, turn on him.

The only solace he has now is that he did not resort, as the other millowners did, to shooting the protesting workers.

Instead, he shuttered the mill and tried to find another way to make his wages.

To stay afloat until things got better and maybe open the mill again.

But it is George and Napoleon's world, not his.

The war demands ever more money, ever more taxes.

Only those born with that great stabilizing anchor of old money seem to be able to avoid debt and unemployment, the insidious, magnetic pull of the only legitimate business currently booming in the country: soldiering.

So it is that Job fights in Spain and Portugal and Italy, repelling the French, while Mary stays home with his only child.

He sends them his meager wages, but Mary is nevertheless forced to scrounge for work.

He fights with that hope that is singular to the soldier—

that this battle will be the last, that this battle will break the back of the enemy, and a return home to family is imminent.

But the war metastasizes.

He is sent further afield—to the West Indies, South Africa, India.

He spends more time on ships than on the battlefield, being shuttled in dank, sunless forecastles across thousands of miles of indifferent sea.

All the while, Mary works, and the price of food goes up, and her wages are not enough.

Years, too, metastasize, and soon Ivy is six years old!

How much master of his fate is he now?

He attempts to build an image of his daughter with each letter he receives from Mary—which must be read aloud to him by whatever literate soldier is currently garrisoned with him.

If she was such when I last saw her, he thinks, and I add this much height to her, this much weight to her, then might she look like this?

Mary's descriptions, as read to him, seem to evoke less and less with each letter that comes.

Something is happening.

Even before handing off each letter to his reader, he can see that the penmanship grows looser, more wild, elegant cursive becoming scribbles.

First the letters devolve into incoherence, then stop altogether.

He spends three more years this way, fighting off new enemies—Neapolitans, Batavians, Argentines, Marathans—all apparently in some confused way backed by, or allied with, France.

He breaks three sabers, goes through countless guns.

He kills for country, though that country is a dim, faraway thing that he has conflicting feelings about.

He is a completely different thing than what he started out as, that is clear to him.

All the ideas he had about himself.

He realizes, for the first time, that the entirety of his life is an accident, the by-product of a thousand—a million—greater forces and dynamics colliding.

How could he think what he thought—that it was he and not fortune that determined things, that shaped him and carved his reality out of the universe?

How humbling, how tempering is the upside of misfortune, the blessing of failure.

The ego is shattered into a thousand pieces, and the foul demon of pride is exorcised.

A man is left to humble reality, without distinction, only the day-to-day immediacy of things that conceits like name and station and reputation cannot touch.

We are meant to sleep and eat and survive.

The rest is folly.

No, there is one more thing.

We are meant to get home.

He returns home once the war is done with the rest of the discharged soldiers.

Hundreds of thousands of men returned to a society in which lines had been radically redrawn.

Properties once thought to be owned are now owned by someone else.

Effectively pawned to keep pace with the inflating price of living.

Mary and Ivy are nowhere in Yorkshire.

He only knows that the mill was sold off, long ago, and that Mary signed the paperwork.

Last that was heard, she took the child to London and the two were living somewhere in the crowded squalor of a workhouse.

It takes him a week in London to learn that Mary is dead by her own hand.

Rendered mad by the impossibilities of a single mother's existence in a time of escalating prices and no prospect of employment.

Broke and without shelter, you find yourself a man or whore yourself or whore your daughter, and she will do none of these.

She too is proud, and that pride shatters her.

So now she is buried in a pauper's grave, one of dozens—anonymous, without pomp, already fading into the nothingness of history as the grave's mound sinks level to the earth. The grass grows full over it, and what lies beneath—unmarked by a stone—is only a whisper, a secret, and soon will not even be that.

Ivy, however.

She has been sent to an orphanage, he learns.

He finds her, and she is a scared thing.

She does not recognize him. Her mother—before her faculties went—told her stories about him, painted pictures of how he looked in her mind, but the war has changed him, and there seems nothing in the stories that matches this man.

She will not at first go with him, preferring instead the familiar, if traumatic, tumult of the orphanage to this strange man that has appeared in her life.

It wrecks him—it's as if his world has steadily calved off around him since the war began.

It's one thing to lose money, to lose business and station.

Another to lose the woman you love.

But even with all that, there is still a place to go, a reason, an axis, however fragile, upon which your existence might still turn, if your child is still in the world.

A last refuge.

But when that child looks upon you and rejects you, it is a pain beyond shattering.

Job has not wept, not through his losses, the horrors of war and the loss of countless comrades, not at the tragedy of Mary.

But the impassive look in nine-year-old Ivy's eyes is too much.

His own blood, for whom none would care more, denies him as if he is a frightful beast!

And because of it, Job falls apart.

He barely makes it out into the alley outside the orphanage.

Masculine affect stripped away, he pulls himself into an unseen corner, and it is not so much that he sobs but that the sobs sob him.

He is powerless. It's a wave a long time coming, the culmination of five years of unrelenting perdition.

It all pours forth from him, eyes and nose and mouth streaming unimpeded.

He is as a child—this is something he realizes in the midst of it with a strange sort of detachment, as if he is watching himself from on high, within the same body that convulses with heartbreak yet somehow separate. A child just like those on the other side of the walls, terrified in the face of the great overwhelm that is life.

In need of solace, of the hand of the mother or father that stills the pain, buffers the fear.

He, of course, has no such solace, his parents long since passed, his friends or comrades all dead or scattered to the winds.

He is just a homeless, penniless man in London.

Ah, but that is why there is God.

Otherwise, how would any man or woman get up from the ground after the whole of them has been shattered?

This would be half this country and half this world.

Half the beings ever born into the hardscrabble chaos of humanity.

Yes, everything subtractive, a process of loss, either gradual or abrupt.

Why, then, go on?

Unless we convince ourselves of an unseen reason, why go on?

Was this what Mary saw in those final moments?

He understands his wife now more than he ever did in their time together.

She saw this truth too.

Tried to find God in the squalor, tried to reap hope from disarray.

And like him, in this moment, no matter how hard she tried, to which her final act stood as testament, she must have found nothing.

No great eternal being that embodied love.

That promised fairness, deliverance.

That by its very presence assured her the scales of the universe tipped inexorably toward the good.

No, she must have seen the opposite, as he did now.

On balance, it could only be that suffering was god, and

that the weaker strains of good, of hope, of peace, were in perpetual rout before him.

A door was closing in Job's mind then, there in the muddy alley.

Henceforth, there would be no light, because there was no god.

Because the god he had seen in church in his youth, the Christian God, the same he'd seen upon the talismans of faith his fellow soldiers had clasped as they'd died, the same he'd seen engraved and painted by the finest artists in England and the world everywhere he went and fought, was a lie.

There was no wizened old man in the sky reaching down with a benevolent hand when you needed him most.

This—this moment—was proof.

So it is the door closes in Job's mind, and the light is no more, and God is no more.

Only.

God is somehow here.

Not the impossible old man high above.

But instead, a moment.

This moment: a realization of footfalls—timid—two sets of feet shifting before his broken form—an adult and a child—looking down at him.

Despite himself, he looks up, and standing in shimmering constellation before his tear-streaked eyes are the orphan master and Ivy.

Ivy clasps the orphan master's hand uncertainly. Both consider the broken wretch before them.

Job is so spent he can do nothing but look up at them, pathetic.

And that is when God appears—or what God would be.

The orphan master reaches his hand down to Job. There is pity in his eyes, compassion.

Job takes his hand because he must at this stage, must feel the warmth of another, a yielding in a universe where there has been none.

As the orphan master pulls Job to his feet, and Job stumbles, young Ivy reaches out too, and with earnest—if still fearful—eyes, steadies him.

The orphan master, himself an orphan, knows the boon of a father.

The boon of a daughter.

Knows the death sentence that is loneliness.

He arranges visits so that Ivy will come to know her father over time.

Job and Ivy find a rhythm over the coming days and weeks.

He comes to her each time as desperate as he has ever been in his life, though he must hide this from her, must present paternal strength.

For if she, in the end, denies him, he knows with certainty he will end up beside Mary in oblivion.

In these days, as a homeless man in London, she is his polestar, the one point of reckoning he has.

He moves tirelessly for her but does not show his haste.

He must be a father, a polestar, in turn, unto her.

Funny how it works, that reciprocity, he thinks.

The circularity of relation.

In her vulnerability, she is God.

She would deliver him if only because her vulnerability required that he move past himself and his needs, become something greater, and make the whole of his life about delivering someone other than himself.

She finally surrenders herself to him, leaves the orphanage in a supreme leap of faith, and joins him on the small bit of floor he's found in a St. Giles tenement for a shilling a night.

The last of his money was gone, and on the eve of her release, he'd panicked.

Until then he'd been content to sleep wherever shadows fell and others were fearful to tread for the night.

He'd held vigil like that in the neighborhoods surrounding the orphanage, homeless, penniless, each morning washing and composing himself at the standpipes before appearing at the orphanage with the appearance of respectability.

But now she would know.

What sort of man would he be to have her leave the four walls of an orphanage for the shelterless grime of the streets beside him?

In desperation he took the first work he could, work that even the night soil men, who climbed into cesspools and emptied them, looked down upon.

That night, before her release, he dug up his first body, apprenticing, as it were, to a bilious man who made his keep by raiding paupers' graves and pulling out four and five bodies at a time, irrespective of their state of decay.

Job found himself in possession of fifteen shillings by sunup and a space—however small, beneath a roof, surrounded by a dozen other tenants in the same room—by ten in the morning.

By noon he had picked up a chaff mattress and a new dress for Ivy.

And by the end of the afternoon, he'd appeared at the door

of the orphanage, the perfect image of propriety, and Ivy was released to him.

It took her three weeks to hold his hand.

EIGHT

JOB

"If your daughter is as intelligent as you say, she should be in a proper school."

The man Job shares an ale with is a dandy, with manicured hands that suggest a reality so far removed from the one embodied in Job's own grimy nails that one would scarcely believe they'd be sharing a table and conversation as equals.

They are seated together in the Fortune of War pub, where Job has come to drum up more business.

The dandy, Reginald Taplin, is a physician at St. Bartholomew's, just up the block.

They are, in fact, equals here in the Fortune of War, if not out in the streets of London.

For arrayed around them on the benches of the back room are the things that make them so: the dead.

Waiting patiently for deals to be brokered.

The anatomists buy, the sack-em-up men sell.

But none are in a hurry, for the most part.

They negotiate and network over drink.

They are kindred in the way that the rest of society would never understand.

Fraternal if not by class, then by livelihood.

Though the bodies have begun the inexorable process of decay, they have been brined or doused with cheap perfume, and any odor that they would otherwise give off is lost to the clouds of tobacco smoke and the permanent stench of spilled ale that suffuse the place.

"She's a woman, she's not of the first circles, she's got no prospects," Job says.

"Aye, Job, but what if I could get her into one of the private seminaries?"

"That's not schooling—they teach 'em how to enter and quit a room, how to sit. Fashion, not character."

No, he will not have her suffer the slums in hopes that she will finally master the art of crossing her ankles on a divan.

The slums, to Job, have always been a way station.

A detour from that life interrupted, shattered by circumstance.

What he dredges up from the earth now, alongside the cadavers, is a prayer for renewal.

Not for him.

Whether he dies in the slums or not, his lot is cast.

But Ivy, she should know what it is to be a Mowatt.

To live again with that hard-fought dignity and rectitude.

May it be that she is one day free of the cage of St. Giles.

He has a way to make this so.

He has been developing the idea for years now.

It will take money, the real sort.

Of which, for the rank sack-em-up men here, soakers to a man, spading up graves that will one day be their own—himself in that number—there is never enough.

Taplin is subtly casting a glance at one of the subjects across the room.

Job knows the dance.

Taplin has been watching this one since he first arrived and took inventory of the dead on hand.

It is an obese gentleman.

Another potential buyer now circles the corpse, surveying it as one would something shiny in a shop—intrigued, but remaining coy, as a good shopper must.

The resurrection man nearby, in turn, extols the virtues of his corpse as any good shopkeeper would his wares.

The buyer, hearing the price, politely moves on.

Job eyes Taplin, sees the subtle relief on his face. Yes, this is the corpse he's set his soul on tonight.

But he must play indifferent until the last minute to get the price he wants.

There is commotion in the back.

More stock coming in.

The anatomists stand, ales in hand, to survey the newly arrived corpses.

In through the back door comes a "short"—a boy of perhaps six.

A premium object that subtly gets the swells around Job atwitter.

Like the rest, the short is unclothed. Any and all sack-em-up men know that to remove anything from the grave beyond the body turns a misdemeanor into felonious larceny.

Such are the vagaries of law in this country, the tangled jungle of statutes.

For years they have just accreted and confused things, Job thinks.

It is worse to steal a jacket than a body.

For a jacket is the personal possession of a family.

And a body is a possession solely unto God.

For the former, the punishment is in man's hands—the latter, the Lord's.

That is Job's assumption, anyhow.

He does not understand the workings of government or God.

They are unseen things with logics he cannot comprehend.

Next comes another subject of great girth, the sight of which again immediately captivates Taplin.

So engrossed is he that he fails to register the pair who unsack the behemoth.

Job, however, does—Beauchamp and Gray.

These two dark currents come in from the night.

They unceremoniously deposit the body on a bench.

An arm flops to the floor, and they do nothing to correct it, which suggests two things: they care not a whit for appearances, and the body is not yet tight with rigor mortis.

And as such could not possibly have been in a grave.

Beauchamp nods to the assembled anatomists. "Finest example of corpulence ye'll find in the city. Don't none of ye beefwits come at us till yer offers for Lord Puff Guts there are real."

With that, he grabs a copious bit of Gray's ass and pulls her over to the bar.

Job can see in Taplin's smitten face that the previous object of his affection—that obese corpse across the room that had been so singular to him—is long forgotten.

The subject before him is so perfect, so round, so fresh, that he is nearly blind with yearning.

"Don't," Job whispers. "That one was never in the ground."

Taplin looks at him.

"They met up with him somewhere tonight is my guess.

Either poisoned him or smothered him once he was drunk," Job says.

Taplin looks suitably shocked.

"To them, digging in a cemetery is too much work, too dirty," he continues. "Easier just to kill the weak, clean out their purse as an extra bit of frosting."

"This . . . should be reported," Taplin manages.

"And who of us standing here in this corpse market would be the one to do it?" Job asks with a wan smile.

The night is at its zenith.

The great pairing off has begun.

Stoked by enough pints, buyers and sellers are beginning to concatenate—a word courtesy of Ivy and her books—and, like heretofore shy ladies and suitors, find common ground. In this case, a price that will leave neither feeling ill treated.

Not much different than the brothels up on Haymarket.

Men, in the company of men, with money in their pocket and liquor in their veins, invariably find a dark outlet for the money.

Bodies are carted out, bound for dissection benches, brine barrels, one form of dismemberment or another.

Job drinks.

He is on his way to becoming a four- or five-bottle man himself.

It is otherwise hard to look on the stark endgame of things so nakedly and without filter.

We become the diet of worms or cut into pale, eerie chunks suspended in specimen jars.

The endgame is not the dignity of the suit we are buried

in, the stateliness of our tomb or headstone or crypt, the decaying legacy of memory.

Those are passing things just as much as the body.

No wonder man needs God.

Because otherwise there is only dissolution.

The thought troubles him not for himself.

He would welcome oblivion.

Should the ruse of God prove just that.

He has suffered enough.

But the illogic of parenthood precludes him from applying the same to Ivy.

He won't—can't—frame her future that way.

Something irrational in him still wants to unlock golden eternity for her—a life ever ascendant, full and worth living, forever oblivious to and untouched by the real endgame.

It takes him no effort to see himself one day—just as he sees these before him now—as a corpse being unceremoniously wheeled out of a place like this.

A pale specimen with a biography soon effaced.

But not her.

That is the problem, isn't it?

As a parent, your head understands that you are meant to die.

But to your heart, your children will live forever.

This is why he drinks.

A dark hope comes to Job just as he is finishing up his last pint.

The money is done, and he will have to dig again.

But not tonight.

Tonight he will stumble home, and he will do his best not to awaken Ivy, and he will pass out, and another night's worth of thinking will be done with.

The patrons of the Fortune of War—living and dead—have steadily bled away into the night.

There are perhaps a dozen left.

Including Beauchamp and Gray.

The haggard duo are drinking as if they are landed—and on credit at that, given that they have not yet found a buyer for their Lord Puff Guts, who lies silently across the room, a few of the remaining drunk anatomists still eyeing him.

Beauchamp and Gray are up to new schemes, Job knows.

The man they have befriended is not coincidentally the drunkest man in the entire tavern.

Not coincidentally alone.

He has been rendered so lazy-limbed and boneless by drink, it's likely he's a six-bottle man that's stumbled into this place fully unaware that the half dozen or so remaining patrons lying in the back were dead rather than passed-out drunk.

They treat him like a lord, ply him with more drinks.

He will be dead before dawn, Job thinks.

If Job were a hero, he would save this man.

Would intercede on his behalf.

But Beauchamp and Gray are not enemies he is willing to make.

He is of no use to his daughter dead.

That is his justification for inaction, anyhow.

He is not alone in this sentiment.

Neither the bartender nor anyone else speaks up.

Death is too common here, life too vain.

This is when Quinn appears.

He is a creature wholly foreign to the Fortune of War at this hour, upstanding, sober, energized.

He comes straight for Job.

"I was hoping I would find you here," he says.

He sits, lowers his voice, which Job finds amusing.

Of all walls, and Quinn should know this as a regular, those of the Fortune of War have ears that know no judgment.

"I have an assignment," he says furtively. "Perhaps the one you've been looking for all these years."

He smiles a smile that is curiously both zealous and admonishing. "In all likelihood, it will kill you."

Quinn tells him of the dead pregnant woman.

Tells him also of his dying wife and unborn child.

It is a window into another man's life not often availed here, or anywhere in London—certainly not across classes.

Quinn is more anxious than usual, more forthcoming, his word choice not as studied.

As if there is no longer any time for appearances or any interest on Quinn's behalf of constructing them.

"If I can obtain that subject, there's a chance, I don't know, however small it may be, that I could use it to help Neva."

It is a strange feeling for Job. They have worked either as equals or with Job as subordinate, the desperate one of the two.

And now this, the walls of formality caving away such that for the first time since the war, he is truly in the unvarnished presence of another man.

It discomfits Job, but he will help, must help.

The world is better for Quinn.

Despite his purple cravat.

"She is to be buried in the churchyard at St. Mary's," Quinn says.

They are both old hands enough to know that this constitutes bad news. The space at St. Mary's is narrow, tiny, with high walls, and stands flush against the side of the church, which remains well lit throughout the night.

Sack-em-up men avoid St. Mary's for these reasons.

To raise a body from that churchyard is like trying to steal a horse out from beneath a rider in broad daylight.

The well-heeled know this.

That is why they choose St. Mary's.

"You should know about her husband too," Quinn says with some hesitation. "His name is Marcus Beddoe, and over the last several years, he has cornered the hair market in England."

"Hair as in wigs?"

"Deplorable, isn't it? It is one thing to do what we do—but at least it is in the name of science rather than vanity. Coercing peasant girls to be shorn like sheep, deprived of their beauty, that birthright of youth, all for a measly shilling, all in service of repurposing those locks for the vainglory of rich women long past their prime? Bah."

"Makes one almost ashamed to be upper class, doesn't it?"

Quinn eyes him knowingly. "There are different measures of class."

They share a smile despite themselves.

But that mirth is slowly lost to Job as he swallows a mouthful of ale and again lays eyes on Beauchamp and Gray and the nearly insensate mark beside them.

"He is apparently a very violent man," Quinn continues.

"Worked his way up from the docks. Figured out a way to bring in hair by the boatful from China. He's managed to undercut the market in this way, for apparently he can get hair for a tenth of a price from the peasants there, to whom the value of money is apparently completely lost. God alone can imagine what conditions he subjects them to."

"You said he was violent."

"Not he himself—he has too many pretensions. But apparently some of the other merchants came to him once they learned of his scheme, and how it might disastrously affect prices, and impressed upon him the need for a floor in said prices so that everyone might thrive. Upon his response—he effectively told them to go hang—they, in turn, told him that he left them with no option but to commission ships to China themselves. The idea, of course, was to illustrate how a price war would play out to everyone's detriment and he would finally see clear and reconsider. Instead, each and every one of those merchants received a visit in the next few days. Most were beaten, one was found drowned in the Thames, another dead of drink despite being a teetotaler. The visitors, of course, were Beddoe's men. The group of prignappers and longshoremen and hackums that came up with him from the docks."

Job absorbs this but says nothing.

"He is apparently going to take every measure imaginable to make sure that his wife is not dug up," Quinn says.

Job nods, his eyes still on Beauchamp and Gray.

They have found a buyer, one that apparently will bend to their rigid price.

As they briefly abandon their mark—his head drooping toward the bar in their absence—to consummate the deal with the buyer, Job looks back to Quinn.

"Hazard pay, I'm assuming?"

Quinn nods. "Hazard *and* expedience."

He proffers a small sack to Job, within which are twenty gold sovereigns.

Job barely manages to conceal his surprise. The amount is twice the going rate of a standard subject.

And this is just opening money.

"There will be another fifty at finishing."

The number is so astronomical—so many degrees higher than any other assignment he's ever had—that he can scarcely process it.

"It will not be for the faint of heart," Quinn says. "And it must be now. Given that it is summer, that body needs to be on my bench within forty-eight hours. Neither that body nor the body of my wife will hold out much longer than that."

Job nods, still trying to suppress his shock. It will get done.

Quinn stands, offers a hand.

The men meet eyes, shake.

Again Job is struck by the vulnerability in his friend's eyes, the need.

Then Quinn is gone, and Job is left there with an empty glass of ale and the foreign feeling of twenty sovereigns in his palm, the cold gold of which slowly warms in his grip.

For a long time, he doesn't move.

Another fifty at finishing.

Good Lord.

Beddoe must be a real piece of work.

He gets up then and, instead of moving immediately for the door, detours by the bar.

He puts his hand to the shoulder of Beauchamp and Gray's mark.

The man's wretched head bobs up, glassy eyes finding Job.

Beauchamp and Gray are busy squeezing a few final shillings out of their buyer.

Job leans in to the mark, whispers quietly.

"So you know, they're going to kill you."

And with that, he, too, is gone.

NINE
BEAUCHAMP AND GRAY

IT'S CLEAR THE old soaker's scared of them. Despite this, he's agreed to come back with them to the accommodation house, if only because his greed, his need, is greater than his fear. They've sold him on things too good to be true: that Gray's a prime trollop, one that can be had for a shilling, and that they have laudanum.

Like them, he is an opium eater.

That is where the similarity ends, Beauchamp thinks, as he watches Gray guide the beefwit into the room. The man's made proper cake of himself and can hardly stand.

Ye got no sense, beefwit. Being out at all hours, falling into a put-up affair like this.

God on high, I understand ye sometimes. Ye makes the stupid so for a reason. Just as ye makes the small fish small. So they fit nicely in the maws of the big fish.

No one has seen them come up.

It is just the three of them and the night swollen up with liquor. The old soaker, as soon as the door is closed, crowds Gray. "Gimme some, ewe," he says. "Gimme some of that purest pure."

He reaches to put a hand up Gray's dress, ignoring Beauchamp as if he is just a cock pimp and expected to bear witness indifferently.

Gray guides the man's hand away with surprising delicacy, holds it briefly with a sidelong glance at Beauchamp. She manages a coy smile for the soaker. "Maybe we'll have a few drops first?"

The man fashions what he perceives to be a rakish smile. As if he is exciting and dangerous and without boundary all at once. "Yeh," he says. "Let's climb up there into the sky."

He wants laudanum.

As it always does, the hate comes on quick for Beauchamp. Surprises him, as it always does. There is no halfway, or quarterway, no small bubbles to announce the larger ones, the oncoming boil, or the subsequent eruption. It is all, up until then, a circus, as it always is, a naughty romp; he is almost never unhappy, never angry. There are dark ideas—yes, Lord, dark plans, but ye know me. Ye know me. I like a good time and I give a good time. The world is better for my cheer. It needs a bit of unwinding, and I am the unwinder. The unworthy will go down, we all know that, but we can smile as we send them there, can't we?

The hate, then, in that moment, he understands for the first time. Ah! It is ye!

Because left to my own devices, I don't have it in my constitution. So ye announce yourself. And through my hands deliver judgment.

Like lightning, my hands. Your lightning.

These are the thoughts that accompany the jolt of fury that comes into him sudden and unbidden, that make him cosh the soaker on the back of the head—squarely above the hairline so there are no bruises—with dumbfounding ferocity.

It happens so fast that even Gray, who knows what's coming, is shocked.

Still, as the man pitches forward onto the bed, she knows

what to do. She is on him instantly as Beauchamp lunges forward, rolls him over.

The booze has done most of the work, the blow on the head nearly the rest. Now it's a matter of Beauchamp restraining him, lying crossways atop him, while Gray covers the man's mouth, pinches his nose shut. The old soaker pitches as best he can, but compared to the others, it's hardly a fight. Like a one-pound fish on ten-pound line.

"No marks," Beauchamp hisses at Gray. "*No marks.*"

Now comes the magical part. As the man's eyes bug (don't worry, friend, they all do), and he wets himself (most do, some before the big moment, some after), and the large convulsions of resistance in his body give way to smaller, curious tremors of resignation and the exodus of life, Beauchamp studies him—seconds like minutes—searching his eyes, trying to see that moment, the exact moment, when something becomes nothing. When what was here isn't anymore. When what was mine becomes yours, Lord. A transfer of ownership.

But still, in that moment, we are equals, aren't we, sir?

Just as I am equal with those neck-or-nothing anatomists when we finally agree on a price. We. Not them. It takes two of us to make the transaction. Two.

A man works hard to be equal to. Neither class nor church will subordinate a man who demands equality, earns it by the efforts of his own (*our!*) hand.

And I can't think of a finer soul to be equals with, Lord.

They ready the laudanum afterward. Watch as the dark liquid splashes down into the water in the jars before them. Watch as it coils, suspended there momentarily, a fantastic, somehow sentient creature they've summoned.

Where in their early days, it was ten and twenty drops in an evening, it is now in the hundreds—what is counted presently is no longer individual drops but instead dropperfuls. Where before the tincture was a horrible thing whose acrid smell was best avoided at all costs, the concoction consumed as quickly as possible, now Beauchamp and Gray revel in the smell of cinnamon and cloves it gives off, a nice touch added by the apothecary to cut the pungency. Cinnamon and cloves, exotica—promises of far-off shores, if only in the mind.

They drink.

All the while, the soaker lies behind them, folded over double (with not a little effort from them) in the tea chest they've expressly bought for endeavors such as this one. The tea chest is not the standard unvarnished cargo box you'd find stacked floor to ceiling in some East India Company frigate, but instead a highbrow affair some fop must've commissioned somewhere along that line in Asia or India, then grown tired of and sold. They'd picked it up at a secondhand fair when they were feeling particularly flush after delivering two subjects at once. It was the inlaid peacock that did it. Gray'd found it beautiful (and she found nothing beautiful), and Beauchamp just plain liked peacocks. You go as far as the plumage you put out there.

It's a nice bit of craftsmanship, too nice for this room by so many miles one couldn't even count, and a painful outlay—two quid!—but feeling flush is feeling flush. And as tended to be the case with Beauchamp, even his ill-thought-out mistakes proved genius. The anatomists loved it. It gave class to the operation—the knifemen were all the more likely to buy a subject without questions on its provenance if the packaging was nice.

And it's better that no questions be asked on this one. They'd gotten a little heady, hadn't they? More than a few of the regulars at the Fortune of War would recognize the soaker if he showed up again tomorrow night, this time as one of the subjects in back. Usually they picked up marks with a drinking problem (like this one), no family to speak of (like this one, at least according to his drunk-as-a-wheel-barrow drivel), no profile in the community (again, this one), but they'd always solicited them away from the knowing eyes of the sack-em-up crowd so no lines could be drawn between them and the dead. But after doing it up so many times now (fifteen?), it starts to come easy, and you just sort of do it before you know it, right?

No, this one would have to go somewhere else. Not to the open market of the Fortune of War. Maybe up to one of the private anatomy schools. Direct to buyer. It tended to be if you showed up to their door, at night, the knifeman who answered couldn't say no to the convenience. In a town starving for cadavers, having one show up on your doorstep is manna from heaven. No haggling, just a body brought directly to you, transportation already provided, the world none the wiser.

And tell me we don't provide a service.

A thousand years from now, when the history of medicine is written, Mal Beauchamp will be right there, front and center. Like Prometheus, the only one brave enough to steal fire from the gods so that mere mortals could unlock the secrets of the universe.

Gray, on the other hand.

Look at her. Fat as a sow and growing ever fatter. Turning

into a frowsy old fussock before his eyes. And sick all the time on top of it. Coughing into her hand. Spreading around that miasma.

"Cover yer mouth," he hisses. "Got ye no manners?"

"Oh, get off it," she says dismissively, swallowing the last of her laudanum with a wince.

All she wants at this stage is for it to hit her. The great tingle. The doors to everywhere, opening all at once. For the night to be done, its wages secure, the deeds that earned them cast into the abyss of yesterday.

More, she wants it to hit Beauchamp. He is still tight from the kill. She knows him well enough. The Unflappable One. He Whom Nothing Touches. Incredible he still sees himself as such.

But he has never been one to learn a lesson, to evolve. She should have known it then, all those winters ago, when she'd first laid eyes on him, being shamed through the streets, whipped at the cart's tail. Like the rest of the people in her neighborhood, she'd come out at the first sound of the cryer below. Public whippings were on the decline, and when one came around, it was not something to be missed. It was drama, authentic, unpredictable, unlike the sanitized, censored repeats forever on offer at the local theater. And free, on top of that!

Who was that girl that came out into the street that day? She was neither rich nor poor. Pretty nor ugly. Happy in general nor sad. If there was one thing to be said for Gray then, it was that she was polite, perhaps even on her way to being refined. She was literate and even enjoyed writing, and like many young women around her, studying to be a governess, a path in life she had never questioned. It was what was expected of a woman.

And yet here came Mal Beauchamp, bound by the arms to the back of the cart as it was led through town, already shook of the skin on his back thanks to the lurcher behind him with that nine-tailed scourge.

Gray had asked one of the hangers-on who dutifully trailed the procession what the criminal had done. What horrible transgression had earned this man these thirty-nine lashes, thrice applied, that none of us God-fearing cits would even think to do?

He'd spanked a glaze, Gray was informed.

Spanked a glaze?

The hanger-on spelled it out for her. The young man before her, blight upon his family, had pulled a smash-and-grab job at an uptown shop, the machinations of which apparently went something like this. Upon spotting an Italian greyhound puppy he particularly fancied in the shop window—the shop in question being a pet shop, the sort that trafficked in all manner of animal exotica, from monkeys to parrots to more prosaic offerings, such as cats and dogs—young Mal Beauchamp had bound the shop door with a particularly strong cord, smashed the window, retrieved the coveted pup in its small cage, and bolted before the bewildered shopkeeper could unbind the door. He'd spanked a glaze. That it was for a dog made the spanking a decidedly unusual one, but it was, technically speaking, still very much a spanking.

Unfortunately for Mal, it seems, he attempted the same trick a few days later—on the same shop—the owner having coincidentally only replaced the smashed window that very morning—and this time with a decidedly different result. Mal made off with an adolescent bloodhound this time. The owner, however, not to be twice fooled, had a knife ready, slid it between the doors, sliced the cord, and proceeded to run his thief down. It did not help that Mr. Beauchamp was trying to run with a confused and resistant bloodhound in his arms. He was caught in short order and held at knifepoint until the constable arrived.

It was all so ridiculous that Gray found herself smiling, despite the fact that the man himself was being split open before her eyes. She quickly caught herself. Tried to see him with the eyes of a Christian, as she had been raised, rather than with the eyes of an entertainment-hungry theatergoer. How stoically he endured his punishment. His flesh was a lattice of blood and exposed muscle, and yet he bore it all unflinchingly as his fellow citizens jeered him and the lurcher continued to flog him.

So it was they went their separate ways, Beauchamp and Gray, after this brief interlude. But Gray did not forget the pitiful thief. While he spent two full months in the awful confines of Newgate Prison, she found herself thinking of him. More specifically, her thoughts centered around one thing: What sort of man steals dogs?

It occurred to her that there might be material here for the novel she had always fancied writing but for which she had never found proper inspiration. She was certainly capable with a pen; her education had given her that, if nothing else. She had read Susan Ferrier, Maria Edgeworth, Jane Austen. Women authors one and all. Why not her? And not that the book would be all about him—he was almost certainly not that interesting—but it could very well prove a starting point. A window into a different world. The life of the streets.

She was, she realizes now, frightfully bored. Seeking out anything that would awaken her from the grinding tedium of her days.

She had summoned all her courage and met him on the steps of Newgate when he was released. She was the only one.

He was understandably confused about why she was there. She had worked out a speech she would give—how she only needed a few moments of his time—but she realized that his confusion was not merely due to the fact that he didn't know the strange young woman before him. He had been beaten so badly by both gaolers and prisoners over the preceding two months that his face was misshapen, his body stooped and cowering, his brain foggy.

Her first instinct was to walk away. He was grotesque, non-responsive—she would get nothing from him. But by the time she'd crossed the street, that Christian upbringing was beginning to assert itself. Another block and she knew she had to turn around. Such a man, who seemingly had no friend or kin, could not be left to wander helplessly into the streets. He would in all likelihood die, either by winter cold or at the hands of the dark men that wandered the lanes and alleys at night looking to do a bit of bumfucking.

So it was that she rented a room for him at the cheapest accommodation house she could find, up near Seven Dials. It was not much—she could not afford much—but it was a place for him to sleep and hopefully recover without fear of being mauled in the night. She went away after supper and came back the following day after breakfast. He was lucid, if only marginally so. She asked him if he had family that he might go to. No. Friends? No. He, like so much of poor London, was at sea in the city. She put him up for another night, because it was the good and right Christian thing to do, though somewhere in the back of her mind was the thought that another night of rest might put him right enough to recount his story to her. She was doing the Lord's work as much as her own.

She came back on the third day to learn that he'd been well enough to go out earlier that morning. With him now was a man with whom he'd apparently shared a cell at Newgate, a fellow prisoner who had been released a few weeks prior. This was the first time she'd been exposed to laudanum. Mal and the man were midway through their preparations when she entered. Mal was solicitous to her, grateful as he had been since he gained lucidity, and introduced her to the man, who, while frightening in countenance, proved to be, like Mal, solicitous and grateful. Uncomfortable, her first thought was to retreat. Yet despite herself, and in part to make small talk so that she seemed at ease and not afraid of them—which she was—she asked what it was they were partaking in. They told her of laudanum and its magical properties. How it straightened out Mal's broken body, chased away the infernal pains that otherwise ran unchecked through him day and night as a result of the beatings in Newgate.

These, then, were living, breathing opium eaters, those vile subhumans she'd heard about in church. Only they seemed hardly that at all! Yes, they were smartly poxed by life, nothing to look at or hold up as a moral ideal, but they were kind at the end of the day, inclusive and grateful. They carried no pretense or expectation, only a desire to knock up a lark here and there, have a laugh before the world inevitably pulled them under its stony skin once and for all. How refreshingly authentic it was. There was none of the false preening of London society. They knew their lot—that they were criminals, unimpressive and without prospect. But how they could smile in the face of it!

She went home that night pleased that she had done this

absurd thing, that she had sought out the pup stealer—though she still didn't know why he'd done it! Indeed, new worlds were opening up to her. The world of opium eaters.

She decided she would pay for the room up at Seven Dials for one more week; in that time, she vowed to herself, she would glean all she could from them—the abundant untold stories of how the supposed subhuman world of criminals live, all the details of its presumed subterranean depths. For what was coming into stark relief for her was the fact that for all the women writers out there, none were writing about the poor, the ones driven by their poverty into small-time crime—not, at any rate, in a way that made such humans, well, human. Jane Austen was writing aspirational stories, but for a good quantity of the world, no amount of aspiration would get one anywhere. It would be the good and Christian thing to do—hold these people up to the light so that the world could see them, understand them, sympathize with them rather than demonize them.

What a week that proved to be. She gained their trust enough that they allowed her to follow them as they effected their petty crimes, witnessing, for instance, one of their favorites—the dining room jump, in which one of them entered a finer neighborhood in London masquerading as a lamplighter. Usually this was Mal's partner, who she now knew as Gunny. Gunny would move contemplatively through the streets with his ladder until he'd found a streetlamp that had gone out. Then, as if forgetting something, he'd momentarily lean the ladder against a nearby house and move back up the sidewalk in order to retrieve whatever thing that was supposedly missing. It was a classic execution of misdirection, sleight of hand. If anyone were watching, they'd watch the lamplighter as he walked away. What they'd fail to see in the process was the man who simultaneously slipped into the shadows beside the ladder, deftly ascended to the second-floor window of the house in question, slipped inside, and made quick work of any silver or other valuables to be found there. If, for any reason, the lamplighter was challenged and told to take his ladder and quit the neighborhood, the thief in the house—usually Mal—was stuck. Hence the term "dining room jump." He'd have no choice but to leap to the sidewalk below, hopefully holding on to his wares in the chaos, and make a run for it. It worked surprisingly well.

She was starting to understand Mal as a boy governed wholly by impulse. He hadn't yet developed the facility of inner debate. What struck him in the moment, whether it be an emotion, a thought, or an idea, was followed without question. Even when the result came back pear-shaped, his instinct was not to review the path that had led him to such a place, to learn from it, but instead to follow the very next impulse that struck him. There was no plan. There couldn't be.

Soon the boys were bringing back enough rag, after hawking their goods in fence, that they themselves could afford the weekly rent for the room. Gray realized they no longer needed her. She had decidedly mixed feelings about this. On one level, the right and wise thing to do was to retreat back to her terrace-house life, continue training as a governess, and use this bounty of insight to write her novel of underground London's sinners and damned. And yet, and yet. Something was happening within her around these men. The heavy burden of expectation, of having to *become* something, was lifted. Every night and every day was not meant to be a building block to some future ideal, but instead to be inhabited forthwith, to be explored, savored, used.

She asked to take laudanum.

The implication was that it would be a sort of recompense for the rent she'd paid on their behalf. A favor for a writer so that she might know firsthand of what she was later to write about. But in truth, she was trying to stay in the rig of it all. Without knowing it in that moment, she had made a choice—governessing as a future was done. She would be leaving society and its confining rails and henceforth be an unconstrained soul in the city. She would see and do everything. Gain the wisdom found in excesses otherwise forbidden by the constipated architects of English civility.

And what wisdom was found in laudanum. Mal and Gunny consented, mixed her the weak glass of a novice, and it was not long before her body started to dissolve. Her flesh and skin felt as if they had turned to a sort of mist hovering untethered above the floor. Neither gravity nor time had purchase on her. Everything became incidental and curious. Especially the idea that one could contain anything in words. There just *was*. Everything being everything all at once. No need to write anything down, to cage anything in thought. Just stop just stop just stop. Stop willing yourself to be separate. It all washes through you and you through it. Just stop.

She and Mal made love that night. He was a tentative thing, still bruised in body and spirit. She sensed she was filling him up with a thing he had never had before. Family was not a thing he talked about. Even his episode with the dogs was taboo. If she so much as made an inference about it, he darkened. Still, for all this, he seemed to grow strong in her attentions. More confident.

The days grew seamless; she was too busy recording the men's nocturnal adventures, too busy chronicling the strange, sweet inner landscapes that availed themselves to her in the laudanum sessions. What pen time she had previously devoted to her governess studies was given over to chicken-scratch notations here and there detailing these boon days without boundary. She planned ultimately to sit down at one point and collate them, organize them into that larger narrative she envisioned, but that point never seemed to come. Always there were more notes and more sessions, more petty crime and more lovemaking. More material, a mountain of it building in her notebooks. She removed herself from the governess school and her family. There was, of course, a great row over this. They were good people, but they were blind to the cages they lived in, blind to the chains they bound both themselves and her in. She was seeing clear through to infinity, and it was her duty to write something that would show them, and the world, what she'd experienced.

At this point, she was still measured in her usage of laudanum. Mal slightly less so. Gunny was the worst. He was a man of appetites—everything was better to him in volume: food, gin, opium. The money was spent as soon as it came in, often beforehand. He'd run accounts everywhere, from the brothels up on Drury to the apothecaries that were all too willing to dispense the ever greater dosages of laudanum the trio required. There was not an apothecary to which he did not owe money; whenever one finally said "Enough," he simply went further afield. Finally there were none that would do business with him until he brought his account into good standing.

It was then, in a perhaps premeditated final orgy of opium eating, that Gunny finally had too much and piked off for good. Upon awakening that morning to find him lifeless and cold beside them, Beauchamp and Gray knew almost instantly that they were hell-boned. Not only had they lost the mastermind of their criminal enterprise, Gunny had managed to use the remainder of their considerable supply of laudanum to ease himself into the great unknown. Thus they found themselves in painful need of a drug with which no pharmacist in London would provide them. The devil was dancing in their pocket, as was the saying; they had no money and no way to get any, at least not the sort they needed to procure their opium and bring stability to their world once again.

With Gunny gone, they tried to dream up new crime schemes to replace his, but all were dismissed as either too small or impossible to effect without him. They discussed legitimate work, but this was an absurd proposition because there was no legitimate work for people like them, and even in the decidedly impracticable case there was, pay still would not come for weeks. They needed money now. Their bodies, so golden and mist-like and without repercussion until now, were growing denser by the hour, as if they were constricting, being transmuted to lead in the most painful manner imaginable, being drawn with a great and angry hand into the depths of the earth. This was how women became whores, Gray thought. She would not do it. She would not be one of those girls up on Drury. Beauchamp, to his great credit, did not even suggest it. Nevertheless, there was much soul-searching in that first day of suffering. They split up and wandered the streets looking for things to pinch.

She came home that night to find Beauchamp sitting over Gunny's body, which yet rested, oyster gray and indifferent, on the chaff mattress. He was staring at it, into it, with a disconcerting look.

He'd heard something earlier that day, he said. From a long-tongued cackler up by St. Bart's. Bodies could be sold.

There were doctors that would pay for them. Good money. This, of course, made Gray uneasy. They had discussed getting Gunny a proper Christian burial just that morning, and she reminded him of this. Beauchamp countered that, like everything else they currently longed for, this would cost money. They could not afford anything whatsoever, not even food, which at this moment seemed nearly, though not quite, as important as the next glass of laudanum. They simply could not afford to do everything. They needed to choose. They could put Gunny in a pauper's grave if they could first raise the meager money required, but then they would have to find additional monies on top of that for both the belly timber and opium their bodies so desperately needed. Wouldn't it be easier just to sell Gunny? The whole of it compounded the subtle nausea Gray was already feeling.

As that sense of nausea grew in the intervening hours, combined with a gnawing hunger, and no other prospect of a quick return availed itself, Gray began to tell herself, though she scarcely believed it, that with proper perspective this could be more material, even more illuminating, astonishing, and incendiary than anything she had so far recorded.

They sold Gunny for five guineas the next morning. They ate pork pies and drank large glasses of laudanum for lunch. The acrid swill had never tasted so sweet.

With Gunny gone, Beauchamp subsequently felt a need to take charge. He felt that if he were to live with a woman, an ideal that was formalized after Gunny's death—it was just Gray and him now, living in sin, as man and woman were originally intended—he had to be able to support her, to pay for the food, rent, and opium. It went without saying that he also had to keep her out of the whorehouse, the imperative of any proper gentleman.

Gray swam through these days, her world becoming more ethereal. The trappings of the material world grew less important to her, for they paled in comparison to the longer and longer flights she took upon her fascination and imagination into the great mists of laudanum. She no longer kept up her dress, no longer fussed over her hair. Juvenile things these, attempts to impress. And who out there was worth impressing? What was gained? Soon even her notebooks were forgotten.

A few weeks later, with much secrecy, Mal led her to a weedy patch by the Isle of Dogs and showed her a body he said he'd found there, a vagrant who'd apparently drowned in the Thames, though there was not much to suggest, to her eye, that the body had ever been in the river. She challenged Beauchamp on this, but he steadfastly denied he'd murdered the man. She didn't believe him. What was incontrovertible was the fact that they were looking at something valuable—the same as an errant purse full of coin, a necklace—and to leave it there was folly. The body was a body, and it could either go to waste here or be of benefit to the medical community. Within hours they had another five guineas.

She tried to get a sense of how she felt about this. Was Mal Beauchamp indeed capable of murder? Of course he was a prig and an opium eater, but all that meant was that he was desperate, not inherently bad. Murder, though. This was not in the grand scheme of things ideal. They had a great row about it. It was not the first great row they had; the laudanum habit had created a new cycle of extremes for them, periods of great, silent, opium-fueled beatitude alternating with shocking outbursts of melodrama. It was as if their emotions, held in abeyance during the laudanum sessions, had not really gone away in that time but instead hardened for lack of expression, marshaling themselves, growing like gases under pressure, waiting for that moment to shatter the vessel that held them if they did not otherwise find release.

What would come during these outbursts was both bad and good, usually in that order. They would fight, scream, occasionally hit each other. His problem was jealousy. Which, of course, meant fear. He was certain she was going to leave him, though no such thought ever crossed her mind. After they had spent themselves in battle, they would subsequently apologize, cry with soul-rending guilt, express love and need in a way so naked and pure that the world had almost certainly never seen its like. The ecstasy of their lovemaking rivaled that found in opium. Almost.

They killed their first man together a few weeks later, once the money and laudanum had again run out and they were exhausted from fighting each other. The act, strangely, was not one of aggression, as one would expect, but rather resignation. They could no longer fight the world, each other, bear the staggering weight of their need. They were spent. They found an old rumfuddle at one of the public houses in the East End, the man so old and decrepit, so far gone in his drink habit, that it was a good bet he'd be dead within the year anyhow. He'd spend a few more months wandering in his pained stupor, his body bent permanently at the waist at a right angle, as if the hinge there had rusted and become locked in position, his brain withered by booze and no longer able to process the world or be in any way a part of it, other than to be the thing that even the most lowly people in the streets shunned and ridiculed. And then he would die. She convinced herself that they were angels of death, mercifully waging war on suffering that could not otherwise be salved.

Gone would be an existence of unremitting anguish. What would be gained—beyond the laudanum sessions it would afford—were the things the anatomist found once this man was under the knife. The world would advance for this man's sacrifice. Best of all, she and Mal would dispatch of the man in a humane fashion, clean his body, and conduct it to the anatomist with the respect it was due. They would not be like the infernal sack-em-up men Mal told her about. Tearing bodies from the earth. Desecrating God's acreage.

One murder, of course, became two, two became three, and soon the precise number became unimportant. But always it was the ones that were better off dead. The ones they would send off, with a little coaxing, into a final, sweet nap. It was a service, really. And so many benefited.

Through all of it, she never got any closer to knowing why Mal had stolen the dogs.

They consider their latest work together now. The soaker from the Fortune of War. Wide-eyed with death on their floorboards. Without question he is in a more peaceable state than he was just moments before, when he was still in the throes of life, still led by the nose by desires that could never be sated.

"What if I wasn't here?" Mal asks after a moment. "Ye'd'a taken a flyer with him, wouldn't ye?"

"*Him?*" Gray almost bursts out laughing.

"I seen it—you took his mitt away from you, but you kept holding it all the same."

"So you could get him, you mutton-headed granny!"

He eyes her in that way that unsettles her. She knows this look. As if he doesn't recognize or trust her anymore.

She quickly dispenses two more droppers of laudanum into the jars. The first round has not yet had its way with them. The world is still fraught, too serious with itself, and Mal is still tethered to it. Another drink and he will be released and all of this will be forgotten.

But it's too late. He cuffs her hard in the ear. The high-roaring squeal that rips through her head is so excruciating that she collapses back onto the floor, pulls herself tight into a ball, gasping.

Beauchamp comes around the small stool that holds the undisturbed jars of laudanum, slowly kneels, putting his knee directly onto the side of her neck, letting the full weight of his body sink into her.

"What do you think you're doing, pulling caps with a man like me? If ye and yer little doxy face hadn't been around so much, weren't so recognizable to the knifemen, it'd be you I'd be rolling into the Fortune of War as a subject."

She waits for the fatal blow, when he will rise up, then drive that knee down into her neck with so much force that the bones within will snap and she will be no more.

Instead, for a moment, there is nothing, just horrible silence. She doesn't dare open her eyes. Swims instead in the horrible ringing in her ears.

He lets up on her neck. She can feel the floorboards flexing as he walks away and sits on the bed.

"But I'm stuck with ye, ain't I?" he says. "Can't sell you off dead. Can't let you walk, let you turn king's evidence."

She knows what's happening. Because it's happening to her.

The feather's here, thank God.

It's just shown up.

Spreading out from the opium in her stomach. She can feel its onset, a lightening, as if the earth is relaxing its insistent hold upon her. As if a divine feather moves through all her veins and capillaries at once, turning her once again into mist.

She opens her eyes. Yes, he's on the bed. Looking at his hands. But the energy that usually animates him is not there. Those hands do not habitually touch his face, don't pull at his sleeve or briefly seek out a pocket. Knuckles aren't cracked, fingers aren't drummed on a tabletop; there is none of that perpetual nervous movement. There is no movement at all.

Mal Beauchamp is still.

It's that he's not trying, she thinks.

That's it. That's Mal in a nutshell. He is perpetually trying. Always reaching for something, trying to get it or become it, scheming, dreaming, in a fine frenzy of desire and endeavor.

He cannot just *be*. (And neither can she.)

Except now.

She pushes herself up to a sitting position. He doesn't look up.

She crosses to him. He doesn't look up.

She sits beside him.

He meets her gaze. There is nothing in it. Neither pain nor pleasure, neither hate nor love. Only a great, perfect stillness. And that, she knows, is reprieve for him. Life wrestled to a standstill. A victory in that draw.

They are damned, she knows. Have been. Since that first one they smothered those couple years back. But that means they're playing with the house's money. Thou shalt not kill, and you did. So what then? God can only condemn you to hell once.

You make choices in this life. Some are more binding than others. A marriage you can get out of. But kill someone together, that is a bond that can never be undone. What's consecrated in the spilled blood of another—the mortal sin and damnation—is eternal and links them in a way a shiny bit of tin wrapped around a finger never can. She has married him in a different way, one that is limited not by class or law or church or etiquette or expectation. They are outside those fences. They are free.

So, yes, he is part devil, this one.

She kisses him. He is dazed by the laudanum but returns the kiss, if only a little.

A lot devil.

She takes one of his hands—the right one, the one that did not strike her—and puts it to her waist.

Those eyes, somewhere in inner eternity, come back to her. Bring some of that eternity back with them. These are the eyes she knows.

Together they fall back into bed in numb perfection. Time will dissolve, and light will evolve in uncertain degrees from a place of darkness to a place of light, and outside the more legitimate strains of civilization will once again come to life and fill the streets with a busyness that will be forgotten by time almost as soon as it happens. Everything for naught except this, the immediacy and certainty of flesh against flesh, the intertwined slow climb to climax, the even greater twinned ecstasy and vulnerability found in sins shared, which only grows deeper and wider the more mortal the sin. And lastly, the liberation found in another that is willing to do anything, fearless of God or society, for he has unshackled you, just as you have unshackled him.

TEN

BEDDOE

THEY WILL WITNESS what love is.

He thinks this thought again and again as he looks upon his wife. How does one otherwise deal with this moment? With the finality of it, the realization that this will be the last time he ever looks upon Ella's face? It is up to him now to give the word to the furnisher, and the coffin's lid will be secured, and she will become a thing sealed away forevermore, will embark on the long, cold process of becoming a memory.

They will witness what love is.

This vow furious, holy, deep, bittersweet.

Oh, what has been taken from me. What has been taken from you, Ella.

The world is made of injustice, I know that. It is a corrupt riot of takers and loss. But that so perfect a creature as you—bearing an even more perfect, innocent creature—should be taken!

They will witness what love is.

Bear witness here, to me, the aggrieved, in this room alone with my wife in her coffin. From my gloves to my cravat to my hat in my hands, not a shred of color. Only black, for I am Mourning. This room, in our house—*our* house—fully draped in black, the finest baize, the funeral furnisher sparing no expense at my decree. No color. And she in her coffin, the interior around her padded and lined with the highest-quality crepe—black, as is the specially made pillow and mattress that cradle her. Even the glorious radiance of the gold chain esclavage necklace I gave her upon our first anniversary—the finest they had at Stedman and Vardon up on New Bond Street, a singular piece that she alone in this city deserved and that I alone could afford—is tucked away beneath her dress, its inlaid amethysts and pearls and diamonds too sublime for the mood of this tragedy now upon us.

I will snuff color from the world so that you understand.

How it is to lose as I have.

I will show the absence of a love most perfect.

What the utter totality of that loss looks like.

The coffin made of the finest, knot-free elm.

The lid, as it goes on now, covered in black silk anchored by a double round of the finest nails, japanned in black.

But it is in the streets that you will know.

See, all of you, from high windows and low, this procession, these half dozen black-lacquered vehicles, drawn by twelve of the finest, pure-black Friesian horses. See the black jobbers and feathermen and pages and mutes and bearers that move solemnly with us. See the universal black in their gowns, sashes, staves, hatbands, gloves, truncheons, and wands. See the elegant black ostrich plumes on the bridles of the horses.

This is what pain looks like. The absence of love.

Hear the knell of St. Mary's. I have paid for that bell! Little did I know that my insistence that it be made by the hands of the finest bellfounder would come back and touch my life so personally, so soon. Hear this, London. Hear the perfection of its bronze tone. The solemnity of its ring out over the rooftops. The anguish of loss carried to all four corners of the world at once.

I will show you what love is.

You will not follow me into the churchyard at St. Mary's for the final moments. It is consecrated ground, not to be besmirched by the unclean. Women, with your delicate sensibilities, shall stay outside the high walls as well, for you cannot bear the final emotional tumult of burial.

No, in the end, it is just the trusted, the worthy. The men that knew her and know me. We are small in number but forged in the same dies. We have come up from the infernal world of bone-picking and rag-gathering, destined for ruin as all poor, unlanded bastards are in this city—born already half dead, then living a life intended to complete the rest of the job as quickly as possible. But there is fury in these men, in us. An unwillingness to be broken, to give away the life that is our only birthright. They are knights, my paladins—their fury their swords, their indifference their armor. We have fought back at every turn. Every attempt by comers high and low has been met by the fist. No matter how much you bleed, as long as you fight, and never stop fighting, the other side will weary. They will either kill you—and the struggle will be done, and you will have won—or they will come to fear you, for they will behold the madness in you, that your body means nothing to you, and you will forever move forward through the pain until you best them.

Of course, fists have given over to finer instruments of battle, and the shreds we wore as bone-pickers are now waistcoats and cravats. Still, know this verily, friend: we are as elegant a menace as the world has ever known.

My paladins stand with me and know my pain. A dozen of us in the churchyard as their queen is put in the earth. They would be given to keening if I allowed them, but this is an upper-class affair. I must remind them of that all the time.

But there is one—Wheeler—who nevertheless outthinks himself, and as the coffin is seated in the earth and the liturgy is about to begin, offers a wisdom that is not wisdom. His voice is what he perceives to be a tactful whisper. "Not wantin' to walk the black dog on anyone, specially you, bein' my Cap'n Tom, and on this day of all days, but you know they'll come for her."

He's bringing up the sack-em-up men, and the liturgy hasn't even been read!

"I'll cheese it after this, master, but time's pressing. Last chance to protect your lady before they seal her up."

I know where this is going.

But I want him to say it.

"Say a word, master, and the furnisher's got quicklime, vitriol, sulphuric acid . . . "

Which is enough. As I said, Wheeler is the stupidest of the paladins. The weakest in the litter that's come up with us. He secretly fancies himself the brains of the operation, I know. But he's a small, scared thing that has gotten fat off the rest of us. Off me. I indulge him. I indulge him because I am a good and just man.

I pull him aside. As I said, this is a highbrow affair—to cuff him hard on the ear as he deserves is beneath the dignity of this event. Of Ella. So instead I say, quietly, "You expect me to deface my wife with acid."

It's not a question. But Wheeler being Wheeler thinks it mandates an answer! "It's done now, often," he says in his nervous, pleading way, "just before the lid's down, so that the body's of no use to the anatomists—"

I give him a look that is as good as a cuff on the ear. Good as two! He shrinks back appropriately. I whisper again. I want it to be as pointed as possible because I will not dishonor this day any further with such unconscionable conversation. "Quit shitting through your teeth, you long-tongued monkey. It is only because we are on God's soil I don't split you wide. Go away from me, or I promise you, a second grave will be dug today."

I pat him on the head like he's a good little boy, though he is not.

He looks at me with the proper amount of fear and a certain amount of dejection. Like he loves me and is sorry beyond measure.

Yes, I love him too. As the devil loves holy water.

Then he gets proper clearance from me, and it's time for the liturgy.

I hear none of it. It is a minister's presence rather than his words, after all. The rise and fall of his voice, the calm certitude. He could be swearing like a sailor and it would seem the whisper of angels.

All I see is that coffin. My world stripped of color.

So this is it, how love ends. You will go away from me now. They will put dirt on you, and you will take all the color with you, the heat, the heat of what we were. You will take our child. You will take our secret, which only you and I knew in that final moment. I'm sorry. That was not what our love was.

I am making up for it, love. I am showing the world how much I truly loved you.

And don't worry. They won't come for you.

Wheeler is a fool. I would never in a million years deface you.

There are other ways to protect you and our baby.

I have taken measures.

ELEVEN

JOB

AS SOON AS the sun goes down that night, Job is at the churchyard.

Better put, he is just on the verge of it.

He knows the area well, has scouted it innumerable times.

The best vantage is from the elm he currently sits in, just outside the walls.

He briefly feels the pleasant buzz of youth in his veins.

Climbing trees, sitting in secret shadow among the leaves.

A world of one's own, the rest of the city unaware.

Yes, he is old, and his body complained during every inch of the climb up the trunk, but oh, to be here now.

Something emancipating about being twenty feet above the earth, anonymous.

The churchyard visible over the wall.

Many things are going on simultaneously in his head, because this one has a feel to it. Unlike his efforts in the past, there is a certain monolithic quality in the air on this night—again that feeling of youth—that feeling that this day alone is the only day that ever was, significant beyond measure, filled with illimitable possibility, shot through with consequence.

Past and future collide here at St. Mary's.

With its watchhouse filled with twice the usual allotment of graveyard shift inside.

Men, no doubt armed, keenly watching the tiny churchyard before them.

There have been graveyard shifts since there have been resurrectionists.

Holding vigil, protecting the noble dead.

A thousand years ago, Job had aspired to that—to live a life of such status that he would be buried among the nobility, in elite ground like this.

A permanent valedictory to a life well lived.

Thank God he was disabused of that.

Had the illuminating misfortune to fall to such a station in life that when he did find himself on such hallowed ground, it was as a body snatcher.

To see what happens to the elite once they are ensconced in soil for a few weeks.

To see the beautiful and the famous and the gloriously moneyed, their honeyed veneers sloughed away by decay, given over to the blackening and bloat, honeycombed with maggots.

Everything aboveground is a dance.

All the pomp of tombs and statues.

Of moving epithets and odes.

The truth is below.

He sees that before him now: all the wonderful headstones of St. Mary's, shaped by the finest stone carvers in the land.

Yes.

How badly he had wanted that.

But all of that is in the past, province of mistakes and the unnecessary vanities of youth.

What he sees now in St. Mary's is the future, in a way he never has before.

The sack-em-up game has been one of hand-to-mouth, day-to-day survival.

But with the purse Quinn has offered on this job—as impossible as it may seem—for the first time, he lets his mind stretch into the future and do that thing he long ago vowed not to.

He hopes, in the truest sense of the verb.

Dreams up better things, holds them clear in his mind, and does not dismiss them as airy phantoms that would tease and disappoint and crush him.

He has a plan—the forlorn sort that is distant and desperate, easy to conceive but impossible to execute.

It is the sort born and entertained over alcohol, when defenses have softened, inhibitions rendered diffuse and porous.

When one is allowed brief flights of escape, of emancipation.

It first came to him a few years ago, during long nights in Quinn's study talking with the anatomist, absorbing his knowledge of the cultured world beyond England, the educated world.

From those conversations a plan took shape in Job's head to get Ivy out of St. Giles, to get her out of London, for that matter.

It seemed so far-fetched that he'd been, until now, reticent to even share it with the anatomist.

A woman in London is nothing, he knows; even the moneyed are impoverished by a lack of possibility, channeled into futures within which their souls and brains are meant to atrophy, unused.

The name Mowatt, when it briefly meant something, represented more than that.

More than docilely waiting for fate to pluck you up, make a wife out of you at the expense of your name, so that you might be a wife and mother, or worst of all, a lady.

Furniture, nothing more.

Worse, of course, are the great unwashed.

Something less than furniture, something less even than the floor beneath that furniture.

A thing to be used up, spit out, forgotten.

She is the end of the bloodline, Ivy.

This is his last remaining strain of pride.

That she will be something.

That the putrid toil of his life will yield a single worthy thing.

Just as grass ultimately grows from the torn soil of a grave, a new and better reality will be birthed, an integrity resurrected.

Quinn has told him about the prospects of women elsewhere.

Of universities in Bologna, Russia, and Massachusetts that would take on the fairer sex, institutions in which they have thrived, limited only by their imagination and diligence, uncurtailed by such false gods as station and the passing fancies of modishness, society, and expectation.

How far the mind will take you if it is unfettered.

The earth itself cannot hold you, Ivy.

That I promise.

I have seen you swim in the stars.

I will give them to you, even if I must burrow away from their glittering kingdom into the dark hollow of the earth to make it so.

The problems are legion.

He can see that immediately.

The graveyard shift by itself is daunting.

The men, he can see, are not the standard beadles or dutiful parishioners.

They are not half adoze in the watchhouse, as is so often the case.

They are, despite their finery, ruffians.

With heavy hands and mirthless faces.

There are at least four of them. They take turns going out into the churchyard, circuiting the grounds, returning to the watchhouse a few minutes later.

It is as active and well manned a graveyard shift as Job has ever encountered.

Beddoe has spared no expense to ensure that his wife's grave is not desecrated, that much is clear.

He will have these men stationed here for the usual two weeks.

Until the body has properly decayed and is no longer of use to the anatomists.

Job, of course, only has this night and the next to get his own work done.

He considers the grave itself. Even without the headstone—no doubt still at the stone carver's—it is easily the most conspicuous burial in the churchyard.

Beddoe has made it so with an astonishing display of security that bespeaks some combination of devotion, paranoia, and mile-deep pockets.

Job has seen mortsafes before.

Job has seen slab-stones before.

But never in combination.

And never to this degree.

The mortsafe Beddoe has hired for the next two weeks must be the finest in the land, if such excess can be considered fine.

It cages the grave with thick wrought-iron bars that sink into the earth on all sides of the newly dug grave—no doubt all the way down to the casket, and probably beyond.

The slab-stone—also hired, everyone's found a niche in the grave-robbing game—must weigh the better part of two tons.

It sits atop the mortsafe, driving those bars deeper into the earth so that there is perhaps only six inches of space between the top of the cage and the earth.

It is a fortress.

And will be so for the next two weeks, until nature has done its job and the vendors come to take away their wares.

Lastly, there is the matter of light: the two lanterns that sit on either side of the grave, which the graveyard shifters refuel whenever they come out of the watchhouse and make their rounds.

Beddoe must really love this woman, Job thinks.

But whoever you are, friend, you are living in the past.

Celebrating a thing in decay.

For that body in the ground only benefits the worms.

Risen, she will unlock futures not yet known.

I don't expect you to understand this, for you are still human.

You have not been where I have.

You are lucky in this sense, perhaps.

But it is my hope, when you awaken the day after

tomorrow to find that body gone, you will realize it was no longer the thing you loved.

TWELVE

IVY

HER FATHER WILL be furious. It goes without question. But she cannot help herself. The night is filled with too much promise. She is in Hyde Park, it is nearly eleven o'clock, and the situation she finds herself in is entirely alien—sitting on a park bench, surrounded by the upper crust as they promenade by in the warm night, carefree, beautiful, a wealth of space around them. Best is the fact that they scarcely pay her any heed. In her finest clothes—yes, they are really her *only* clothes, though properly turned out and thrice washed—she is assiduously bathed and groomed and could almost be any one of their number, whiling away the evening in a repose without edges.

It was the mudlark—Adam—who told her to come here.

As always with him, there is a plan. It is a sort of game they play. He devises great epic undertakings—forays into the far reaches of the city, to the habitats of creatures otherwise exotic to them in St. Giles: cats'-meat men, blind fiddlers with dancing dogs, gut spinners, faytors, and faulkners. And tonight, "the nibbiest of the nobs." At least those were his words—whatever they meant!—as he seized her on the way home from the ragged school, whispering so that his sweaty, brash cohort of mudlarks would not hear.

She fancies him a sort of closet anthropologist or, better yet, a zoologist, with the city and its surrounds as a jungle, its inhabitants undiscovered species.

It is a fancy, she knows. His curiosity is an inch deep, fleeting. But how it burns. He has more potential within him than a whole city block.

What he could've been if he'd been raised in the homes of these people, she thinks, eyeing the fops and ladies as they pass.

Likewise, take him, with the waistcoat and the watch. How would he fare in the flats of the Thames, the mud sucking at his boots, his back laden with fifty pounds of rubbish?

All of it random. The dice of existence.

He'd said one more thing before he let her go that afternoon. "Tell me tonight what you want me to become, and I will be that."

There was a steadfastness in his eyes when he said it, a humility and vulnerability that had not been there before, and it unsettled her. It gave her a sense of power over another she had not previously felt in her life. A feeling of responsibility, however unreal. No doubt it was glib, a passing sentiment, as was everything he said, but still. There was something else going on beneath the beauty and pluck.

Zoologist, Adam. That is my answer.

These are her unspoken thoughts as she looks absently skyward. Here in the western reaches of the city, the haze from the factories, mills, and tanneries is nowhere to be seen, blown east by the prevailing winds that buffet the metropolis.

Perhaps that is the greatest division in the city: the West Enders get the stars, the East Enders get perpetual smoke.

The working class unfailingly complain about their meager wages, but they don't realize they're deprived of a greater bounty—wonder available with but a glance heavenward. A sense of boundlessness rather than the sort of half-understood existence they inhabit beneath the brume that acts like a lid on their perception.

She draws lines between the stars with her eyes. Doodles with the heavens. Each time it's something new—freshly birthed constellations, gods, myths. She is, for a moment, as old as time, a shaman, no less steeped in wonder and bewilderment than the first of her human forebears that looked upon this same firmament. The stars are beyond language, that's it. They evoke currents within that cannot properly be named, only felt. It takes a mystic, not a scientist, to understand them. The stars are unimpeachable companions, warm murmurs in the soul.

Lord, what it would be to live around here. In Mayfair.

And not one of them looks up, she thinks, eyeing the handsome promenade before her.

When he appears, she at first does not recognize him, mistaking him instead in half a glance for one of the well-off promenaders moving past. It is not until he deviates from the rest of the strollers and moves intently and unmistakably toward her that she realizes the man that approaches, in a new coat, fine buckskin trousers, and a grand, high-collared shirt is, almost impossibly, her mudlark.

She is so stupefied she can barely speak. He stands before her, somehow taller because of the garb, a fine box under his arm, his newly shorn hair glistening with pomade, his rogue's grin never greater.

"Witness the frisk," he says, presenting himself proudly.

Still agog, she can manage little more than a few syllables of chuckle in return.

"And if I look an eejit," he says, leaning in with a knowing smile, "have mercy and don't tell me just yet."

He presents her with the box. A gift.

"Open it."

She considers the box, looks to him briefly, then undoes the bow. Within, a pair of pumps made of soft kid, trimmed with a rosebud, a pair of long silk gloves, and a shawl, which he nods toward proudly. "Made up in Paisley. Reversible."

It's said in such a way that it's clear he's regurgitating what a shopkeeper told him.

"Where'd you get this?"

He shrugs. "Shoes were from up on Cornhill—"

"I mean the money."

"It was a good day today."

She gives him a look.

"What can I say? After I saw you this morning, me and the lads went upriver to have a poke around the Isle of Dogs. The India docks were a madhouse what with all the recent traffic and spring tides. Hundred fifty ships got turned around just this last week, they were saying. Most ever. Everything was in the flats. All their rubbish. Dingables. What the sailors didn't want now that they was home. What the lightermen dropped by accident. Just the usual big mess that's left behind, but five times as much. And 'cause of them spring tides, it was all just laid out in the mud for the industrious fellow to set upon.

"You should've seen how many of us there were! People come off the banks, trudging and sloshing everywhere—couldn't tell one from the other with all the mud. Just a bunch of mud people digging for treasure. And I'm right there with them. Just a nobody mud person. But guess who was the one that landed the treasure? Sure, they all got something, everybody got something, there's always something if you're persistent. But I didn't get *something*. I got the *one thing*. At least on this day.

"I get my hands on a box. It's out there toward the middle of the river, so there's still some flow there, and the mud's worse, so people are busying themselves with the easy pickings nearer shore. But me, I'm seeing that wood box, maybe as high as my knee, sticking out of the mud, and something just says I got to go. So I trudge out there, and it's heavy and sealed, and something's shifting around inside, and I know I got something. Not rubbish. Something dropped and not meant to be in the river. Which means the sky's the limit. So I get it away up onto the bank, which about nearly kills me, with all the mud and river water trying to suck me under with that big muddy box on my back."

He nods to the gift box in her hand. "Something about a box. Turns the world wherever you are, whatever day it is, into Christmas, doesn't it? Suddenly you got a mystery before you, and it could be anything. Anything. You might be a king after you open it, might be the same old ninny." In this moment she understands for the first time her puzzling attraction to him. Yes, he is beautiful, but it's more that he and she, shackled by the hardship of class, know and embrace, for better or worse, the maddening resilience required to hope. To endeavor daily in earnest, as if your efforts will yield something other than a return trip to the same chaff mattress that night.

Yes, Adam, we are persistent.

But we are waiting for fate, one time, to smile upon us.

All of it random. The dice of existence.

"So I open up that box, and all the packing linens are soaked and muddy, as they should be. I push 'em aside, and there's my prize: dishes. *Dishes*. I'm properly bobbed, right?

Dead cargo. Completely dead. It's gonna earn me something, but not what I'd hoped. So come lunch, tide's changing, and I do my rounds. Take my lot of rags for the day up to the rag shop, bones to the bone boilers, and the dishes, I take up to a thimblecrib I know—good man, usually takes the metals off me, silverwares I find, but he'll also take plates and cups and such. I'm hoping I'm lucky and pull a few shillings for the lot. But his eyes get real big when he sees it, and I know right then I've got something. Turns out it's *Imari* porcelain."

He gives her a presumptive look, as if it should be as clear as the nose on her face how significant this is. She knows that once again he is regurgitating someone else's words, pretending that his worldly understanding of Imari porcelain somehow predates the meeting he'd had with the thimblecrib earlier that day.

"He figures it's two hundred years old, and a complete set at that. Being a round-dealing man, he says he can't with good conscience give me less than *twenty quid*." He looks at her expectantly.

Ivy feels herself flush. It is a lot of money. A windfall. He is nothing if not a good storyteller. Whether it's true is another matter; it's just as possible he and his cohort of mudlarks had taken a crow to the door of a warehouse somewhere and liberated its wares, something oft rumored among the girls she walks with. They will make their due one way or another, whether it be in the flats in the morning or the warehouses at night.

But tonight, everything conspires to tilt her toward positivity: the stars promiscuous above, the foreign but sweet caress of the cashmere shawl she's absently put round her neck as he's told his tale, and most of all him, this flawed godling that stands before her, fully intent upon her, whose story suggests that either there is providence, however small—that the universe does sometimes smile upon the abject—or that, in covering for a more objectionable crime, he has conjured a story with such aplomb (Imari!) that it betokens a deeper talent and imagination than even she thought him capable of possessing.

She considers the pumps, his jacket, his haircut. "You've gone and spent it all on us, have you?"

"God, no. Woe be the eejit who spends all his money on *things*. We, angel, are going to live."

Before she knows it, they are on the wide sidewalks of Pall Mall, their shadows orbiting them as they pass first one gaslight, then the next. Gaslights! Carving civility out of the night! So this is how the night can be, cleansed of shadow, free from the fearful unknowns lurking therein.

Adam's hand is in his front pocket, her gloved hand resting lightly in the crook of his elbow.

"Look at us," he whispers, "*promenading*."

It is all absurd, too rigid and peacockish by a mile for either of them, but how wonderful that absurdity! If only for a night!

There are few others around them at this hour, in part because the quality that inhabit the mansions and town houses of this street have repaired to the coasts or, now that the season is turning, their country houses for grouse shooting and foxhunting. Only the occasional passing carriage or couple suggests that this spit-shined paradise in the center of London is not completely abandoned. Which is not lost upon Adam, who laments, predictably, that there is this entire, empty tract of city, the massive residences of which could hold a hundred people each. He is lapsing into revolution-speak again, she thinks, the reheated, failed arguments of the Blanketeers and the Luddites and the Cato Street Conspiracy. The kind of thing that got a great many of them shot.

"The privies alone," he says, marveling at the mansions.

"I beg your pardon?"

"Oh, my apologies," he says, catching himself, remembering his role. "My lady."

Which elicits a smile from her. This boy. This blessed boy. After a moment, once they've passed another couple—with complete success, they are spies of the highest order—she whispers back, game, "What about the privies?"

"Forget I ever mentioned it. It slipped my mind I'm a gentleman."

She looks at him flatly.

He shrugs, philosophical. "Well . . . they're magical, if you give it a proper think. For the rich, I mean. A porcelain throne. You do your duty, flip a lever, and it goes away forever. *Forever*. Doesn't just sit out there in the dung heap looking back at you. Or in the cesspool stinging your brain with its stink."

"That's why you want to have a revolution. So people can have proper water closets."

He meets her gaze, and in that moment she knows without question that he knows he's full of more shit than all the cesspools in London.

"It's as good a reason as any," he says with a knowing smile.

He finds the place he's looking for. A few blocks down, they step off the sidewalk before one of the mansions—darkened, its owners apparently gone like the rest—and approach an unassuming door along the side. Painted on the brick above the door, a small but elegant rose, the size of a woman's fist.

"What is this?" Ivy asks.

"Where the nibs do their nobbing and the nobs do their nibbing." He opens the door, revealing a long, narrow side yard stretching away from the street, lit only by a few intermittent candles.

"You are now *Lady* Ivy. From somewhere far off. Dorchester. Both of us. And this one," he says, aiming a thumb at himself, "is Lord Adam Hadthwaite."

Which sparks a realization in her. "Is that your real last name?"

He looks at her, some of the mirth in his face giving way to dispassion. "Wouldn't know my real last name if you told it to me."

And with that, they're through the door and moving along the dim passageway. The mansion proves not to be a mansion at all, but another thing entirely.

Disembodied laughter caroms toward them from a well-lighted quadrangle ahead. Tavern rooms become visible, framing the space on all sides. People spill out of them; they are beautiful and loud, their collective laughter a thing in its own right, a massive invisible beast, ecstatic, aggressive, and unrestrained.

The rich at play.

"The thimblecrib put me on to it," Adam says, looking on at the reverie with a curious mixture of excitement and revulsion. "Cock-and-hen club of the highest order. It's how the other half live, darling. It's how the half of the half of the half of the half of *that* half live. The ones the angels gave birth to. Or at least shat out."

The patrons, on the midnight side of an evening drinking binge, pay the two newcomers little heed. To them, it seems, Ivy and Adam are merely the latest of the well-dressed that would descend on this place, bestowed with the selective knowledge of a darkened door with a rose above, beyond whose inscrutable veneer lay this raucous redoubt.

The great stiffness of the upper class—that exclusive front Ivy has always seen whenever in the presence of the moneyed, as recently as the studied propriety of the Hyde Park promenaders earlier that evening—is nowhere in evidence here. People roar with laughter, argue. Men grab women, women grab men, and all of it, indeed, is *loud*. Nowhere is the phenomenal din met with a "Cheese it!" from a high window, or threats of violence, or visits from the night watchman. They are free to bellow and sing, cackle and howl. As if they are on an island far from the moderating forces of civilization and no one can censure them.

So, too, does it seem the convention of personal space has broken down—a thing she once considered a hallmark of the upper class. Till now it seemed beneath them to be among a crowd, to be intruded upon. Rather, to be rich was to be *landed* in a more hermetic sense—the greatest property one owned was not the soil beneath one's feet but the space that afforded, the space around one's self, the space to be free, unperturbed by the chaos of the world, untouchable to violence and pestilence, an untarnished being. Here, arms are around shoulders, around waists, lips to necks, fingertips to lips. They are sweaty in the collective heat. A beautiful tangle of bodies.

Ivy can scarcely take it in. Adam nods to her, cognizant

of the fact that while they have entered successfully, anonymously, to continue to stand as they do now surveying the place with doe eyes will only flag them as outsiders. "How about we get a couple brandies and join in?"

Ivy nods absently, for above all what she feels is a strange sense of guilt—yes, she is a trespasser here, an interloper—but the sin seems somehow deeper, inculcated into her on a more primal level, such as a domesticated animal might feel on the doorstep of its master. As if it is one thing for said creature to walk, equal to that master, under the communal light of the sun, but another thing entirely to drag one's muddy paws across his unprofaned floors and befoul his personal space.

And yet, with Adam's coaxing and the numbing promise of a brandy, she moves her paws. Moments later, she is upon the master's floors.

The brandy flows, and the night with it.

An uninterrupted stream of cricketers, actresses, intellectuals, and rakes wash through her vision and conversation.

Adam has them talking to people with titles.

Nobility.

Though none of them seem any the wiser that the pair before them are imposters.

They are either too drunk or simply cannot conceive of such creatures as the great unwashed in finery equal to their own, slum dwellers with audacity.

They only see what is before them—a couple as striking as any here, as hale, as outwardly refined.

These, it seems, are the only criteria.

For they hardly seem to listen.

Rather, it seems that the game played here is one of seeking out the most estimable company at the affair, then talking *at* them.

No sooner have Ivy and Adam presented themselves—Lady this and Lord that, Adam keeps changing the names—than their fellow magpies take the reins of the conversation and steer it invariably toward themselves, toward the fascinating number of grouse they bagged on their hunt, the two-hundred-seat chapel whose construction they humbly financed in the name of the Good Lord, their seat at the coronation (one could have practically reached out and touched the queen consort), their critique of the latest offering at the opera, the mysterious tracts on the far reaches of their summer estates (it takes one a half day to walk across, you know, and then one is utterly done in and not at all interested in exploring dark forests, and moreover, if one doesn't head back, one is likely to miss supper, so it's a bit of a conundrum, isn't it, owning an estate one simply hasn't the time to explore?).

Gasbaggery, all of it!

But at the same time, at least initially, a welcome reprieve!

Ivy was so anxious over the prospect of being discovered that she drank her first brandy in a single go, something she'd never done before.

And it was wonderful.

Just to sit there, brain marinated in liquor.

Listening.

With no interest, unlike the people around her, in proving anything at all.

And instead being, alongside Adam, exactly what these people seemed to want above all else tonight—a beautiful sounding board.

The men prominently display their watch fobs and bring quizzing glasses to their eyes whenever the appearance of consideration is required, though they are both much too young and drunk for such optics to have any use.

The women appear to be living, breathing versions of the porcelain figures she's seen in shop windows—skin impossibly milky and smooth, uncheapened by the sun. There is nary a freckle in this place; such imperfections, which would suggest toil—the necessity of toil—are no doubt chased away with Gowland's Lotion, buried beneath studiously applied powder and vegetable rouge. The effect is unsettling. They are beautiful, yes, but somehow unreal. Museum pieces.

The greater dissonance lies in their behavior. These objets d'art are loud with booze and, despite their finished accents, as crass as any of the hedge whores up on Drury Lane.

Ivy finds comfort in that. You add liquor to someone, and the edifice comes down. We are all one in how we slur and swear and make a horse's ass of ourselves, aren't we? Rich and poor alike, infantile at our core, pulling on our wares, becoming our wares, believing the whole presentation. But with booze the presentation falters, the pretensions that have taken so long to polish, all the years of vainglory and studiously insecure self-obsession begin to come undone by the first glass of claret and are destroyed by the second.

Ivy is no different. When prompted, despite all efforts to maintain the front of sophistication—to be the dress that she wears—she lapses into their cluckery, swearing right alongside them, gossiping, sizing them up, giving false praise about their dresses, tresses, bangles. Such artifice would otherwise sicken her, but tonight the novelty is so great, the wild energy in the air so infectious (I am among the well feathered and purse-proud! And they are as shallow as the rest of us!) that she surrenders to it. It is a game, a lark, a privilege, and for a few hours at least, the broken world outside does not exist. The ever-present, invisible sense of foreboding that permeates the streets of the Holy Land is, if only for tonight, a curse for others. And for that she is grateful.

A moment comes. It is fleeting, between conversations, when the latest couple merrily pardon themselves and the round-robin resumes—a sort of great, jumbled dance—everyone searching anew for virgin marks they've not yet regaled with the same stories. Ivy and Adam are briefly alone.

"I've never seen anything like this in my life," she says.

"That was the idea."

"Even so. The amount of money. You could've put it toward better things—better certainly than impressing a Holy Land mot like me."

"Wasn't trying to impress you. Just wanted to show you the highest of the high." He looks at her briefly. His eyes, glistening with liquor, are radiant with the light of a nearby lantern. "And for you to see that you are a higher thing still."

Dinner comes.

It is long past midnight, but out come beef, venison, turtle, eel pie.

People repair to tables, and soon the linens are soiled with claret, dishes are broken, and the laughter is so loud that conversation beyond the person beside you is almost impossible.

Then there is a tinkling of glasses, someone calling for a toast.

Ivy looks up to see one of the eldest attendees rising to his feet at the far end of the table. The man, in a sash, epaulettes, and brittle gray mustachios, seems a thing from engravings—a relic of the British wars of long ago. He must be nearly eighty. Adam relays to Ivy what he's just gleaned from the person sitting on the other side of him. The man's apparently a general of some renown, a widower too old and infirm now to leave the city as most of the rich do, and as such is known to occasionally haunt cock-and-hen clubs like this one—even if he is at least forty years everyone's senior—if only to have someone to talk to.

The din of the place settles enough that the general's voice can be heard.

"A toast," he says, raising his glass.

Ivy and Adam, along with the rest of the room, dutifully raise their own.

"To rape, riot, and revolution," the general says.

Which elicits chuckles from the group and an amazed gasp from Ivy. She nearly spits up the claret with which she's been numbing her tongue.

The general continues, his voice as elegant a vessel for words as Ivy has ever heard. But what words!

May prostitution flourish, may virginity cease.
May son-of-a-bitch become a household word.
Bees do it and die, birds do it and fly.
Dogs do it and stick to it, so why can't you and I?

By the time he is finished, the room is filled with so much laughter and exhortation Ivy can scarcely believe it.

Before the guffaws and shrieks have even subsided, another man is standing—as dignified and ranking a swell as one could imagine—his glass already in the air, his countenance as demure as a priest's. His toast is delivered as if it is a liturgy.

When the frost is on the pumpkin, that's the time for
dickey-dunkin'.
But when the weather's hot and sticky, that's the time for
dunkin' dickey.
May bloody piles possess you, may corns adorn your feet.
May crabs the size of lobsters sit on your balls and eat.
And when you're old and gray and in a syphilitic wreck.
May you fall right through your arsehole and break your
feckin' neck!

The place erupts, the air filled with hoots and cackles colliding, with every manner of chortling, chuckling, and tittering. Like a forest full of songbirds, Ivy can't help but think. Mad songbirds.

At once she can feel the pull of the collective mirth and a sort of queasiness as well. Yes, we are all one, she thinks, beautiful when unshackled from the affect of class, free to be a fool—to be authentic in one's imperfection and as such a member of the human race—but these are the people that we would let lead us? This is the top of the heap? Maybe she understands Adam all the better now, his angry—if ultimately feckless—calls for an uprising from the unwashed, which until now she has dismissed as the frustrated diatribes of a boy facing the very likely prospect of making his living in the sewage- and filth-ridden flats of the Thames for the rest of his life.

Could it be that a mudlark might see a better way forward for England than the monarchists, the landed, the educated?

Could it be that these people have not known struggle and are in a sense more deprived than any of us in the Holy Land?

Lord, how terrible to have everything!

To have beauty and station and wealth and endless mirth.

How the dimension must fall from your life!

Moving from pleasure to pleasure, to know nothing but.

Hence this. Everyone in a perpetual reach for more. They are beautiful, yes, but they are just as truly five- and six-bottle men as the tosspots up in the Holy Land. They have had so much pleasure they cannot be fulfilled.

Such people are broken and cannot lead us.

She has much to tell Adam now, once they are free of this place, how until now she has judged him from her bookish knowledge, how she's looked down on him because—mistaking this knowledge for wisdom—she's assumed an unlearned individual such as himself, no matter how passionate, cannot have appreciable insight into the world.

All these thoughts, telescoped inside the peals of laughter around her, a whole universe of illumination—and shame—inside a few scant seconds.

Yes. She just wants to leave. With Adam. Throw herself at his feet and admit these things that he probably doesn't even know, or care to.

How great it will be to breathe the soot of the tanneries, smell the stink of the Thames at low tide. To leave the cocks and hens and their hunger and never look back.

And yet.

Beside her, as if in a dream, while the rest of the patrons compose themselves, take their seats, Adam rises. He clinks his glass with his spoon. He is the only person standing in the whole place.

And for a moment, she thinks she has never seen him look so heroic. He scans the crowd, this mudlark.

A more fully perfect human than any of them. Unafraid.

Here, then, they shall know his defiance. The revolutionary will speak.

But this is what comes out.

To Honor.
I offered my honor.
She honored my offer.
All night long.

He stretches this last bit out suggestively, lays his hand on Ivy's shoulder for all to see. Knowing oohs and aahs rise from the crowd. Almost instantly, the color drains from Ivy's face.

I was Honor and off her.
Here's to
Spying Honor,
Getting Honor,
Staying Honor.

By now Ivy, scarcely able to breathe, feels as if an icy dagger has been driven through her chest. The place has broken out into such bawdy cheers that Adam must nearly shout his finish.

If you can't leave your seed in her,
Leave your seed HONOR!

The room explodes. People roaring, rising to their feet,

madly applauding. A man reaches over the top of Ivy, claps Adam on the shoulder.

For a moment Adam is the center of their universe. All eyes on them.

He stands there beaming, drinking up their adulation, as proud as Ivy has ever seen him.

She finds herself out in the street before she knows it.

For a moment she is alone beneath the gas lamps.

Though she'd attempted to make her departure in a measured fashion, waiting a good ten minutes after Adam's speech before pardoning her way out quietly as still more bawdy toasts were being delivered, she no doubt caused a scene—a thing she has been brought up from childhood to understand is beneath a woman—or a man, for that matter. Still. It was worth it. To be away from that horrid sound of laughter.

In short order, Adam appears.

He is drunk. They are both drunk.

This will not go smoothly, she thinks.

Rather than causing yet another scene, she opts to move away up the sidewalk. Back to Hyde Park, from where she can properly navigate her way back to the Holy Land. It is not the most direct route home, but given how lost she was in the promise of the evening as they walked here, it will be a minor miracle if she can retrace the path they originally took from the park.

"Stop," says Adam.

She does not.

"Quit carrying the keg, will ye? It was a black joke, that's all."

Even so she does not stop.

He follows her, still trailing the adolescent glee of the place as he does. "You know I'm just good and shitten. We're all just shitten, every one of us in that place, good and shittenly, even you."

She does not want to argue. Knows full well that liquor is an accelerant when it comes to matters of the tongue. Better to be silent than to ignite an inferno.

But Adam is not one for silence, for being ignored. He seizes her arm a half block up the street, turns her around to face him. He instinctively summons all of his profuse charm, unfurls that beautiful, insouciant smile.

"Come, let's do something else," he says. "I'm sorry."

But all she can see in that smile are the streaks of claret that give his teeth and gums the appearance of rot.

"I'd like to go home," she says, pulling herself free.

For a short while, it is almost comedy. Ivy attempting to navigate her way back through the unfamiliar neighborhoods while Adam—who she is desperately trying to ignore—trails behind, intermittently calling out to her which way she should turn so as not to get lost.

He is playing the long game, she knows. Allowing her the requisite space, despite the fact that he could catch up to her with scarcely any effort. Instead, he dutifully remains a good fifty feet behind, calling out directions when it is necessary, but otherwise remaining largely silent.

He is trying to wear her out. She cannot decide if this is

the tack of a conscientious and astute lover or that of a patient predator aware that its surpassing endurance will ultimately win out over that of its prey.

The kid pumps he's bought for her do not help in this regard; they are not made for treks like this. Already she can feel the hot sting of blisters developing atop her toes, ringing her heels. Still, she is resolute and continues onward.

Before long, they are in familiar territory. The smell of the Thames is upon her, and with it comes the welcome sight of recognizable buildings and streets. She knows her way home now.

With this realization comes a sense of relief. Yes, until now she has felt herself trapped in a sense, prey in a sense. Panicked.

But she is free now. Not beholden to him or constrained by the city.

She turns to face him, passion subsiding. She can make it home. She *will* be home. Soon. Then she will be able to sort all of this out in her head once she has had a proper sleep. It may be that she'll decide that she overreacted, that she invested too much in a boy that is, at the end of this and every day, a mudlark, and so the real fault lay not with him and his actions but rather in the unrealistic expectations she'd foisted upon him.

"Thank you," she says. It comes out terse, though this is not the intent, and immediately arrests the smile developing on his face. That smile, so cocksure, so certain his quarry, in stopping and turning to face him, had finally acquiesced. And then this—this cold, unctuous phrase accompanied by eyes that broker no emotion whatsoever.

A look of betrayal crosses his face. "Thank you," he says, not so much in return, but rather in a way that suggests he is weighing the two words, weighing what they mean and what they are worth in this moment to him.

If the sum of the evening, and all he has done, is worth a trifling thank you.

"So you're going, then," he says, considering the ground rather than her. The frustration in him is palpable.

She feels strangely removed from herself. Whether it is the claret or something else, there are impulses within her that are at once implicitly hers and also those of someone else she is bearing witness to, someone more frank, someone who would cut to the heart of things because to shade it in any manner would be dishonest.

"Yes, I'm going," she says. "You gave me an evening I'll never forget."

"You don't plan to see me again, do you?"

"I don't know."

He absorbs this. Petulance there. A child silently recoiling. The man of strength and charisma, suddenly reduced.

"Because I got shittenly. And made a few fat culls laugh."

"No," she says—and here is where that parallel impulse in her, that spirit-fueled candor—takes the reins, despite a nagging awareness somewhere deep within her that less should be said here, not more. "I'm leaving because I misjudged you."

With that, she tries to take leave of him, but once again he stops her. "Misjudged me how?"

She considers.

"I thought you were something that you are not."

"And that is?"

"All your talk of revolution. That was just swagger and vapor, wasn't it?"

"How so?"

"You were never happier than you were with them. When they accepted you as one of them. You would do anything to get them to slap you on the back. Even call me a whore."

He eyes her unsteadily in the darkness.

"I don't mind that," she says coolly. "They like their whores. But hypocrisy is a different thing entirely. Good luck to you, Adam."

She pulls her arm from his grip, which is surprisingly light, as if he has been enervated by her words. She offers him a wan smile because she doesn't know what else to offer him, then heads up the path along the Thames.

She walks and does not look back.

She hears only the scuffs of her pumps on the paving stones, her heartbeat in her ears.

Part of her is sorry for him, though she knows she is right.

She will keep walking, and she will return to her father and take refuge in his simplicity, his earnestness, his utter lack of need for society and its approbation.

Yes. Less. Not more. Society is a lie. Family is not.

Nor is the sky.

The stars, she thinks, as she once again casts an eye heavenward, do not perform. Their majesty is true, for and of itself.

Humble companions. The best sort.

Then the sounds come behind her.

Footfalls. Someone coming on fast. Adam.

Before she knows it, he rams both his palms into her back, driving the wind from her. Her blistered, tired feet lose purchase on the path, and suddenly she is falling, tumbling helplessly down the riverbank toward the mud.

The next thing she knows, she is a few inches deep in the shallows. Her left foot cold—one of the pumps lost in the fall. The chill of the river seeping in through her dress. She is lying on her side in the mud, and the world around her is a dizzying spiral of shadow and starlight.

Adam quickly descends the bank, sloshes across the shallows to her. She tries to get up, but he pushes her back down. She can feel the mud ooze into her hair, and a many-sided nausea washes through her stomach and limbs.

"I gave a whole year's wages for you. You cracking shit fire!"

He waits momentarily for her to respond. But she cannot. The nausea and shock overwhelm her. She tries to find words, but instead the whole of her threatens to shatter into tears, and it takes all her strength to prevent this from happening.

"Give me what I gave you," he says, pulling at her. At the shawl, the gloves.

She tries to ward his hand away, but all she feels is the cold of the mud, the cold of the dirty river water. All she sees through tear-fogged eyes are dancing streaks of light—the stars high above, fractal, attenuated, interrupted only by this angry, dark form that looms over her, pulling at her, shaking her.

"Give me what's mine," the form hisses again.

He is on her now, and the sweetness of the claret on his breath clashes with the stink of the mud around them. It is not just the shawl and gloves now but her dress, which tears as he yanks at it and pulls her hips from the mud. Again she tries to fight him away inside of that star-streaked madness, but her hands are no match for his. Those hands—monstrous things that take what they want, no longer interested in nuance, but only in taking.

The world reduces, simple indeed.

There is darkness and light, misshapen stars bearing witness to this commotion that spasms madly, anonymously, in a place that no one in this sleeping city would think to look.

Except a mudlark. For whom this is home.

She tries to focus on the stars. The stars. Their perfect, innocent whiteness, even if it is stretched gossamer and near to breaking by the pain.

Then he is on top of her completely, and the stars are no more.

THIRTEEN

JOB

JOB HAS WALKED for miles.

Aimless in direction, if not in intent.

For it is not the streets of London he treads but instead the imagined spaces of St. Mary's churchyard.

It is ghostly and gigantic in his head.

He wanders through its grounds, tiny, anonymous, invisible, trying to pinpoint a weakness in the graveyard shift's scheme.

Speed, silence, and secrecy will not be enough, he knows.

Nor will, he suspects, the next arrow in a resurrectionist's quiver: bribery.

For no way are his pockets as deep as Beddoe's.

How then to circumvent two thousand pounds of slabstone?

And the thickest wrought-iron mortsafe he has ever seen?

All the while not arousing the ever-vigilant eyes of the thugs?

In some ways it is titillating, like a game or puzzle that must be solved.

And yet if it is not solved, perfectly, it will be an exercise in self-slaughter.

He wonders briefly, as he nears home, if the wisest solution is simply to say no.

But where will that leave Quinn?

The anatomist would not have enough time to secure another resurrectionist, certainly not one as adept as Job.

And that's part of the problem, isn't it?

The esteem you are held in.

The esteem you have for yourself.

You would not be bested by any assignment.

You refuse to be.

There is always a way.

Pride before the fall, Job.

Pride before the fall.

It will take another.

At least one more.

Someone long on skill or short on wisdom, given the challenge.

The only one he can think of is the boy, the freshman anatomist—Cager.

These are the thoughts he thinks as he enters his house.

They are the last thoughts he has on the matter.

His daughter is here.

He hears her before seeing her.

Her breaths abrade the darkness of the cellar, weak in volume but strong in pain.

He puts on a lantern.

His throat constricts at the sight of her.

She lies on the bed, misshapen, streaked with mud and blood, eyes swollen and half lidded.

Her gaze seeks purchase but finds none; she is somewhere between this world and another.

He sets upon her, cradles her, asks her what happened.

She provides no answer, just gazes impassively into her half-world.

For the briefest of moments, it is as if the ground has opened up and he is falling, the order of creation shattered.

He must do something or he will fall forever.

Instinctively he goes to the barrel.

There is still water there.

He finds a rag, begins cleaning her, whispering to her all the while.

"We will get this off you," he says. "We will get this off you."

Her clothes, foreign—finery beyond anything he knows or could afford, and yet torn, bloody.

They are part of the story, he knows, and so he removes them, undressing his daughter until she is in her familiar undergarments and not this horrid, unfamiliar visage he has stumbled upon.

His hands tremble.

He has trafficked in mud and blood his whole life.

But it is another thing entirely to squeeze a rag and have the living blood of your daughter run through your fingers.

This is what it is to die, he thinks as he wipes the dried blood from her lips, her nose, revealing once pristine, now purple flesh beneath.

Hell is not oblivion, but this, he thinks, as he patiently rinses the river muck from her hair.

Truly there is no greater agony than that of the parent in the presence of a child in a pain that cannot be solaced, cannot be undone.

A parent that would take on that pain a thousandfold themselves if it would but release the child.

But there is no bargain to be had here.

Though that is Job's prayer right now.

God, let her be free of this.

Give it to me.

I will carry it.

For all the days of my life, if you would but let her rest easy tonight and be back to what she was before the sun set.

But such deliverance does not come.

His daughter moans and stares into infinity.

He will clean her all night if that is what it takes.

Until this is gone from her.

And she is back to what she was.

He holds vigil over her once he is finished cleaning her.

He keeps her hand between his and whispers stories into her ear, about how she used to be, about how he used to be, about when she used to be small enough to pick up, about the words she used to mispronounce.

He finds himself smiling all the while.

It is less that the memories are sweet, though they are, but more that in not knowing how or if she will recover, he wants to fill her remaining time with warmth, with smiles, even if she cannot see them.

Because she can hear them.

The way a smile carves the sharp edges off words and renders them soothing.

He knows she is listening.

Because her hand, weakly, pulses in his.

By first light she is capable of speaking.

From those swollen, split lips come a weak, staccato account of the evening.

Mostly he is glad she is back, that her focus has returned to things in the cellar, to him.

She will be sore for a long time and perhaps scarred in places.

But she is back.

She cries, apologizes for her intransigence.

Which is, of course, nonsense.

Your transgression is tiny, he thinks, and to any realistic person expected.

Youth strains at the bridle, or it is not youth.

But he, the one who did this . . .

She has told Job everything.

About the surreal night at the cock-and-hen club.

About the mudlark.

She has told him his name.

When she finally sleeps a sleep that is not tattered and restless, he takes leave of her.

The sun is a different sort of thing this morning as he sits in the courtyard, contemplating.

Redder, more intent.

He is thinking about the Thames, that it is not far from here.

Surely the mudlark is there, to be found with a little industry.

This despite the facts that he has not solved the conundrum of St. Mary's churchyard and that it must be solved by tonight.

It is the wrong time for anger, he knows.

It is always the wrong time for anger.

But anger chooses its own appointments.

The where and when of fury.

The boy is found, without too much work, on the far side of the Thames in the shantytown just upriver.

It's high tide, so there is no work for him in the flats.

Instead he idles in his shanty, working up a pile of snuff on a foraged table.

He is so consumed with working the carotte against the snuff-rasp, building a growing pile beneath it, that he fails to notice Job standing in his doorway.

Job clears his throat.

The boy squints up at him, gives him an inconsequential look.

Then goes back about his snuff.

"What," he says flatly.

"You're Adam," Job says.

The boy nods, considers Job again, the look on his face this time indicating that he senses this visitor hasn't come upon him by chance, for trivial reasons.

Job can see the boy quickly inventorying a list of past transgressions, spats, tangles, and slights in his head, as if trying to determine from which this visit might be born.

He is made of guilt, this one, there can be no doubt—his misdeeds so manifold he cannot tell them apart.

Job would pity him save for the one misdeed that cannot be forgiven.

He approaches the boy, and the boy knows his intent immediately.

"You come for me, I'll split you," the boy says.

He stands.

There is a knife in his hand.

"What's this about?" he grunts.

Job rounds the table, silent.

The boy will get no answers, only comeuppance.

Not justice, because there is no justice.

Just a share of the pain.

A larger slice than the rest, because he has earned it.

What he has given, he will get.

And he will get it again.

And again.

Until Job has no pain left to give.

Job knows the boy is stronger than him but afraid, rotating the knife too much, flashing it too much, relying on it too much.

Suddenly he is calling out to his mates down the embankment—more mudlarks, more youths like him, arrogant with freedom, unconstrained, powerful in their number like a pack of wild dogs.

"Got a peck of troubles, lads!"

The boys, roused from their midday idyll, squint up into the sun, up into the shadows of the shanties from whence the boy calls, and Job knows they are confused, if only momentarily, by this sudden disembodied outburst.

"Best run back off to the Holy Land, if you're who I think you are," the boy warns. "You do anything to me, they'll come for you. And your daughter."

Job moves for him.

Everything becomes hot, half blind, primal.

There is no longer thought, no longer sense of time or sequence.

Rather, everything happens at once, an overwhelm of violence, of blood, of flesh tearing and teeth breaking.

Everything is noise and pain.

Job, in this moment, a vessel of ruin.

The boy beneath him screams, thrashing wildly up at Job, his mouth shattered, his blood choking him.

Job knows the other mudlarks are coming—struggling their way up the steep embankment.

He should run.

But he is not finished here—he is not yet again Job.

He moves to strike the boy again, as if one more will finally exhaust the pain in him and absolve his daughter of hers.

And in that moment, the boy's last-gasp flailing knife strikes true.

Job feels it in his gut.

He recoils, blood spilling from him quickly.

And the pack of dogs is nearly up the hill.

He gets to his feet.

The boy is done.

Rolled over and curled fetal, crying, his own blood pooling on the floor of the shanty.

He will live, but he will be a different thing for it.

Job does not think beyond this.

He runs.

Up the bank, through the trees, and quickly into the streets.

He does not look back.

Surely the dogs are back there somewhere.

Surely.

But they do not come, though they would be faster than him, old and broken as he is.

Some blocks later, he ducks back from view behind a building, scans the streets behind him.

No, they are gone.

Perhaps the shock of finding their comrade was enough to hold them up.

It could be any number of things.

But they're not here—that's the important thing.

He clutches at his belly instinctively, if only to hide the blood from the passersby in the street.

When they are clear, he looks to his wound.

What he sees is not good.

FOURTEEN

CAGER

CAGER HAS SCARCELY been in London a month, and the things he has seen.

From corpses to classrooms to the inner sanctums of the rich, in those short thirty days, whole new horizons have availed themselves to him—horizons that a few scant months before, as a naive country joskin in Lancashire, he had no idea existed.

That's the thing about the world, he is learning. The horizon is not a singular thing, a *there*, but instead a wavering promise beyond which lies infinite horizons, each circumscribing a world of heretofore unknown possibilities and truths. They come upon you like a sequence of waves, each original, each enthralling. One need merely sally forth and let the waves wash over him. Edify him. Nourish him. Expand them. In motion is discovery.

What lies before him now is as titillating, confounding, and mortifying as anything he has seen: the rookeries of the Holy Land, the tangle of alleys named for St. Giles, patron saint of beggars.

The resurrectionist has summoned him here.

Earlier in the day, Cager had stopped in at the Fortune of War, as was his wont now, eager to soak up as much of the culture as he could, to learn and, of course, scrape up a few shillings if the opportunity arose. He was told the resurrectionist had been there an hour before, asking for Cager explicitly. Cager was to come find the old man. There was an opportunity. A significant one.

The Holy Land astonishes him in a way the rest of London does not. Upon first arriving in the city, the traffic and crowds took his breath away, but those outer boroughs have nothing on the crush of humanity that is St. Giles. There is no space here. Hogs and dogs vie for ground space with every manner of shagbag and pickaroon; the wails of newborns compete with the nonsense spewed by drunkards spilling out of noonday flash-houses. Everywhere is the scourge of cheap, readily available gin, opiate of the poor—dram shops and chemist shops and strong water shops all selling the genever for a shilling to ten-year-olds and old men alike for takeaway or to drink standing up. Everywhere are whores and coiners and fences offering stolen silk handkerchiefs.

Good Lord, the world. Trying to numb and distract itself from the crushing flood that is modern life.

But where else, he supposes, would a sack-em-up man live?

They stand in the doorway together. The old resurrectionist has invited him into his cellar, but curiously only partly so. His daughter, it seems, is sleeping. Her form visible farther on in the dark interior of the place, unmoving. Strange, Cager briefly thinks, given it is noon. But this is the Holy Land, and for that reason, one could imagine a whole slew of explanations for her torpor. At the same time, Job seems not to want to step outside either, to speak in the presence of the dishclout and her sizable family in the courtyard. So instead they stand here, in the shady between.

He tells Cager of Ella Beddoe and St. Mary's churchyard.

Of the sizable payout. Of all the considerable complications. He tells him frankly that none of his other collaborators are willing to take on the ordeal. That he finds himself in somewhat of a bind and must make this happen. Must find a man to second him in the effort, one who is strong and fast and bold to the point of being foolhardy. Job will pay him a princely fifteen pounds for that foolhardiness tonight. It will be required.

It is all thrilling to Cager. Perhaps most thrilling is the fact that the resurrectionist thought specifically of him, thought that he above all the rest would have the gumption to do such a thing as this. He already has a reputation! And it is perhaps that burgeoning notion of reputation—the desire to live up to it—that makes him say yes, despite all the apprehension that begins to unfurl in his head and gut at roughly the same time. No, this will not be easy, or perhaps even smart.

Job tells him it must be tonight.

Cager flushes. Surely they'll need more time than that to survey the place, make a proper plan, if it's as challenging as Job says. "Tomorrow would be better."

"I won't be here tomorrow," Job says. "I cannot be here tomorrow. Tonight, sundown, come to the alley behind this house. And if my daughter should for any reason be up and around at that point, she's not to know our intentions."

He nods. Job offers him a companionable, if weak, smile, then moves off into the dark interior of the cellar and the inert form of his daughter.

Cager dithers briefly. He has met this man all of once and yet feels bound to him, if only in a dimly understood way. Back in Thundridge, they'd gone together to a place few others humans go, and so they were members of a select, probably ignoble, breed. Job had buoyed him through his horror. Was certain where Cager was tremulous, afraid.

And yet a dynamic now suggests itself that is decidedly different. As the man ambles away into the shadows, his gait is inexact, his shoulders slightly hunched. His face had been pale, his movements gingerly. That certitude was gone. Something has changed.

FIFTEEN
BEAUCHAMP AND GRAY

BUSINESS IS LIGHT in the Fortune of War today, so much so that, given the lack of active pipes and cigars filling the air, one can see clear across the pub. It seems more spacious to Gray than she remembers. Even so, the smell of the cadavers in back seems particularly crushing today. She and Beauchamp are whiling the day away, awaiting a proper bid for their latest mark, who lies mostly ignored beside a few other corpses over by the privies.

Strange, this. Seems the more people they dispatch, the worse her reaction becomes to their stench. She wonders briefly if this is the work of God, recompense. It permeates her. Compounds the nagging physical unease her body has been experiencing these past weeks. It's getting worse too. Could it be some sort of miasma taken on from the putrid dead? Maybe so. You swim in something long enough, you can expect to get some of it on you sooner or later.

She takes in some rum—imported from Rhode Island, properly distilled and good for the constitution, unlike the infernal gin of the ill-informed masses out there—and watches Beauchamp across the way, ceaselessly regaling the publican with half-flash tales of his exploits, out-and-out lies neither man believes but the latter indulges. The rum, despite her best hopes, does not steady her. She feels the world slowly pivot every so often, careen.

Her biliousness is apparently evident enough that a kindly

looking man, one of the physicians from up at Bart's, takes pause at the sight of her.

"Are you all right, madam?"

She loves this, being called "madam." It's happened perhaps a half dozen times in her life—her second life, since she left the terraces and took up with Mal. "I'm not sure," she says.

He raises his hand to her in a way to which she is not accustomed—slowly, the backs of his fingers toward her, supplicant, in the manner one might offer a hand to a horse to sniff. A sign that no harm is meant. He wants to feel her forehead. "May I?"

She nods, at once amused by the timid civility and beggared by it.

He puts fingers to her; they are cold in comparison to her flesh. "You've a fever."

"If that's all it takes, maybe I should be a doctor up at Bart's. I could've told me that." It's supposed to be wry, but she knows almost instantly this man does not speak wry. It comes off crude, and she feels a curious pang of remorse. What is happening to her? From whence come these sensitivities?

He smiles politely as if not registering the slight, or perhaps having chosen to tactfully ignore it, and moves his attention to the rest of her. Her skin, the quality of it, seems to interest him. She considers it as he does: the swelling in her hands, the pale quality to her flesh there, interrupted only by the deep crimson that congregates in the creases of her palms.

"Do you have nausea?"

Her first instinct is to tell this man—this stranger with the temerity to come into her space uninvited and *assess* her—to piss off, turn up this nonsense, but instead she says, "Yes."

He is good, that is the problem. And the good have not looked upon her like this in a very long time.

He is also a man, which presents its own problems.

As he asks her further questions about whether she knows if she's been exposed to contaminated water or food, she becomes intensely aware that she cannot be doing this, sharing this space with this kind, bang-up-to-the-mark doctor. Beauchamp is across the pub, behind her and, for the moment, out of her line of sight with the publican, but she can feel him. The great crush of his presence, the everywhereness of him.

It will go like this. Beauchamp will materialize, invite himself to the conversation with a knightly smile, boon fellow to all, and as always, all present will be smitten. How apparently jocund and cosmopolitan a soul, this Beauchamp, even if he peddles in death and worm-ridden pestilence! He will dominate the chat, and all will go away impressed. Then, once away from the light of the world, he will properly discipline her for being a whore, as he always does, for her confounding inability to resist the temptation to solicit the attention of men.

She tells the man to go away from her, that she'd prefer her own company at just this moment.

"You're sure, madam?"

You and your "madam." Say it a thousand times more!

"I'm sure. Leave me be."

He tactfully nods, readies to leave. "Should you change your mind, come find me at St. Bart's. Randall Sims. I specialize in working with the disenfranchised. It will cost you nothing."

She nods. No longer makes eye contact with him as she's certain Beauchamp is staring her down at this very moment.

"Better we find out what that is and address it before it becomes something worse."

A moment later he is gone, pulling on his hat and stepping out into the street.

She is unsurprised when Beauchamp appears beside her. But he is not the wrathful thing she expects. Instead, he's brought two pots of beer. He puts one before her on the table and sits across from her. He's got a look in his eye. Things are afoot.

"What," she says.

He keeps his eyes locked on her, but subtly nods his head left, across the pub toward the windows. To two men there having a conversation.

"The young one, recognize him?"

She doesn't.

Beauchamp casts the briefest of glimpses back at him. "We saw him out at the knifeman's house a few nights back. With Jobber."

She drinks the beer, more than anything else relieved that her interaction with the physician seems to have gone unnoticed.

"Old toast he's talking to's been sackin' 'em up almost as long as Jobber. Buck's asking him everything he knows about St. Mary's churchyard."

"Sleeveless errand, St. Mary's," she says. It's common knowledge in the trade that St. Mary's, province of the rich, does not yield corpses, ever. Too many eyes, too tight a space, too many precautions. "Too young to know if he goes in there, he's putting his head in a noose."

This only seems to enthuse Beauchamp all the more. "He's going with Jobber."

"Jobber wouldn't do St. Mary's."

Beauchamp is positively beaming now. Briefly childlike in his enthusiasm, if childhood encompassed among its many splendors madness, butchery, opium, and drunkenness. "There's a knapped woman in there. Still crisp but going putrid fast. Quinn wants her by tonight and going to pay top iron for her."

She eyes him, dubious. "You thinking of getting into the sack-em-up business, are you?"

He gives her a look of pure disdain, raises his palms to her. "These ain't paws. Digging in the dirt's for animals."

"What scrap you working on, then?"

"You heard of Marcus Beddoe?"

She has not.

"The dead thing's his wife. And he's as plump in the pockets as they come."

SIXTEEN

BEDDOE

THERE IS BLOOD everywhere, and the men roar for it.

They have not accepted me all these years, the landed. I have come to the countryside with good intentions and open arms; I have bought the Meynalls' estate and made every effort to be neighborly. But they have shunned me as if I am something less; my money is new, they say, my manners coarse.

But I have earned my money, unlike you, whose only claim to it is that you've been suckled since birth by it.

And now you would come to my property, crowd my drawing room, and scream into my beautifully constructed cockpit as the birds fight. We are friends, suddenly. All it took was to turn my home into the site of this battle royale in which sixteen of the finest cocks in the county fight to the death.

The earl of Sefton is here, the earl of Derby, deep in their cups, foul in their tongue as they shout imploringly at their birds. On any other day, they would not even make eye contact with me. But they drink my wine, piss in my privy, let their horses begrime my driveway. I am their *friend*.

At first I sought you out, your approval. Now I just want your birds.

Each of you has bred and trained your bird as I have, for two, even three, years. Brought them up to the ideal weight of four and a half pounds so they would be at the high side of the prized middleweight class. Bigger than the other birds, but still middleweight, because that's where the money is, the prestige.

I, too, have trained my bird. Trimmed him for the fight, his tail cut into the shape of a fan, his pinions carefully manicured, each quill cut at a slant so that a lucky stroke might take out an eye. On his legs are the spurs that all the birds here are fitted with. Those spurs more than anything tell you about the swells around me. Though they are sharpened to a needle point, weapons above all else, the various birds bear versions made of steel, of silver, even one poor creature's of gold, though it is the most feminine of metals and not a thing for war.

They would be beautiful first, effective second. That is the problem with people, isn't it?

My bird wears bone. Sharpened and true against its flesh. A thing it understands intrinsically as a beast. The rest wear collars, baubles. My bird is here to kill.

And kill it does. Witness. How sixteen birds become ten. How ten become eight. How the highbrow screams when his bird goes down, as if the mortal wound that has befallen it has somehow struck the man himself.

They have never been in a fight in their lives, these men. So they do it through their birds. Those cocks are possessed of a hundredfold the courage of these swells, indomitable, the concept of retreat an unknown thing to them. They gash each other with their spurs, take each other's eyes, their feathers awash in blood. They fight to the very last moment, ruffle their hackles furiously, attack with claw and beak, even if in the next moment they drop dead. Even twitching, crossing over to death and insensate, they lash out once more. The life is out of them before the fight is.

I watch as my bird bleeds but wins. I watch as other cocks fall. I watch as my bird loses one eye, then another.

But even blind, in the end, he bests the last remaining cock, the earl of Derby's.

Then there is silence. Fifteen dead birds. And one victor.

I have made a lot of money. And I don't care a whit.

I drink with them afterward and do not try to conceal my gratification. They know who I am now, intimately. Whether they like me or not, I do not care. They will no doubt go away from here and wag tongues, they will no doubt begrudge me. But that means I have something on them. Have something of theirs. Respect, even if it is sheathed in jealousy.

They bid me empty condolence for the death of my wife, then go away in their growlers, with their legion of footmen and coachmen. I am left alone with fifty empty wine bottles and a quarter ton of manure in my drive. It has been a good day.

Until Wheeler comes to me. Infernal Wheeler, with his ever-thinking mind. His *conscience*. Forever throwing the snot and sniveling about.

He's concerned about my bird, which I've just put in the pen and given a celebratory feed that includes bonemeal, sugar, and honey. The cock eats ravenously. He's earned it.

"If I may say, my lord," he begins, fumbling ever so subtly with the designation. It's only recently that I've instructed my men to so address me, and it's clear it displeases him beyond measure, as if it is beneath him or I have somehow not earned such appellation, though he does his best to hide this fact.

But I know, I can see it in his eyes—he thinks I've somehow changed.

He nods respectfully to the cock. "The most humane way would probably be with the hatchet."

"I beg your pardon?"

"The bird, valiant as he's been—is—can't go on without sight. You have to agree."

"You care about the bird now, do you?"

"Above all else, in this case. He's of no value to you anymore and destined to an existence of permanent suffering at this point."

Blast this man. He tries for pragmatism at the expense of loyalty! He thinks of tomorrow at the expense of yesterday. Forgetting what this bird has been groomed for, what it has endured, what it has delivered! And he would think of tomorrow?

"Wheeler, sit still and cheese it for a moment. Look at the bird. Look at it properly." He does, though clearly he doesn't like having to. "Not once did that bird peck my hand. Not when I cut its feathers to the quick, not when I set it up against larger birds time and time again. Because it knew. Somehow it *knew*. That it was being guided, trained, improved. And so, after all these years, it is a champion."

"That doesn't change the fact that it's blind."

Wheeler. It was this very reason I did the same for him back in the day. Brought him up from the wharves with us. He was eager, if young, an asset that could be guided, trained, improved. He wasn't afraid to speak truth, and for it added a perspective—if naive and not fully formed—that the rest of the set didn't have.

But now he is just a nag. A worrywart. Forever the devil's

advocate. I am tired of the devil. There are some truths that don't have two sides. I tell him this.

Wheeler receives it with his usual deliberative pause. "I am who I am, my lord." And again, he fumbles with it—he hates it! "If you love that bird, it should die."

Now I am angry—not so much because I love the bird, though I do, but because I love loyalty, unquestioning loyalty, as it is embodied in the bird. I tell him this. This is what loyalty is! "Not some simpering fool who is always second-guessing me. Every once in a while, it's good to hear 'Yes, you are right.' I was right when I lifted you up from the docks, wasn't I? And maybe I'm right now to keep that glorious bird alive so that he might breed, so that he might yield more of him, creatures of perfect enthusiasm and courage you and your like cannot even conceive of. Could you fight on if your eyes were taken, Wheeler?"

The question makes him uneasy—he is trying to determine whether it's a threat. I am not quite sure myself at the moment. But I want him, as I said, to cheese it. I am tired of noise. I am tired of conflict. I want peace. My peace.

"You look like you want to quit this place," I say to him quietly after a moment, surveying his face.

His reaction, supremely subtle as it is, instantly tells me I have struck the nail true.

But the conversation does not go any further.

Because we have visitors.

It is a most unusual pair that shambles up to the manor house a few steps behind Watts, the gateman.

Another of the whip-jacks I've liberated from the docks,

Watts is apologetic for the intrusion. "Sorry's for interruptin', milord." He, unlike Wheeler, seems to revel in saying it, as if it elevates his character. "But they bear most disturbing news about the missus. May or may not be grub, but I thought ye should hear for yourself."

I take inventory of the couple. They are derelicts. A man and a woman, sunken-eyed, nervous in my presence, their hair, manner, and clothes absent a shred of pride. Street people.

The man introduces himself as Mr. Beauchamp, and the saggy, corpulent piece beside him as Miss Gray. He tries, it should be noted, and fails miserably at it, to infuse the appellations with dignity.

I hate them immediately, if only because they remind me of the thing I was years before. I hate them because, unlike me, they have done nothing to become something more.

"Good bit of terry firma ye got here, sir," Beauchamp says, surveying the place.

"If you have something to say, say it."

"There's a villainous scrap afoot, sir. Involving your recently departed wife."

Something dizzying passes through me. The horror is supposed to be past. I ask him politely what he means.

"Surely ye know of the resurrection men."

Something inside of me tightens.

"If you have something to say, say it," I repeat. This time more sternly.

"Well, as I say, there's a scrap to happen, and I thought perhaps given we know the names of the principals involved, there might be room for a barter."

"You want money."

Beauchamp smiles a sickly smile. "I want the sanctity of

yer beloved wife's grave to remain." He nears, trying for the kill. "I can give you the name and location not just of the shovel man, but more importantly, maybe, the man who's pulling his strings. You'd have it all, if'n you see fit to pay what's right."

"And what's right?"

"My understanding is the shovel man's to get seventy pounds for his work. Being upon the square myself, I couldn't accept any more than half of that for this information."

"Thirty-five pounds," I say quietly, if only because I want him to acknowledge this is truly what he is asking of me.

"Thirty-five pounds," he says. He is a small man, one who mistakes the depth of the water he swims in.

I summon Alister, who is close by. He is always close by, close as God's curse on a whore's arse. Alister is good value in situations like this, if only because he is tall and his ears are scarred and swollen from a lifetime's worth of fighting. I tell this Beauchamp that I am not interested in paying for information. What is right and good and on the side of God is for him to tell me the names of those who would dare desecrate the grave of a woman and her unborn child.

Mr. Beauchamp, though, tries to bollocks his way forward, negotiate. If not thirty-five, then perhaps twenty-five—

I give Alister a sidelong glance, and he punches Beauchamp in the throat. What is funny is that the woman cries out rather than the man. He, breathless and in abject pain, collapses on my drive in silence.

Alister and Watts descend on him and give him the proper Turkish treatment—kicks all around, tip of the boot, no stone on the body left unturned.

The woman cries out again—we are savages! But have you

seen yourself, guttersnipe? You and this wild-eyed, foul-smelling cretin that have come here to extort me and besmirch the hallowed memory of Ella?

I have the men hit her too. This time it is Wheeler who calls out! What is happening? You hit one person, and it's another that screams!

"Need we really do this, master?" he asks in his desperate voice. Oh, Wheeler, you sniveling, slack-jawed puppy mamma! You do not know it, but you have challenged me in public for the last time, you vaporing, cowardly dunghill!

I squat by the fallen couple, briefly allow them reprieve from Alister's and Watts's boots and fists.

Amicably, I ask the man if he would like to reconsider and see this not as a situation in which to bargain but instead one in which magnanimity is the right and only path.

"Just names, that's all. A few short breaths, and you'll be on your way," I say.

He is properly horrified, as he should be. He stammers a few things. I look to Alister and Watts. They help him to his feet. Grab the woman. In short order, both of these wastrels are through the front gate and off my grounds.

I have what I wanted. The names.

An execrable grave robber from the Holy Land named Job. An anatomy student by the name of Cager. And most important, the ringleader, who unlike the others has a last name the cretin was able to recall, meaning I can find him in the tangle of London with much greater ease.

A man named Percival Quinn.

I have other things on my mind, but even so I seek Wheeler

out shortly thereafter. This will only take a moment. He looks shaken, which is not a surprise. He is always shaken. He averts his gaze at my approach.

I tell him he is done. He is no longer a paladin. He and his puny stomach are to leave the grounds of my property and never return.

And does he respond as he should—having known me all these years—having known my decisions to be the immutable things that they are? No. He smiles on the wrong side of the mouth, his face puckering with tears like a bull beggar scarechild.

It all comes a-stammering out. Surely I'll reconsider, he's been the loyalest of the loyal—

As I say, I have other things on my mind. This is not a thing for words, and he is incapable of understanding that.

I yank him hard by the scruff, some of his hair tearing off in my fingers. I drive him good against the first hard thing I can find—a wall.

There will be no more talking, and he understands this now. There are only two alternatives: more violence or departure.

He nods. Attempts to suppress some of those doxy tears in a vain attempt at dignity and soon is off the grounds of my estate. His sunken posture tells me he properly understands he is never to return.

Thank God.

As I say, I have other things on my mind.

The air is stretched taut around me, silent save for a buzzing that may or may not be there.

I have left Alister and the others to rid my drawing room of the blood and carcasses of the birds and otherwise return the grounds of the estate to their usual pristine condition.

I am alone. Away from the manor house, between the formal gardens and the park, in the studied wilderness the Meynalls developed before my purchase of the land. It is a muddle of trees and trails, bushes and brooks. A romantic "recapitulation," they said, of the land as it originally was and wished to be. All I see is an unkempt mess. Insects and slimy crawlers and creeping molds and pestilences waiting to be born. I have vowed to tear this wilderness down and make the finest, purest gardens imaginable in its place. Everything visible, known, clean.

But I can think of nothing else in this moment save those beasts out there in London—this anatomist and his ilk, this vile grave robber—can there be anything closer to a beast than that? To burrow into the earth and find subsistence in the rotten—like a dung beetle, a maggot, a black-eyed vulture?

Can we at least let the dead be pure for a moment, while their memory is still true and pristine in our minds, the pain of their absence everywhere in our heart?

I do not want to look at this, think this—that is the real problem. I have shut this out, found freedom in distraction and drink, and now these foul men reopen the wound, cast wide again a door I'd slammed shut—

—and I see, I *feel,* that fleeting moment that seems of another life—

—another man's life, truly, not mine—

I see those final moments of life in her eyes, my hands around her neck, squeezing tight that airway to seal away her words, her harmful, hurtful words—to shut her up—to save both of us from the indignity of what she is saying to me—

—no, I chase that away, I chase that away now—

It was a row that any and perhaps every man and woman

have had since biblical times. Men and women fight. And sometimes it becomes physical, as it must, though never murderous. Never murderous. Only the evil would think to kill their beloved. I never thought that, Lord, never.

But I held on too long. I was angry. And by the time I let go, there was no breath in her. It was not my intention. I only wanted the fight to end. For her to cheese it, give me a moment to think. But I held on too long.

That is why I took her from that morgue in Bart's as quickly as possible. For if they gave her more than a cursory look, and they would, they would know she is too clean—as she was and should be forevermore—too clean for the story of falling from a horse. There was bruising nowhere else, scrapes nowhere else, fractures nowhere else. The very purity of her would be telltale. The lie would be revealed.

It will be the last lie I ever tell, Lord. The last.

Just help me. Help me.

If they dig up her body, they will know.

What.

What's that?

Yes. If you want to kill a snake, you start with the head.

And so it must be.

Yes.

I will start with Percival Quinn.

SEVENTEEN
QUINN

FOR THE BETTER part of the day, it has been Percival's strong inclination to climb inside a bottle of claret and languish there, numb to the weak, fitful moans that come with increasing frequency from Neva's room. The studied detachment of the physician, well earned and so long a sort of armor for him, has been stripped away. Every wince she experiences, every dagger of pain that cuts unannounced through her body, shoots through his own at twice the depth. But better to feel, to be present for her, than to flee into selfish oblivion. Every moment in her presence a fugitive, bittersweet blessing.

He has already decided he will not do as she says. He will not cut into her living body to free the unborn child, killing her in the process. This decision damns her, he knows, to more pain, a greater protraction of that pain, but the irresponsible hope within him mandates that he blind himself to what would otherwise be the clear-eyed truth of the situation, the need to think in palliative rather than curative terms. Funny what that admixture of pain, horror, and hope do to us, how rationality falls away as its first victim. We go mad with hope, with prayer. And what does he think will come to pass, the highest version of things that he is holding out for? That somehow the resurrectionist will bring him the body of Ella Beddoe; that it will not yet be rendered putrid by the hot, wet soil; that he, in turn, will somehow find, with his scalpel, something in her decaying physiology that will magically deliver Neva and Oliver from death's door?

Brewer comes upstairs. She tells him he has visitors. He divines in her voice, despite her usual dispassionate propriety, that they are an unsavory sort. Which heartens Percival. Perhaps the resurrectionist has news.

He makes his way down to the door, yet rather than finding Job standing in the foyer, he instead sees a couple of well-dressed men, one with a face that is vaguely familiar to him. Something frozen and edgy briefly moves through Percival.

The nib from the morgue. Marcus Beddoe. The husband of his mark.

A look of recognition, in turn, assembles itself on Beddoe's face at the sight of Percival.

"Afternoon to you, Mr. Quinn," he says. "When your name was given to me, it didn't occur to me that we had met. But now it makes quite a bit more sense." This man is made of fury, Percival thinks. It is amazing that he can bind it up in such civility, as affected as that civility might be. It seems to want to leap from him, unceasingly, to mete itself upon everything before him.

"Is there something I can help you with?"

"I inquired after you at St. Bart's, but they told me you were home with your wife. She's apparently ill and lying in?"

The mention of Neva at once chills and angers Percival. "She's unwell, yes. Perhaps we could step outside to allow her a bit of quiet?"

Beddoe quietly assents, nods to his colleagues. The trio steps out into the bustling energy of Leicester Square.

"I hate to be rude," Percival says, "but I should really be by her side. Perhaps you could tell me the nature of your visit?"

Beddoe, not a man to yield control of a conversation, opts not to answer and instead casts his gaze around the square. A studied pause to reset things, so that it is he who shapes the conversation rather than Percival. "An expecting woman is an extraordinary thing, isn't it? She becomes another thing entirely to you, reveals to you in her form alone that you are no longer the man you were and that many great evolutions await you. That you will become something more than you were, better. All of it no doubt a hardship and sacrifice, and not always pleasant, but she and that child together are a sort of crucible, a test. A holy test. To see if you can properly evolve toward humility, honesty. The world advances because of women, not just in generation, but insofar as they soften men, pare away their baser instincts, and thus civilization is that much more civilized."

Good Lord, this man is a whiddler, Percival thinks. But he nevertheless opts to be yielding, if only because he hopes that Beddoe will run out of sermon and get more quickly to the point so that this whole thing can be put in the past.

"You are a beast," Beddoe says, leveling a dark gaze on Percival.

Percival briefly formulates a retort, some form of deflection, feigned innocence, but ultimately thinks better of it; Beddoe can only be here because he knows something.

Beddoe takes a subtle step toward him. "So you know, if my wife is dug up and dissected, we will return the favor and take a knife to yours. Most assuredly."

Percival has been on the receiving end of ire and indignation ever since he began his public curriculum in anatomy a few years back. All manner of the aggrieved have come forth and assailed him—on street corners, at Bart's, even here at his front door a few times, so such a visit here at Leicester

Square is not without precedent. But unfailingly they have been moralists of one form or another—clergymen, zealous parishioners, the odd apocalypticist imploring him to cease his godless ways for fear that they will make manifest the inane prophesies of John's gospel—that in disinterring the dead, he would somehow give them unholy life, and the horrors of Revelation would be visited upon the whole of the world. Such bedlamites were in the end easy to dismiss. One merely needed to slip back into the assiduous calm of the physician, play the role of forbearing listener as they had their say, then, once they'd worn themselves out and seen that you offered no resistance, no argument, no fuel to sustain their flame of outrage, the sum of the encounter would be that they'd ultimately go away, usually with a frustrated epithet or two as punctuation, and the world would go on as before. But this is different, personal, the stakes something far more insidious than merely a tongue-lashing. It is the first time in Percival's well-heeled life he's felt the sting of mortal threat.

He is pleased at what arises in him because of it. This is his territory. And his own are upstairs.

"I encourage you to listen, Mr. Beddoe, because I haven't time for inconsequence," he finds himself saying. He is half this man physically. Less than a tenth of the collected strength before him. Still. He steps wide of Beddoe, casts an arm toward the crowds around him, the neighboring houses. "You and I, we are both men of public standing. We are *known*. So much so that people see us on the street and make note. As is the case now, as is the case before you arrived here, as will be the case when you leave. Unless you kill me here, now, it's my intention to go upstairs, pen two letters outlining your threats, and have them ready for dispatch both to Bart's and the constable. In killing me, or my wife, you would bury yourself, Mr. Beddoe. So I encourage you, let the dead be so—and let the living live."

He has never felt so upright. He is pretty certain it will get him killed, perhaps momentarily.

Beddoe reflects on it ever so briefly, then leans in, whispers, "You talk to me as if I can be reasoned with." He turns to go. His men instinctively know to follow. Before disappearing into the crowds, he looks back a final time at Percival.

"I pity both you and everyone you've dragged into this, sir," Beddoe says. And then he is gone.

EIGHTEEN

BEDDOE

THE ANATOMIST, LIKE myself, is a romantic.

He will make choices with his heart rather than his head and, as such, cannot be prevailed upon to do the rational thing. And his point about the two of us being public figures cannot be dismissed.

Generally speaking, the problems I have done away with have been the ones nobody misses—the low-level screwmen and housebreakers, the nappers and conks. The people born anonymous, who subsist in the sunken, unknown spaces of existence for all of their wicked lives and are never missed when their meager, incorrigible flames are snuffed out forever. They die unceremoniously, as they should, nameless to history, like rats in the sewer.

Yes, physician, perhaps you have too much of a name.

But your resurrectionist does not.

NINETEEN

JOB

IT IS HIGH tide, and the waters of the Thames can scarcely be seen beneath the myriad ships that crowd the river.

Everywhere sails, a forest of masts and canvas, ships jostling for position with lighters, barges, pleasure boats.

There is more timber and rigging here than river, Job thinks.

And that is good.

In those ships, somewhere, is hope.

They will load and unload overnight at the quays and, with insatiable appetite for profit, will weigh anchor once high tide returns and sail for the next port of call in the morning.

The world in those ships.

The entire world.

Attainable.

Full of tomorrow, escape.

He moves through the chaotic energy of the tobacco docks, dying.

Blood continues to ooze from the wound the boy inflicted upon him.

It is invisible to the people around them, should they look, by virtue of his soil-darkened jacket.

The blood has slowed but remains stubborn, consistent, refusing to clot.

He dabs at it occasionally with a rag clutched in his fist, but by now he knows it will not stanch the flow.

It does not help that he has been constantly moving since it happened.

Another man would go to Bart's, have the surgeons there do their best to fix him.

But then this coming evening and its opportunity would be lost.

And they would not fix him anyhow.

A gut wound is a death sentence.

He knows this from the battlefield.

It would be surrender of the worst sort to die in that hospital while the mudlark and his boys hunt Ivy down in his absence.

Exacting revenge for what Job in his unthinking fury has done to the boy.

And Job will not be there to do anything about it.

No, there is another way—this way.

Providence, he knows, has visited itself upon him in the last couple of days, with a face imperfect and squalid, and he must act, must seize upon the terrible opportunity he's been given.

Deliverance, he knows, has never been announced by angels on high, ethereal and comforting, but instead by tribulation, the hammer strike of pain.

Only then are you quickened into that most supreme understanding of life, in which all narratives fall away, all trivialities, and the singular imperative of what must be done comes clear.

You are nothing, Job.

You never were.

Even when you briefly had money.

That was taken from you by circumstance.

But what did you truly give?

You are nothing until you give yourself away, all of you, and you have not done that yet.

You have let your daughter grow to womanhood in the slums.

You could have done more.

But the world wounded you, and you quit.

You shrank away so far that you sank into the earth itself and dealt in carrion, your business a reflection of the rot within you.

But now you have this one last chance.

To deliver her as you should have years ago.

The pain has awakened you—maybe you sought it.

It is grinding, horrible, but also thrilling.

The world wears its colors now as it never has, its smells, its sounds.

You are suddenly and wholly in creation because of this slice in your stomach.

That bleeds and is poisoned by the cess in your perforated intestines.

There is no coming back from this—either loss of blood or infection will kill you.

Can you use it?

Go, Job, move with haste.

For you can see it, can't you, through the snarl of masts and canvas?

The sunset—as bittersweet a salmon color as you have ever seen.

He finds a packet ship bound for Boston that would get Ivy and himself within coach distance of Bradford, site of one of the academies that Quinn told him educates women, but the transatlantic passage, at forty pounds a head, is too expensive.

He carries with him the twenty gold sovereigns advanced to him by Quinn, and though he has made it a hard and fast rule never to count money in his pocket that is not yet there, plans on having another thirty-five once he has paid out Cager for his share of the night's work.

He would never make such a presumption—that the job will be done, that it *can* be done—but all things are staked to this evening now, this evening that is likely the last one over which he will ever again exert any control, so he must will the future he spoils for into existence, must become the reckless, overconfident thing he was in youth, the thing he vowed never to be again.

Night burgeons around him, begins to constrict things, squeeze away the horizon and outer reaches of the city from view.

There is no time.

Every minute spent haggling here is a minute not spent on the greater task, the job at St. Mary's.

So it is he finds himself on the gang of a well-rounded brig he's learned is bound for Italy.

As the crew takes on dozens of bales of wool from the Great Floor nearby, he negotiates with the captain.

A cabin is available, slight and without porthole.

Twenty-five quid a head.

It is scarcely bigger than a closet.

But it would get them to Genoa.

Again, coach distance to a city with a university that admits women.

Bologna.

After paying for their passage, Ivy and Job would have all of five pounds to subsist on.

Reckless, presumptuous.

He agrees to terms, even when the captain insists upon the whole of his twenty sovereigns as down payment.

The rest is due at first light, when the brig sets sail.

Job tells him it shall be paid.

The captain informs him he runs a tight ship, that the vessel will weigh anchor on time, irrespective of whether paying passengers are present or not.

Job says it's understood and a minute later is up the quay, chasing away the inner voice as he does, the one that tells him he is a fool for giving away twenty pounds—real money—in hopes of trading up to a castle in the air.

Better, if you are to die tonight, the voice says, to leave her with twenty pounds than destitute because you gambled, a desperate old man, and lost.

But he sees something—as he moves through the sea of laggers and dockers around him—that confirms to him that this is the only ploy now.

There is a boy, strong and most of the way to manhood, that seems to trail him.

He's an urchin, a feral thing of the quays, cap pulled low.

Though the flow of traffic is thick in Job's direction, this one stands out.

Job thinks, though he cannot be sure, that this boy was back at the Thames this morning.

One of the group that witnessed his assault on the mudlark.

Yes, they are looking for him.

Job wends through the crowds, trying to disappear.

He cannot fight this one, not in this condition.

Better to channel all of his faltering energy into St. Mary's churchyard.

As the quays give way to the city, he entertains the possibility that in his dizzying blood loss he is being paranoid.

But when the boy appears again, some blocks back, once Job has crossed into the Holy Land, he knows.

They cannot come here, Job thinks.

They cannot know where he has put up Ivy.

And so he runs.

TWENTY
CAGER

Cager squats in the dim candlelight of the Irishman's cellar, considering the broken girl on the divan before him. She is, he has learned, the resurrectionist's daughter and has apparently taken a turn for the worse since enduring a violent attack the previous night. Never has he seen such bruising on a woman. She is swollen to the point that even when her eyes are open, one would scarcely know it. Only the occasional glint of candlelight that flashes weakly off the thin slits of her bloodshot sclerae betrays the fact that she is awake and alert.

Fife, that wry, pungent boglander who'd coached them away during the Thundridge job and scarcely a half hour earlier tonight pulled Cager off the street upon his arrival in the Holy Land, has told him everything. "Mr. Mowatt's got a peck of troubles."

Cager's been made to wait. The resurrectionist is expected back at any moment.

He surveys the wretchedness around him—his second time in the Holy Land in a single day!—the tight quarters, dirt floors, general foulness, the windowless stench. The seemingly limitless supply of boglanders of all ages crammed into this tiny back slum, all apparently begotten by the industrious Fife—a dozen or more children from sty-eyed newborn to broad-shouldered man-boy. Cager has been raised to disdain the Paddies, that scourge of knuckle-draggers from the Urinal of the Planets across the Irish Sea, and yet these days in London, despite himself, he is fascinated by the squalor.

Funny that fascination—he came to be educated, sophisticated, elevated, a gentleman, and the most titillating discoveries and profound revelations have not been of the exalted sort to be found in the airy halls of learning, the opulent theaters of culture, but instead in the hardscrabble, scarcely believable struggles of the downtrodden—the darker and more desperate the straits, the better. It somehow insists he participate, that he get his hands dirty alongside them, however horrid the toil. As if the real aim of education is not to rise above and become something more, not to inhabit an impossible ideal or impress your fellow man, but instead to find what is most real and true and become a wholehearted citizen of it. In short, to be human, imperfect, and striving, rather than a two-dimensional model.

And here before him is what the vast, real scrum of imperfect humanity looks like, notwithstanding the swells and highbrows he has thus far sought out and occasionally consorted with. The family before him persists, above all else, taking a sort of roughshod pride in it. They live on nothing, their needs winnowed away by privation to the point that only the true essentials of life are considered and pursued. And first and foremost of those essentials in this moment is dutiful, compassionate ministration to the resurrectionist's daughter, though the broken girl before them is a Protestant and they themselves craw-thumping Catholics.

They clean her and hold her hand and tell her ribald jokes. Cager is nearly moved to tears by how some of the youngest of them, without guidance, instinctively cosset her, whisper sweetnesses to her. Like they are trying to will her back to life, to wellness, because that is what one does for another human being when that human being is shattered and failing.

Good Lord, how sick of himself he is. Sick of that vainglorious gasbag that he was when he arrived in London a few short weeks ago to make his mark on the world. What a waste. What a misuse of the momentary, tremulous time one has on the Earth. Hoping to be noticed, celebrated, all the while missing the real goings-on of the world, the beating heart of turmoil and pain beneath all things, which he, like the rest of the world, has worked long and impressively to avoid. Witness this girl given respite in the darkest hovel of the darkest slum, the subhuman hell of St. Giles that any civilized man would be wise to bypass. Witness firsthand a child's soft fingertips put compassionately to the split lip of a stranger—there, truly, is the work of cherubs, nearly otherworldly and pure in their love, rather than the nonsense of frescoes in the high and inaccessible walls of churches. Witness, in the end, pain and what it evokes. You cannot know the holy, truly, until you have languished in hell, properly languished, and not merely passed through as a tourist. Only then will you yearn with appropriate understanding for the light of the world, its smallest mercies and embrace. Every day aboveground, properly understood, is rich with the work of angels, the ones that are here and present and walk the streets with us.

He goes to her, this girl he does not know. He feels a great shame in his modishness, his clothes, his affect. He looks ridiculous here in his breeches and vest, he knows. But hopefully these people will see that beneath this jester outfit is one no different from them, one that has been confused by opportunity and all the roads it affords.

He asks for the rag so that he might take a turn cooling the girl's bruised brow. The eldest daughter yields it, and Cager sits beside Ivy, tending to her with one hand and soon, unconsciously, holding her hand with the other. He's never held a girl's hand like this, under such circumstances. Always there was another agenda. Now it's just him and her and the warm silence of the place, the quiet availability and presence of Fife's family. How strange. How perfect.

He wonders what she looks like under all the disfigurement and bruising. A brief bolt of righteousness shoots through him knowing that Job has administered a nasty beating to the brute who's done this. But that is soon past. All he wants is for her to feel his hand, hear his voice, be solaced by the cool water on her skin.

For as long as he can remember, he has wanted to be a physician. But he has not understood, until now, the true nature of that calling.

This, then—his hand certain around hers, his presence as unwavering as that of the people around him, as if they will stay with her unfailingly until every shred of her pain is gone—is perhaps what healing is truly about.

Job returns, a grim sight. He greets Cager with a warm, if weak, smile, then turns his attention to his daughter. She is aware of him in a way she is not for the others. As if their link in blood connects them on planes Cager cannot understand. She doesn't open her eyes, but at his words, unlike those of the others, she stirs. Her split lips form a barely discernible, woeful smile at the sound of his voice. With it comes a small, laborious nod that seems—strangely, to Cager—to suggest strength, an attempt to assuage her father's unspoken anguish from inside the locked box of her own pain.

"I am going to go now," Job says to her. "Sleep. I will come to collect you before morning light. You will need all your strength."

Again that tiny, blind smile and nod in response.

Yes, she is strong. No doubt Job's daughter.

Fife, until now silent in the dim recesses of the place, speaks up. "Need to show ye something." He motions for Job to follow him deeper into the back. The back slum of the back slum, as it were. Job nods to Cager. They follow Fife through the dark warren that wends beneath the building above, past even more desperate abodes down there in the darkness—more families, further even from the world of light than Fife's—until they reach what Cager perceives as the adjoining block. There they rise up into the sleeping house of another family. Fife gives the patriarch—a man with freckles and a shock of hair so red it leaves no doubt that he, too, must be a craw-thumper, a knowing nod. The trio move to the single, paneless window on the far wall. Fife nods out to the street. "Got the wrong sort looking for ye," he says with a glance to Job.

Job says he knows, that the mudlark's contingent is no doubt combing the blocks of the Holy Land as they speak.

Fife shakes his head. "Don't get the sense they're river lads," he says with a nod toward the window.

The three men peer out. Visible is a site uncommon to St. Giles. Swells. A half dozen men in finery, more than one bearing a polished lantern, moving among the population, stopping people, peppering them with questions.

"They're asking for ye, Job. They know your name."

Job considers them, as does Cager. Yes, they are dressed

in varment hat and coat, cavalierly flashing pocket watches despite the thieving reputation of St. Giles, all of them collectively quite a go, but tawdry as St. Audrey. Too much pomade, too much silver, too many clashing colors among their cravats, gloves, kerchiefs. Men with money but without a clue how to spend it. And men that are blithely unafraid of these streets.

Job says he knows these men. He's seen some of them before. They are Beddoe's men. Killers.

"I've got the full breath of the devil on me now," he says quietly, more to himself than the others, then turns away and moves back into the darkness.

Before they set out for St. Mary's, Job kisses his daughter on the forehead once more. A moment later, they are out on the streets. Better put, they are out into a maze. Job guides Cager through byways he's never seen; the two men bear directly away from the ruffians on the other block, their path a footpad's dream, weaving in and out of an interconnected network of passageways, alleys, slap-bang houses, cellars. Cager quickly gleans that this is one of the boons of living in such tight quarters with thousands of people, all steeped in the ways of the street. If one has accumulated enough goodwill, as Job apparently has, then collective passage is his. Your neighbors' byways are yours, as long as you reciprocate, and your movements are unknown to authorities and interlopers alike. If you have earned this goodwill, this trust, then your business—whatever it be—and the memory of it vanish like the smoke that rises from the makeshift hearths, candles, and rushlights that are everywhere down here, trying to carve dignity out of the threatening darkness of a St. Giles night.

Once they are clear of the Holy Land and Job seems convinced that Beddoe's men won't find them, he turns to Cager. Something is bothering him. "You shouldn't come," he says.

Cager tries to hide his surprise. "Why?"

"There are people out there mean to kill me. You shouldn't be involved in this, not for fifteen pounds."

Cager is briefly beset by a strange panic, one he did not anticipate. A fear that he is being abandoned. Left in London alone by the one man he feels any true, abiding kinship with. This desolate body snatcher.

Job nods darkly, deciding. "Walk. I don't want you anymore." It is said categorically, a send-off. No eye contact. He turns to go.

Cager, despite himself, blurts out, "You won't be able to do it alone."

Job does not respond, continues to move off.

"You are bleeding to death, Job," Cager calls. Job slows but doesn't look back. Cager goes on. "Let me take you to Bart's. Let me get you treated. Properly."

Job shakes his head as if it's an impossibility. But he doesn't move. When he lifts his gaze to meet Cager's, the look in his eye suggests somewhere, deep down, a fear that he cannot reconcile, cannot inhabit.

Cager catches up with him, again feeling that calm sense of duty suffuse his veins. He puts his hand to Job's shoulder, deepens the gaze they share, his flesh once again in tremulous contact with another's. This, then, is what he seeks—this country boy alone in the city with only the great uncertain future as company—companionship, amity.

Communion.

"Tell me," he says with a voice that seems to solace himself even as it seeks to solace Job. "So I can help you."

TWENTY-ONE

BEAUCHAMP AND GRAY

GRAY IS FORTUNATE. Beddoe's men have gone comparatively lightly on her, and she shows no bruising. Beauchamp, however, has managed to bring home an admirable collection of weeping lacerations and widening bruises from the visit to the estate. She insists on going out for plasters. He tells her it's not worth the fuss. But she doesn't listen and is soon out the door.

Fine, then. In her absence, Beauchamp will be allowed some silence in their room at the accommodation house.

He draws the last of the laudanum, enough to fill one entire dropper, and deposits it in a glass of water, stirs.

They will need more money. He had been banking on Beddoe taking the bait, emptying his flush pockets as any upstanding man would've if presented with the same information.

See what magnanimity does? Entire bloody human race bites the hand that feeds them.

Like dogs, really. Surprisingly so.

Nowhere to turn, is there? All your life, you try to fit into the world, and it just doesn't let you.

Dogs. It amuses him that he tried it, thought it would work. Funny and sad, the way that kids try to squeeze a bit of happiness out of life. Seems a couple of lives ago that he was that foundling on the sidewalk, spanking that glaze to get that greyhound. His fellow urchins were out there around him spanking jewels, silver, and there he was, nipping curs! Absolutely no money in it, but that wasn't really the point, was it? Money meant nothing to him then. It was the bloody look in the dog's eye the first time he passed outside the shop window. The way it considered him from its rattan cage with a sad, hopeful longing. Something strange came alive in him, a sense that he was somehow needed. That the pooch was beseeching him with its eyes to free it. To adopt it and look after it.

It was an unfamiliar feeling for a foundling, a boy dropped some years before in the street for the parish to keep, an act that said he was anything but needed. The parish priest, of course, had been overstretched, domineering, and occasionally untoward in the way he cared for the children, so Mal rightly took to the streets, and it was not long before he was sleeping in the corner of a back slum cellar, surrounded by a bunch of other unlicked cubs like himself that came in at night after working their schemes, all of them vying for muddy floor space so they might be safe at rug for a few hours before awakening to the whole catastrophe again the following morning.

Nowhere was there privacy—it was like living in a cage at the zoo with scores of other monkeys, all of which would fight you at the drop of a hat, steal your lot when you looked away. You were wise to spend whatever rag you made that day because you wouldn't have it when you woke up. A hand-to-mouth life, as they say. That much he didn't mind. But damn it all, to find one soul on this earth that ran deep on trust, someone piss and fart—sound at heart. And you thought it would be a spindly little sad-eyed Italian greyhound, Mal Beauchamp! God bless you, you fool!

There was that copse of trees then, out past Leicester,

where they hadn't yet put up all those infernal terrace houses. It was surrounded by new streets and would soon be built out with more terraces and populated with that odd breed of well-bathed, contented cits. But for the moment, it was still just trees. Nevertheless, the perception among the rovers, hedge priests, and foundlings was that it was too close to the legitimate strains of society, and so they stayed wide. Surely the night watchmen would come and roust them if they tried to steal a night of sleep there, perhaps even bone them up to the whit for a fortnight. But not so. Mal had his look—he tested it out. He slept first one night there in the thick foliage, then another, and no one came. He had, then, his own place, his own palace of wood and leaf! Now, if only he had someone to share with him, someone that would not steal from him or lie to him or abandon him. And then that damn greyhound looked at him with those august, needy eyes. A dog, yes. Man's best friend.

He stole that greyhound and took it back to his castle of leaf and wood. He fed it whatever meager pap he could rummage up. The dog was alternately nervous and playful. They curled up together that night, and Mal had the wonderful sense of another warm body against his, the reciprocity of heat coursing between them. He felt at once needed and attended to. How miraculous a feeling of drifting off to sleep this way.

When he awoke, the pup was gone. Wandered off or run off, he didn't know. He searched high and low but realized he couldn't call out for the cur because he hadn't named him. He called out for Pooch and Pup and Cur, and finally, realizing the dog was never coming back, Whore's Son and Shitten Arse, but of course, those didn't work either.

He would name the next one—that would do it. So he

spanked another glaze the next day. This time from a pet shop up on Ludgate Hill. It was a terrier, possessed of inescapable and needy eyes that seemed to promise any liberator eternal love in exchange for its release. A few hours later they returned together to his castle of leaf and wood. No sooner had he named the new cur—Ezra, for reasons unclear to him—than the infernal beast turned on him as he hugged it tightly and bit him so hard on the nose that it drew blood. It bolted away into the trees immediately thereafter, never to be seen again.

Fool that he was, he assumed it was the breed of the dog that was the problem. Greyhounds and terriers were nervous sorts, whereas bloodhounds—so he had been told—were calm and loyal to a fault. The problem was that the only bloodhound he could find was in the window of that very first shop he'd spanked. Could he really spank the same shop just a few days later?

He gave it a try. The bloodhound pup, however, proved to be not so calm, not so agreeable, when he liberated it. It, too, bit him as he ran, squirmed from his arms, landed on the sidewalk, and tripped him as he'd tried to make his escape. It was all so ridiculous, and because of it, he was in Newgate a few days later, subjected to beatings at the hands of fellow prisoners so horrible that no man on the whole of the Earth should be made to endure them.

What was it with the world?

For it surely wasn't him. He meant well, damn it all!

Strangely it was this woman, Gray, that could finally see this and give him what he wanted—someone piss and fart. She wanted from the start to know all of him, his soul and his history, including the bits about the dogs. For some reason, he couldn't find it in himself to reveal much of it to her—

the childish vulnerability and heartbreak of the whole affair, the embarrassment. You let on about such weakness, and a woman will lose respect for you. Will see you not as a Captain Tom but instead as a simpering chickenheart. Even so, over the years they've been together, he's seen a change in her, like she somehow senses it in him, this weakness. He sees her looking at other men in that certain way. What is it with the world? Everyone always looking to run off.

Well, they can't run off on you if you run off first.

He chases away all these thoughts because they solve nothing. And things need solving at present. He needs money, because the solution that he spoons around in the glass before him is far too light, half strength, and showing too many of the impurities in the water collected from the pump. Those little bits spiraling, dancing. Living things, probably. He would rather not know. His kingdom for a proper solution of laudanum so the drink would be dark as tea and keep its secrets to itself.

He drinks it all in one go, squints away the acrid train of cinnamon fire that slides away down his throat.

There. The silence will widen now. Soon enough. London will cheese it. The walls will cheese it. The thoughts that tumble into one another in succession, nonstop in both his waking hours and sleep, will stop. Space will grow between the thoughts. Cool space. Not the hot, infernal world of brainwork that is every damned moment of every day. To blazes with all this thought. Most of it for naught. None of it comes to pass anyhow, not as you expect it to.

Why is the entire world not a world of opium eaters? Why choose problems over no problems? The rough over the smooth?

The cut dose of laudanum tries its best to usher him away

into that Great Smooth that he seeks, but it's not equal to his body's demands. So instead, as the minutes go by, he finds himself on the precipice of numbness, unable to cross over, and all the more frustrated because of it. To have a little, to feel that tantalizing tip of the feather in the brain, is worse than to have none at all. It is a tease of the worst sort. Now his body insists that he take it all the way, but he cannot.

There is a knock at the door, short but insistent.

It cannot be the neighbors, for they know better than to involve themselves in Beauchamp's business. Nor can it be Gray. She has a key.

Beauchamp goes to the door. Calls through for the visitor to announce himself.

"I have a business proposition for you," comes a voice on the other side. It is somehow familiar.

Beauchamp opens the door. The voice is familiar because he saw this man just a few hours ago, at Beddoe's estate. One of the swells, one of Beddoe's lieutenants.

Beauchamp decides he's got a fight on his hands, tries to ready himself. But finds that the small dose of laudanum has dulled the fury required to fight. What a terrible halfway state, capable of neither rising to fisticuffs nor shrinking away into sweet numbness. He has become a slab of meat for the moment. Verveless, indecisive meat.

The man, though, seems to have no interest in a tilt and, in fact, seems a bit nervous to be standing here alone before Beauchamp in the dark hallway. He announces himself as Cecil Wheeler, asks if he might inconvenience Beauchamp to let him step inside.

Beauchamp tries to properly assemble a reaction.

The man is small, his gaze indirect.

No, he is not a fighter.

"What sort of business?" is all Beauchamp manages.

"Something to make the both of us good and fat," Wheeler replies.

Some minutes later, they are seated on opposite sides of the small room—Beauchamp on the bed, Wheeler on the peacock steamer. Wheeler is telling him how Beddoe, after the incident at the estate, will no doubt move against the sack-em-up men, perhaps this very night—a thing obvious to Beauchamp—but the real pearl comes when Wheeler suggests that there is more opportunity in the whole affair than the sack-em-up men realize.

"Opportunity?" Beauchamp asks in a barely discernible grumble. His mind is only half present to Wheeler's words. Mostly what he sees is Wheeler and that steamer he sits on. How easily Wheeler would fit inside.

"The sack-em-up men are after a body. But a body can only be worth so much. Specially if it's gone putrid. But what else is in that coffin?"

"Speak without the teases, man. I'm not some rich frump yer selling a thing to."

"Very well. Master Beddoe is a man of passions, as both ye and I can attest. He loved the wife, even if he gave her a dose every now and again when she got obstropulous. Always he was somewhere between hitting her and buying her more trinkets. And by trinkets, of course, I mean the best—to my knowledge, the purchases included a butterfly brooch with emerald eyes; a tiara of diamond; a garnet cross of ivory, gold, and pearl; a choker of aquamarine; and the largest red diamond in all of London. How do I know this? Because

I arranged the purchases. He sent me up to Hamlet's, to Rundell and Bridge on Ludgate Hill if Hamlet's didn't have what he wanted. I know what he bought her. And I know where it is now. On the missus's body."

As Beauchamp mulls this, Wheeler sits forward with a conspiratorial nod. "That woman had a burial fit for an Egyptian queen."

"And you're proposing what?" Beauchamp says.

"You know what I'm proposing. We get in there, you and I, and make use of all that scratch that'd otherwise just sink into the earth. As I said, those are the real spoils in there. Nuff for a man to buy an estate. A couple men to buy a couple of estates."

Beauchamp is inwardly tantalized, of course, though he won't give this little mooncalf the pleasure of knowing it. He wonders briefly if the real bird in hand here is to forgo the two in the bush being proposed to him—this queen's bounty—and instead simply strangle the man and put him on the block in the morning at the Fortune of War. By the look of him, he'd probably fetch five quid. Odd shape. Wide hips. Recessed jaw. Brow of an ape. As Beauchamp contemplates all of this, he keeps the conversation alive by offering a wry thought. "But it's larceny to take something from a grave."

"World's upside down, isn't it? You get caught taking a body, there's no exact law to deal with you. But you take a thing—an inanimate little bit of nothing to be forgotten by the world—and they'll lock you up good. Shows you it's a world of possessions. A world of laws made by rich men to protect their possessions, even if they're locked up in the ground forevermore."

Yes, Beauchamp thinks, I'm going to kill him.

But it would be rash to kill him just yet.

He will still be worth five quid tomorrow. Even the next day.

"I'm interested, maybe," Beauchamp says, "on certain conditions. You got to tell me a few things: Why you need me, why I need you, and above all, why are you bridging your Cap'n Tom like this?"

Wheeler throws off some sad tripe about being sacked by his master, this despite years of loyal service. He whiddles about things like disrespect and lack of severance, whatever the blazes that is. Christ-in-the-sky, just another man painting himself in tears.

"And why come to me?"

"'Cause yer cork-brained," Wheeler says, on the verge of a smile, a thing that seems unnatural on his drawn face. "Ye came to the master's estate thinking you could sell him. Which means yer brave indeed, if stupid. But I suppose being stupid is one of them prerequisites of being brave, isn't it?"

"Just like you coming here," Beauchamp says darkly.

"Just like me coming here." Wheeler nods. It's the first time Beauchamp likes the little grunter. Though he still fully intends to kill him.

"Right," Beauchamp says. "And why don't I just do it without you?"

"I'd tell, of course."

"Not if I milled your bleating arse right here and stuffed you in that trunk."

"True. But then ye'd be racing the resurrectionists alone. Tonight. Because you know they know the missus's body has already been in that steamy ground for two days and the worms are starting to yam her good by now."

"Sack-em-up men don't fright me, not a single fee, faw, fum."

"How about the graveyard shift, the mortsafe, the two-ton slab atop her grave? You think you could handle those alone too?"

Beauchamp eyes him, doesn't have an answer.

Wheeler stands, proud of himself. "I know the men on the graveyard shift. I have a key to the lockhouse. They would not suspect me until it's too late. And I know the man from whom they hired the mortsafe and slab. Where he lives. I arranged it. If yer willing to do the things that you do—and I know the things that you do, I have heard, I have asked around about you—we can get him to take away his wares just as easily as he placed them there. While the master sleeps. But it must be now. His men watch for the resurrectionists, not us. The advantage that is ours will soon pass if we don't seize on it."

Beauchamp feels a brief sting to his pride as he realizes, or at least acknowledges, that this man has come up with a plan far superior to anything he himself could have produced. He hates Wheeler implicitly for it. But he smiles nevertheless, and the words that come out of his mouth are uncharacteristically earnest. "I'd be honored to dig up the missus with you." What's left unsaid, of course, is that he will slaughter Wheeler afterward, or at any point that it seems the mooncalf's plan proves at all bogus. Whether or not he fetches five quid is beside the point now. The man has belittled him with his bit of genius. It's not a pleasant feeling to know that one is not the smartest person in the room.

But you're only smart until you're dead.

Then you're just a piece of meat to be either sold off to the knifemen or dumped into the Thames and lost to the tide, like so much else in this world.

Within a half hour, the two men are on the streets of London and bound for Somers Town, where Wheeler says they will find the man responsible for the mortsafe and slab—an official of the church, apparently, the sacristan of St. Mary's—whatever that is. It seems, in these boom times of digging up the dead and protecting the dead, that the church itself has gotten into the act, having bought a few mortsafes and heavy stone slabs to hire out at exorbitant rates to families fearful enough, and rich enough, to insist upon them.

"Catholics," Wheeler snorts. "Bilk you any which way they can."

As they head out into a city oblivious of their intent, Beauchamp thinks briefly of Gray. Whether he should tell her about this. Whether he should include the mollisher in the windfall, should it come to pass.

She is piss and fart, sound at heart.

But she will not have done a thing to earn this, will she?

And sooner or later, she will leave him.

Better think, Mal. Big rag like this comes once in a blue moon. And you have never seen a blue moon.

No, if he knaps this good swag, he decides, it will be his doing alone. And as such, whatever he lines his pockets with should be rightfully solely his. For while he is once again going bodily into harm's way, she is busy getting plasters.

Which elicits another thought. How long does it take for one to get plasters, anyhow?

Gray is with another man.

She had come to the voluntary hospital at St. Bart's some hours back to collect free plasters but had not made it far before encountering the physician whose acquaintance she'd made at the Fortune of War—the infernally kind Randall Sims. Though she'd indicated that her visit was not for herself but rather an errand for another, that she had no interest in being examined, the good man simply refused to hear it. The way he looked on her as she talked, with such care, was excruciating. Though she couldn't see herself, she could see her condition mirrored in his face in the way he furrowed his brow as he studied her. Yes, she knew she was in bad shape, well before any of the business at the estate. But that was not the reason she was here.

Still, he would not yield the plasters to her until she consented to be examined. Lord, the man was as polite as an angel! (Not that she'd ever met one!)

And so, knowing that the fastest way to secure the plasters and get back to Beauchamp was to accede to his request, she let him give her a quick once-over. Only, it was not quick. One thing begat another, and soon he was asking to see more of her. How supremely uncomfortable that had been, to lift her dress, to allow him to see her in all her heaving filthiness. But how kind he had been, how assiduous. She had not felt that looked after since those dim memories of her childhood in the terraces, when her mother was still there, was still that comforting, godly giant that cradled young Gray, her arms a great, warm fortress that, without fail, beat back the wordless, amorphous pains and fears that stalked the small child as they stalked all small children.

And yet now Gray is here, with this terrible new knowledge.

It's one thing to have someone to look after you, to care,

but it's another thing for them to tell you what she has just been told.

In the back of her mind, she had more than once in the previous weeks suspected that what was now irrefutably occurring to her had been indeed happening all along. She had chosen to chase such thoughts away with laudanum and denial. Mr. Sims, in his sweetness, had shattered all that and made her see the truth.

How can such news come from the mouth of an angel?

Do you not know what this means?

Everything, everything, is ruined.

TWENTY-TWO

JOB

She is there, Job thinks, as he peers in at St. Mary's churchyard.

He is once again up in the branches of the towering old elm outside the walls, hidden to the world by the rich, late-summer canopy of leaves that envelops his movements in shadow, his sounds in its perpetual whisper and rustle.

The earth is already working on disassembling Ella Beddoe down there, though he, of course, cannot see her.

He hopes it's taking its time, as it sometimes does, but you can never know.

It's a question of how industrious the worms have been, how stoutly the body holds out against decay.

Every case is different—sometimes it seems that if a subject was tenacious in life, so, too, is it in death.

They decompose more slowly, as if still encoded into their dead musculature is the hardened resolve and unwillingness to surrender that got them through their lives.

I hope you were a tough one, Ella.

That you have not gone quietly.

And that the whole of you is largely still there, lying in as pristine a state of quietude as a corpse can.

I would rather see you that way, would rather handle you that way, than have to sort through the sludge of you.

No one would be the better for that.

And this errand, already a fool's, would truly be for naught.

The boy, Cager, is with him, crouched in the branches nearby, resolutely scanning the churchyard—taking in the mortsafe, the slab, the lanterns, the men of the graveyard shift that regularly move through the grounds below.

Job had done his best to dissuade him from coming, but to no avail.

He's made the mistake of sharing with the boy, under pressure of time and pain, angrily, begrudgingly, all that is in his head, his great absurd plan.

He's not yielded the secrets of himself to another—and everything is a secret, it's safer and more comfortable that way—for as long as he can remember.

But dormant places are coming alive in him despite himself.

The desperate quarters of emotion that have been sealed up, denied, forgotten.

He is not fully in control of himself.

The rectitude of age, experience, seems now to him more an idea than a truth.

For if it's true—as seems amply evidenced by the lightness in his head, the weakness in his limbs, the sticky ooze of the wound in his gut—that his life has suddenly been telescoped into this single night, then also within that same span are compressed the entirety of the fears and emotions and vulnerabilities that would otherwise have been strewn, half experienced at best, across decades, attenuated to the point that they were never truly felt at all.

In urgency comes life, true, beautiful, horrifying.

Perhaps he's ultimately allowed the boy to come along

because he was stirred by just how moved the boy was upon hearing of his plight.

How idealistic, loyal, and noble Cager's insistence had been that he stay by Job's side, even if it amounted to a sort of condescension. *You cannot do it alone, old man, you are not capable.*

On any other night, Job would have snorted, pride would have been aroused, and he would've dismissed the boy out of hand.

There are many strains of man, that Job-on-another-night would have said, ones that traffic in many things, from bank bonds to jewelry to shit and corpses, but none of those things are their measure.

Their measure, rightly understood, as is that of all men, is capability, how one gets the work of life done, how he manifests it, refuses to be cowed, broken, or denied until his aim has been achieved.

That Job would have been as offended as he had ever been.

He would also have told the boy he didn't want his blood on his hands, that this was his own private fight, and he would have delivered such lines with impossible brio and virtue, even if going in shorthanded as a result would've certainly meant failure.

Better to die for an ideal than live compromised.

Such that Job-on-another-night would have thought, anyhow.

But that other night will not be.

That other version of him.

He is only and will ever be the man he is this night—imperfect, needy, desperate.

So he has taken the boy up into this, for he knows the boy is right.

Even two men are too few to do this job.

But it's all they have.

And solutions must come now.

They watch the graveyard shift, check the sight lines, forge imaginary paths across the graveyard with their eyes, whisper things between them.

They will need time to dig, perhaps as much as thirty minutes, without taking the mortsafe and slab into consideration.

It will not be a top-down job, because that requires the removal of the slab—an impossibility given the circumstances.

Their best chance will be leaving the slab in place, coming in from the side.

Done properly, the heavy steel cage of the mortsafe will support the slab, and they can remove Ella laterally.

That means the mortsafe must be dealt with—either unlocked or its heavy iron bars somehow bent.

They haven't the key for the former or the raw strength for the latter.

Their only option would be a fulcrum of some sort, a pry bar to work one bar against another and widen the cage enough that a man could wriggle in, and thereafter wriggle a body out.

But this will require time as well—perhaps another thirty minutes—to speak nothing of the noise.

An hour, then—they will need a whole, impossible sixty minutes down there, in that place horrifically overlit by a half dozen lanterns, being watched ceaselessly by the graveyard shift in the watchhouse, who even now have dispatched a couple of men into the cemetery to make the rounds.

Job and Cager watch as the well-dressed pair move below.

Each totes a pail, a brush.

This has been happening since Cager and Job arrived.

The men have systematically been circling the graveyard, dipping the brushes into the mysterious contents of the pail, and dressing the insides of the churchyard walls with the curious liquid.

The walls glisten in the lantern light.

Whatever it is, it is viscous and does not dry.

It is only now, once the two men are close enough and work the wall below, that Cager and Job catch a waft of the mysterious dressing being applied.

It is the smell of kitchens, of spent tallow, of soap factories—rendered fat.

The boy doesn't understand at first what's happening, but to Job it's pretty clear.

He leans over, whispers to the boy what he thinks.

They are making it so that the walls cannot be scaled.

But are only doing so on the inside.

Which means only one thing to Job's mind.

The fact that the men came looking for him in St. Giles means they know this woman is his aim.

And rather than futilely attempting to flush him out of that labyrinth, they have simplified their pursuit.

Why chase the man when they know precisely where he's going?

Even now, they blow out one lantern, then another, enshrouding the churchyard in an all-too-welcome darkness.

The sort of darkness a resurrectionist, they think—correctly—would readily get to work in.

"They would have it that we can get in," Job whispers into Cager's ear, "but not get out. The only way out would be through the gate, where those men will be waiting."

Job considers the dark forms of the men in the window.

"They don't know exactly where, but they know we're here."

TWENTY-THREE
BEAUCHAMP

BEAUCHAMP IS NOT in a good mood. His new colleague's plan has not gone as advertised. The sacristan, so central to Wheeler's grand scheme, now lies in a mewling, bloody heap at their feet. The man has not been agreeable from the outset—not since making their late-night acquaintance at his front door, not upon hearing what was initially a kindly request that he remove the mortsafe and slab from Missus Beddoe's grave, this very evening. The request was met with an indignant scoff, the man alone in his house not understanding that what was being proffered was not a question but a demand—an affable, polite demand. The mortsafe and slab *would* be moved. Tonight. Wheeler and Beauchamp were only being properly English about it, but the noddy bastard was not being properly English in return.

And so Beauchamp snapped, gave the man a few quick nopes in the mouth, and the man moved from vertical to horizontal almost instantaneously, his collapse silent, any breath or complaint in his throat swallowed out of sheer shock. For the briefest of moments, Beauchamp had thought the aged fellow dead—which would've *really* gummed the wheels of the plan—but a few moments later, the stricken sacristan managed to finally exhale a long, pained blast of air and, along with it, a tooth, which skittered away across the floorboards as if fleeing, a roach from a burning building.

Beauchamp is frustrated it's come to this, but with all

that's transpired today, he's a positive whorl of conniption. His body's in revolt from lack of opium—his patience, a wisp of a thing on most days, is nowhere in attendance.

The good news is that the violence has apparently appealed to the sacristan's better angels. He no longer scoffs. He's congenial, accommodating. English. He hears out their needs. Agrees to help. Violence, properly wielded, is civilizing, Beauchamp thinks. Easiest way to motivate someone is to reach into them, awaken their survival instinct. Once they understand that you are capable of bringing about their extinction, they become strangely agreeable to you. And thus all the nonsense of violence can be done away with. So much easier just to establish where everyone lies in the hierarchy from the outset. Then collegially get on with things.

And collegial the sacristan becomes. He's quite the conversationalist as he gathers the things needed to effect his part of the plan: the key to the mortsafe, the tack required for the horse team he will use to haul away the slab.

Why are they digging up the body? Are they resurrectionists?

Something thereabouts.

Where do you sell the bodies?

Does it matter?

And on the conversation goes, the man's lips occasionally slipping and tripping on the words as blood seeps from his torn gums. The important thing is that it's all moving forward. They are now behind the man's house and in his stable. The horses are being roused and tacked up.

Beauchamp senses a funny turn in the sacristan. The man is at once dutifully making small talk in a way meant to show compliance, yet at the same time seems somehow liberated, as if the upstanding churchman has been freed from the shackles of propriety by this indenture and is thereby able to indulge in questions never asked in polite society. The man is titillated.

"The decay does not bother you? The putrescence?"

"We live in putrescence."

"What do they look like?"

Beauchamp realizes the man is referring to the dead here but wants to make him say it. "Who?"

"The corpses—is it as they say? Is it the stuff of nightmares?"

The sacristan, Beauchamp knows, wants him to say yes. As if it's somehow a sweet, forbidden horror to him.

"Surely you've seen the dead."

"Only aboveground. They are pristine then. Cleaner in death than they ever were in life. An illusion. I have always wondered about . . . the subsequent stages."

"The soul escapes, holy man. That should be enough for you," Wheeler interjects.

Beauchamp nods. "You'll get your look. Tonight. If you want it. Now keep on. You tack up those steeds any slower, and it'll be sunup before we get out of here."

The man moves to harness the horses to his nearby growler. He is preoccupied, Beauchamp knows. With seeing the dead. Beauchamp can see it in his eyes, the way they stare beyond this stable, beyond his harness, the way they turn over thoughts that unconsciously cause the brows above to grow lax, rise, giving him the same vacant mien of children lost in daydream.

Beauchamp briefly pities him. You are a man of the light, and I am a subterranean thing. But I am free, and you are caged by your rectitude. I fear nothing—neither God, nor sin, nor the stink of the dead. You fear to indulge the dark questions, the dark, irrational currents of desire within. You have ossified, haven't you? You have been in the light too long. You have been upstanding, so much so that you have risen to such station in the church that a thousand eyes now look regularly to you. And so you bury away your humanity, your turgid desire, to be the exemplar they expect you to be. And that is the mistake.

Better to investigate. Better to enter into those black warrens of the earth, of society, or yourself. Better to get your fill. Your answers. It will not turn you into a demon. It will liberate you. You will have gotten your answers. You will not wonder. You will be free to come back to the world of the light, sated. Wiser. Woe to you or any man that thinks the path through life can be traveled only in daylight. Day is only sweet because it is twinned with night. Do not lie to me and say you have no night in you, sacristan. Walk naked into that night, unafraid. It will embrace you.

I will take you there, in fact. I will do so with enthusiasm. I will enlighten you.

In response to the sacristan's unspoken thoughts, Beauchamp nods warmly. "Don't worry. Once you lift that lid and look down, what's in there's just us. Minus the breath and bullshit."

A thought occurs to the sacristan as he nears completion of his work. "What of the graveyard shift?"

"What of it?"

"That's something Mr. Beddoe arranged. Not me. It'd be pointless to even try to undertake what you're trying to do with those men there."

"They won't be a problem," Wheeler says tersely.

The sacristan pauses. "What do you intend to do?"

Wheeler meets eyes with Beauchamp, looks back to the sacristan. "Your work is to get the hardware off that grave."

The sacristan surveys the two men, dubious. "You intend to kill them?"

For the briefest of moments, Beauchamp wonders if this act, too, holds dark allure for him. But it becomes clear this is not the case. The sacristan stops harnessing the horses. "I won't be party to murder."

"Want my friend here to knock out the rest of your teeth?" Wheeler asks flatly.

"You can kill me. I won't participate in murder."

Damn him, Beauchamp thinks. Damn him to hell.

The sacristan defiantly begins to unharness the two horses.

"Don't do that," Wheeler warns. "If you int gonna use 'em, we will."

Beauchamp knows where this is going. He punches the sacristan in the back of the skull, and the sacristan goes down. But the man rises to his feet a moment later. Resumes unharnessing the horses. Beauchamp punches him again. The sacristan slumps against one of the horses, agitating the creature, but again summons some deep reserve of conviction and fortitude, and a moment later, the first horse is free of the harness.

"Leave now, the both of you," he gasps, eyeing Beauchamp and Wheeler. "Find God. Know that he watches everything." And with that, the churchman slaps the rein in his hand against the hindquarters of the already agitated horse before him. The horse is all too willing to flee. Before Beauchamp and Wheeler can respond, it's gone into the night.

Already the sacristan is moving to spook the other.

Shite, Beauchamp thinks. Bastard's all hell hocus with God now. Which is the worst sort of intoxication. These thoughts come sharp and quick to Beauchamp's aching mind. Time has already ground to a standstill. The man unstraps the last horse before them. Wheeler, of course, is worthless, putting feckless hands to the man, protesting in his affected gangster way. The man has the strength of God in him, Wheeler! Your fay hands are about as useful in this situation as a side pocket to a dog.

And so it comes. It rises up out of Beauchamp as it always does, mysterious, primordial, pragmatic, an instinct called to action before his brain can even shape intention or plan of action.

He hits the man so hard he can hear bones breaking. The sacristan's cheekbone, collapsing inside his face. And maybe even within his own fist, that bone of the middle finger exploding.

This time, the man goes down in a very different way, the angles of him unnatural.

He hits the ground in such a way—as if his body is suddenly uninhabited, abandoned—that both Beauchamp and Wheeler know he will never get up.

But in that chaos, he has cried out, has crashed down onto the back of the remaining horse's hock, and the horse, already spooked on account of the other's flight and sensing that something very untoward is happening, responds accordingly. With only a half-fastened strap still binding it to the growler, it breaks free, slipping the strap and following the first horse into the night.

Beauchamp's vision is swollen with fire. He can do nothing for a moment but look down at his work. This churchman, permanently broken before him. Wheeler is somewhere beside him clucking about the lost horses. It takes Beauchamp all he has to abide the fire within him and not turn it on Wheeler. Better maybe just to burn everything down. Destroy Wheeler and himself and let the fire have its way and never think again.

But as always, the cool comes on fast, washing through his veins. Best get rational when there's a dead man at your feet. It seems another sort of instinct. Sit around at the scene of the crime too long, and you're not long for this world.

He rummages through the dead man's pockets, finds the keys to the mortsafe, announces this.

They have the key, at least.

Horses, however, are a different story. Without them, the slab does not move.

Beauchamp has come too far to allow for this outcome. He has endured Wheeler, has killed a man of God. Most important, he just wants to eat opium. Slip back into the Great Smooth and be done with all this infernal busywork that is life. And the straightest line to opium is this cock-eyed affair he's now knee deep in. It can still work. It's just a matter of getting a new set of horses and a gig.

He knows where to do this, though the replacements would be no match for the sacristan's fine team. It would also mean bringing Gray into it. For the animals he now conceives of are the sickly pair that they have long used to convey their goods about London. The sickly gig attached to them. The sickly woman too, who is nothing but a headache.

But that would mean that his share of the swag, already halved with Wheeler, would be halved again.

Yes, he decides, they will go to Gray.

But when this is all said and done, this purse will not be split three ways. Of that he is sure.

TWENTY-FOUR

GRAY

THE ROOM IN the accommodation house is a different thing to her now. The space, the silence, the smells, are suddenly unfamiliar, not the hallmarks of the home she considered this place to be only this afternoon. Instead, in the crushing, post-midnight darkness, they are alien, ill boding.

That is why she's asked Mr. Sims to come up from the street with her. As if his unstinting beneficence might spell the heaviness, might chase away the shadows that have long inhabited this place alongside her and Beauchamp, shadows that were once harmless effects of light but now seem to be living things, crouching, watching, ravenous—as if they might draw her up into their maws and drag her into a world darker even than this one.

The floorboards flex beneath her feet in a way she's never felt before. Yes, they have always been accusatory, the telltale sounds of the malfeasance she and Beauchamp have committed within these walls, yet now she hears them, truly hears them, the way that the creaks and cavils radiate out through the boards and into the frame of the building itself. How the whole of the vulgar, second-rate building ever so subtly shivers at their presence.

We have been such a curse, she thinks. A two-headed pestilence. It is understandable why the shadows would want to eat us. Rid the world of our blight.

Mr. Sims's arm is warm under her hand. Were it not for

him, she thinks, but then does not complete the thought. Because knowing what she now knows, she cannot envision surviving without him.

The body is a mystery. She understands it less even than she understands her head. Her knowledge of both has changed indelibly this day. The rest of her life is dead to her, everything that preceded this moment. She is not a terrace girl or a writer or an opium eater.

The physician will not let her lament.

She is to collect whatever she needs and leave this place.

Beauchamp, when he returns, will never know what became of her.

TWENTY-FIVE

JOB

JOB AND CAGER have come down from the tree.

Have slunk through shadow and silence like the thieves they are, away from the cemetery and a block into the nearby neighborhood.

Fife waits ahead atop his tattered growler, those two dutiful bonesetters idling at reins' end before him.

Solid as the earth, this man and his steeds, Job thinks.

Were the world populated exclusively with creatures so outwardly unclean but inwardly spotless, there would be no need for God, government, or gallows.

It is always the other way around.

We clothe ourselves with gloss, carry our dirt within.

And for that lie—wearing our skin, the truth of us, inside out—the world has from the outset learned to distrust itself.

Not so here.

In this desperation, the sin of this night shared unabashedly, is communion.

There is no malice in it, only imperfect, unsightly, but noble need.

Fife has agreed to be their growlerman.

To spirit Ella Beddoe as quickly as possible from the graveyard to the anatomist's residence.

He has indicated that he will do so free of charge, as a sort of valedictory to the relationship Job and he have long shared.

Both men know Job will pay him anyhow.

"The plan has changed," Job says.

Fife absorbs this, faintly amused. "When don't they?"

"You want to know how?"

"Not particularly."

"It'll take longer."

Fife gestures with his pipe. "I got any duties beyond sitting here smoking mundungus?"

"No, but you may need more of it."

Fife pats his jacket pocket, pleased.

"Got a whole Carolina plantation on me."

He nods up the street to the low industrial fog that hangs ghostly and yellow in the effulgence of the gas lamps, rendered soft and spherical by the light like disembodied, noxious dandelions.

"Better out here smoking than back home sleeping. Can't smoke when you sleep. Man needs to keep his lungs virginal. Now, go. Get on with it."

Job and the boy circle the far side of the graveyard, away from the watchhouse and graveyard shift.

They give it a wide berth, staying a block out, always in the shadows.

Once they are abreast of the church itself, they bear quietly back toward the grounds.

The church looms before them, a bulwark between them and the men on the other side.

For all the sundry reasons that there is no time, they get instantly to work.

Job is not a man of God.

But putting a pry bar to a church evokes a strange feeling in him.

Their plan is to circumvent the grounds of the graveyard entirely.

There will be no walls to climb, no gates to pass through.

No matter how much light the watchmen cast upon Ella Beddoe's grave, it will not be enough, for Job and the boy will quit the world of light entirely tonight.

Job wraps the end of the pry bar with a sack, doubles it over so that the padding is thick and soft, then presses it hard against one of the panels in the lowest stained-glass window of the church.

With enough pressure, the glass flexes and quietly snaps.

Job looks back at the boy, who is gazing up at the larger stained-glass image with an inscrutable expression.

Up there, Mother Mary with child.

Job cannot tell if the boy is troubled by this, breaching Mary, but hasn't the time to wonder.

He quickly reaches in, begins pulling away the other glass panes around the breach.

They acquiesce easily in his hand, alongside the lead came frame that binds them.

Soon he has pulled enough away that there is a gap in the window adequate for them to fit through.

He makes a stirrup out of his hands, nods to the boy, and a moment later the boy is up and inside the dark church.

Job follows, first passing the tools through, then pulling himself up with some effort to the hole in the window.

He leaves behind a telltale smear of blood on the stone sill of the church, hoping that it reads only black in the night to passersby, just another of the thousand sooty streaks of rain that have fallen from poisonous skies and scarred this holy place.

It is a familiar cold inside, the permanent season of churches.

Though it is dry, everywhere is the odor of dampnesses unseen.

They are insulated from the rest of the world for a moment, the stone walls great moats of silence between them and the city.

There are only the sounds of their footsteps, which move parallel to them in the echoing space, manifold and spectral, through apse and sacristy, between pews, around and behind the altar.

As if they are walking with an invisible army of themselves, no doubt nobler versions, closer to God.

Soon they are before the thin set of steps in the transept that descend to the crypt.

It's down there they will do their work.

In a place the watchmen would not think to look.

Out there, somewhere, they diligently watch the grounds from on high, from every vantage allowed.

But they do not think to look in here.

And that is their mistake, for their assumption is that the only direction one can dig is down, from the hallowed world of the living above.

The crypt houses the rich and the holy.

A half dozen of London's finest Catholics.

The walls, despite the brickwork, seep.

And that is good.

Job crosses to the far wall, presses hard against the bricks.

They are flexible, compliant.

It will not take much to pull them and their grout away, set upon the earth.

Job estimates it will take thirty feet of digging to tunnel unseen across the churchyard and get to Ella Beddoe.

He pries away a brick.

The soil beneath is damp, yielding, promiscuous.

It will make for fast digging.

It means if the stars align, they might retrieve Ella by sunup, and the whole of the plan can still work.

It also means that the earth will be unsteady, unstructured, ready to shift and collapse at any turn.

They quickly begin disengaging bricks from the wall.

Soon there is a wide enough space that both men can set upon the naked soil with mattocks.

The earth receives the blades greedily, sucks them into its muddiness, yields them again easily for another strike.

It's as if the earth conspires with them, encourages them, muffles their strokes so that none of the living above can hear.

What should crunch whispers instead.

What should crack instead hisses and grunts.

And such things don't travel far, even in churches.

Only the dead behind them hear.

And the dead, Job knows, do not pass on what they know.

TWENTY-SIX
BEAUCHAMP

BEAUCHAMP'S NOSE RUNS, though he's not sick. His eyes well with tears, though he's not sad. His stomach lurches furiously as if it were trying to tear itself free from his body, that seat of widening pain and unease.

He can think only of the Great Smooth. Escape. It is so far from this place. So far from the roaring, silent onslaught that is his limbs, his guts, his mind at present, an onslaught that only grows with each moment. What he would not give, what he would not do, for a glass of laudanum. Just a glass so that he might just *be* for a moment, his mind wordless and without narrative.

His night has come full circle. He returns to the accommodation house with execrable Wheeler in tow.

He thinks, as the hulking blackness of the house comes into view, that they'll collect Gray, the gig, and the horses, and it'll be onward to Mrs. Beddoe and her trove in a matter of minutes.

Forms assemble themselves in the unlit alley ahead. A man and woman, hurriedly packing the very gig he aims to use!

The woman is Gray. The man is unknown, though what is more important in this moment is the fact that the man has his hands upon her elbow.

For a moment that is all Beauchamp sees—the way that in shadow those two arms create a single, unbroken silhouette, as if they are one thing, indivisible.

His feet react first. He begins to shuffle, then run. Wheeler blurts something behind him, but Wheeler is nothing now.

That horrid indivisible silhouette bounces in his vision as he runs toward it. They see him. Try vainly to mount the gig so that they might escape before he arrives.

Escape! *Him!*

He is on them before they can properly mount the gig. He yanks Gray as hard as he can, breaks the chain of them. She hisses something at him, but Beauchamp casts her aside like the trash that she is and grabs the man. Pulls him hard from the gig and slams him onto the ground, into the cess and rubbish where he belongs.

"Got a flash man, do we? Stealing my twang?"

The man tries to stammer something, but Beauchamp gives him a muzzler that puts an end to it.

The man's eyes quake in his head, dazed, as if trying to find focus, as if trying to access reality. Beauchamp does not give him the privilege. He slams him again, this time even harder, and the man is out.

He pivots to Gray. Wheeler arrives.

Gray, Beauchamp thinks, looks even worse than he must. Sickly as always, but now horrified. Caught. Her leaden face growing pink, tears no doubt about to burst forth everywhere.

Beauchamp briefly eyes the man on the ground. Decent wares. Too decent for this neighborhood. "Trading up, were you?"

"You haven't a clue," she says defiantly.

You petty little crack, he thinks. Your words are tough, but your face is the truth. You are properly scared of me, as you should and always will be.

He calls her a bum-strumming whore but stops there. There are a hundred things he could say, a hundred ways he could visit violence upon her. But a subtle eddy of wisdom swirls within the chaos of his mind. She, what she has done, is secondary in this moment—remember that. To dwell on it will not get you closer to what you want, what you need.

He seizes her elbow, shoves her forcefully back toward the gig.

She protests. What is he doing?

He tells her they are going to St. Mary's churchyard. That she will be participating in a racket there and that she is not to ask any questions. Only to do as she is told, which is to mind and guide the gig while the two men are engaged in a job.

She pulls herself free with such force that it surprises him. That leaden face that had a moment ago threatened to go all feminine and pink and blustery is once again pallid and serious. Only more so. More than he can remember it being since she was that smart girl who'd first met him on the steps of Newgate.

She has regained her wits, he knows. Has seen through the lie of him.

"I'm not going," she says.

"I'll tell you if you're going," he returns and grabs her anew.

She hits him. Hard. It is an unpracticed thing, this punch, the fist not completely closed, her fingernails open and exposed to the world. They slice the bridge of his nose. A moment later, there is blood.

The fury that comes is volcanic. It rumbles and roars within. He tries to suppress it, though he knows it's futile. "Last time, cat," he growls at her, hoping she will relent.

She hits him again.

And so it comes. A hot wave up from hell. Beauchamp

doesn't have to do anything, can't do anything. This is a thing of its own that must be, that already is. His body is only a conduit. He can only witness as his knee goes to her first, then his fist, then his elbows. She is standing, then she is on the ground. He is standing, then he is crouched atop her, mounted atop her, drawing blood from her with his fists. It is a purging. It must be until it is not. Until it is spent. It comes in fiery gusts, one after the other, until the last one passes and there is nothing left. Then the world returns, and there is sound. The cool of the evening on his sweaty forehead. And she lies in a mask of crimson between his knees.

Wheeler says nothing, mortified. Beauchamp says nothing.

The only words to complicate the night will be hers. They come as she chokes on the noxious London air around them. Again there are tears in her eyes. Though, to Beauchamp, they seem a different sort than what was promised before. There is no fear there, nor pain, but instead regret. Her swollen lips seem almost to smile, though the smile seems split through with a sadness bound for eternity. "You have killed two of us," she says.

She says no more, nor will she. Her eyes seize up, not in the way of death, not yet. But as if the muscles behind them have quit, the connections that power them have been fatally compromised.

She breathes, if only weakly, but her face is slack, as if she has died from the neck up. The rest of her body seems not far behind. The breaths grow ever shallower, though they do not yet stop.

You have killed two of us.

It's not until Beauchamp sees her left hand that he starts to surmise what this means. It lays protective over her belly, that swollen aberration that he had heretofore hated her for, which he had thought was a sign of her sloth, her weakness.

The vents in him open again. The heat far below beckons.

But he doesn't know how to do this, to give up on living. It would be easier to die, to just end it, but he cannot surrender like that. Cannot let death cast final, irrevocable judgment upon him.

He picks up her body, finds himself laying it gingerly in the back of the gig. Not *it*. *Her*. He will not let himself think this way. She is still here. She will always be here. Piss and fart, sound at heart. He will make this right and good, and they will again swim together in the Great Smooth. He will finally tell her the truth about the dogs, and he will probably cry, but he doesn't care anymore.

"She's dead," Wheeler says. "Brain quit."

Beauchamp abides this quietly, spent. Everything leaches from him, all impulse, all emotion and reaction. He can only persist now, nothing more. Continue, nothing more. All along the straightest line that will get him to the Great Smooth. "We'll still do it," he says, climbing into the gig.

Wheeler looks uncomfortably at the insensate woman in the rear.

"I'm not leaving her in the street," Beauchamp says without emotion. "I'm not that kind of man."

Wheeler looks at him for a long time, weighing things.

A few moments later, he mounts the gig beside Beauchamp, and they head out for St. Mary's churchyard.

TWENTY-SEVEN

BEDDOE

I HAVE COME to St. Mary's at this late hour because I cannot stay away. I must hold vigil over my wife, my beloved, especially during these early nights of her interment. I thought I could remain at home, but I am strangely more at ease here among the headstones.

Better to be with you, my love. I walk these grounds with you, breathe the air for the both of us.

It is dignified, this place. Befitting you.

I have never until now understood the saccharine romance attributed to graveyards.

But I understand now. One is made eternal in death, fixed to a place, certain. We fear losing people in life, but in death they are steadfast. They cannot be lost. They can always be found—a place has become them, and they have become a place. You will be this place, this air, this grass, forever. If I am ever alone, I know I can come here and inhabit you, and you me. Thank God for that.

I am ready to let go of you. I have wondered about you incessantly since you slipped from my view beneath the soil. I have wondered with each passing day and hour how you look. Are you still as beautiful as in life? Or have you begun the process of giving yourself to the earth, becoming this space forever?

Will you walk with me?

Good. It makes the night endurable to know you are listening.

I wanted you to be clean forever. So that my crime would never seem real to me. So that the memory of you that inhabits me remains a thing of permanent beauty, like the altarpiece angel you are.

This grass is you. This marble grave marker beneath my finger. Even the rough stone of the church itself. You will outlast it.

I wish you would rot now, however.

I have made my peace. Welcome the worms, would you? Let the maggots undo you. Become this place. Go ahead.

You and I both know where to start. Yield your neck first. The bruising. The testament to my guilt.

I will be able to sleep that way. I will not be summoned here from my warm estate out of anguish. Free me of that anguish, will you, beloved? I tremble at night, do you know that? For the first time in my life, I truly tremble at the thought that our shared secret might be discovered. Do not give these miscreants something to see, should they somehow succeed in unearthing you. They are worse sinners than I am, a collective pox on the land—I care not for their opinions. Yet surely you understand that they mean to convey you to an anatomist who would assiduously put a knife to you, study every inch of you. You see my problem, then, don't you? That the anatomist works at St. Bart's—that place where I hold such high station—only compounds the problem. I am a *known* man. And my sin would be equally known. I do not, in the end, deserve to be judged solely by that sin—that single mistake, that single minute of my life—after all I have done, all I have overcome!

Come apart, then. Let go of this flesh. Let go of your

husband, who just wants to sleep. You would not deny me that, would you?

What—

My God, a shiver has just passed through me—

A cold beyond reckoning—

It is you. Your hand. Unseen. Signaling your presence.

The world warps. The church itself is disturbed. Its walls ever so subtly undulate before me. There, that tiny stone by the window. You have announced yourself. You have reached back into this reality and upset things to speak to me in the only way that you know how. Telling me you have listened. That you have complied.

I come to you. My legs can scarcely conduct me.

Why here, why this stone?

Why do you cause it to flex ever so subtly, the mortar around it dropping dusty fragments to the ground below? Is it the stained-glass image above that you have chosen to somehow make your wordless point? This saint astride a dragon?

This is most certainly real. Even the stained glass that makes up that saint is flexing. Something is happening.

Or perhaps . . .

See how it's all a sort of chain reaction? How the panes of glass tremble and flex in the window right above that nervous stone? How if you look close enough, the stones in the wall beneath that nervous stone also shift? Of course you do not see it, because I don't think it's you. They don't *move*, at least not with any outward evidence. But the mortar around them cracks ever so lightly, yields a bit of itself to the ground.

No, what is doing this is a thing of this world, right beneath us. As if the unseen soil down there seems to be quitting the place.

Quitting right here, and nowhere else.

TWENTY-EIGHT
BEAUCHAMP

LONDON IS DEAD with sleep around them as they make for the cemetery. The gig jounces over the cobblestones, Gray's inert body shifting behind them as Beauchamp snaps the reins and Wheeler hands him something.

A pistol. Beauchamp does not acknowledge it.

Wheeler's mouth has been going this whole time, but the words have been crushed to nothingness by all that has transpired. Like they are spoken from a mile deep in the sea.

"Pepperbox revolver," he's saying. "Four barrels, you rotate 'em by hand after each go."

He lays a coat atop the pistol. "Put this to 'em first. Shoot through. It'll get the job done, keep it quiet at the same time."

Beauchamp listens through the man's words to the back of the gig. To that body. To her. Rocking about ever so slightly, without resistance. Indifferent to potholes, to the corners they take. It has that terrible sound he knows so well, that has so often accompanied him on all those recent nights in this vehicle. Lifeless yielding.

A body reduced to cargo.

TWENTY-NINE

JOB

"SO THIS IS what it is to be dead," the boy says.

He seems faintly amused.

Job welcomes mirth in this moment, given that they are surrounded in mud and worms and impossibility.

The small tunnel continues to grow.

It is misshapen around them, uncertain, hardly a tunnel at all.

It is more of a warren, something a creature of the earth would make.

A mole.

The ceiling is scarcely two feet high, the space just big enough so that they might wriggle forward on their elbows and reverse the process with Ella Beddoe in tow.

Truth be told, it's scarcely a ceiling at all.

It seeps and shifts and threatens to come down at any moment.

The men have used all they can as bulwarks—shovels, a stool from the church, slats from the two decaying coffins they've come upon as they've burrowed.

They pulled the coffins apart, left the mud-eaten corpses alone.

But without the structure of the caskets, the graves collapse in on themselves, the bones scattering into the tunnel beside the two men.

The men clear them away like they clear everything away, impediments.

Job works in front, splits the earth, passes it back to the boy behind him, who shimmies back up the tunnel, dumps it in the crypt.

They have placed a lantern halfway through in a small, muddy niche they've carved from the earth.

The quarters are so tight it does little for them beyond rendering them in silhouette, but it is enough.

They can see the edges of each other, golden, the only suggestion of color in the otherwise crushing scheme of blackness around them.

Job continues to dig, push back mud.

The boy continues to dutifully shuttle it back to the crypt, crawling back into the tunnel each time with some wry whisper, some joke Job knows is intended to buoy him.

Keep the dying old man's spirits up.

God bless you, boy, you should not be in this grave with me.

I count the minutes for you.

Maybe sixty, ninety more, and we are to Ella.

After that, maybe five to get to Fife and be gone into the night.

A hundred minutes.

I count them.

To get you out of this.

To end my chapter in your life.

He carves away more mud, passes it back.

The boy reverses himself again, shimmying back to the crypt.

Job strikes the slats of another coffin.

It cannot be Ella's.

They have not yet come far enough.

Besides, its boards are rotten, giving easily beneath his blade.

But maybe it is, in a sense, far enough, Job thinks. Maybe there is opportunity in this.

The boy returns.

"What is it?" he asks hopefully.

"It's her. We're home," Job says.

"Mrs. Beddoe—you're sure?"

"Go tell Fife. I can get her out on my own."

"You need me, don't you?"

"Not anymore. Go tell Fife."

"You can carry her?"

"Carried men twice her size—go."

The boy absorbs it, works his way back out of the tunnel.

Something heavy drains from Job as he does.

It was wrong to bring the boy, to give in to him.

It was a moment of weakness.

But now it has been made right. The boy will be outside the walls and out of harm's way.

It will only be Job and the earth, as it should be.

He digs.

Clears earth.

Progresses further, deeper.

Slides the spent soil behind him like the mole he is.

Without someone to clear it, the tunnel becomes increasingly disjointed, thinner, lower.

He persists, the lantern light fading as the tunnel extends, its aperture constricting.

There is only him and his breath and the darkness, the sound of his blade and the earth.

The world sharpened into a pinpoint, reduced to endeavor only, one endeavor, this endeavor.

The earth yields itself to him, and he takes it, for he knows that soon the agreement will be reversed, when he shall yield himself, and the earth shall take him.

But not now, not just yet.

He still toils.

He takes a brief break, catches his breath.

His blood, he knows, is draining from him, and the toil will not get easier.

But he must rest, just for a moment.

He lays himself in the mud, listens to his breaths come and go.

They do not sound like his breaths.

They wheeze, rasp.

And there is something else.

A voice.

Disembodied, behind him.

He shifts slightly, looks back.

If the boy has returned, he will give him hell.

But it is not the boy.

Far up the tunnel, barely visible through the narrowing aperture he has made, is the small slice of light signifying the opening to the crypt.

A shadow passes before it.

In the dim light of the tunnel, Job cannot make out more.

He is too soaked, his vision too blurred.

But the voice is not the boy's.

It is too angry, too guttural.

It projects into the hole, furious, calling out to him, seeking him.

The shadow crowds the opening, and the light of the crypt falls away.

They are coming in.

Whoever they are, they are coming in.

Instinctively Job presses himself into the mud, becomes the mud, his boots shoving loose earth up behind him in the tunnel in a vain attempt to create a berm, an obstruction, so that he might not be seen.

The shadow, with great difficulty, fills the hole, crawls forward.

He is a big man, and his words are foul.

He swears, disgusted, furious.

"If there's anyone in here, they'd best come out now lest they want to be gutted!"

Job says nothing, remains silent and unmoving as the mud around him.

The shadow heaves, gasps, swears.

Job has never heard such imprecation before, and Job has heard everything.

This man, whoever he is, threatens to come apart in the cramped space, and he is raging.

He yells at the hole.

The hole around Job does not respond.

He yells louder.

The earth swallows his words.

Job doesn't speak, for he can tell the man cannot see him.

Cannot see beyond the glow of the lantern midtunnel.

Cannot see into the shrunken, unlit extension of the tunnel Job now hides in.

Most of all, the man, Job can tell, cannot stand being in the dark, in the mud, away from the world.

He is unnerved by the death around him, claustrophobic.

The man swears once more, looks blindly beyond the lantern, then seizes the lantern itself and begins a frustrated, labored retreat out of the hole.

Job watches him go, watches the lantern bounce and shrink until finally the man reaches the crypt, exits, and the light of that dim space once again outlines the mouth of the tunnel.

The requisite questions flood Job—do they know he is somewhere in here, did they find the boy—but before he can sort out the most likely answers in his head, that slice of light that is the crypt—his umbilical to the world—darkens again.

There is more than one voice now.

They are working together.

And that slice of light is starting to disappear.

Job knows this means they are filling in the tunnel.

He is too far away to reverse himself to get there.

Too far gone to surrender.

The light goes away, bit by bit, until there is nothing.

No lantern, no umbilical.

Just him, the earth, and darkness.

THIRTY
JOB

JOB THOUGHT HE was beyond horror.

That there was nothing to fear, because he had already seen everything there was to fear.

And yet through all that, he now realizes, it is a different thing to behold fear than to *be* it.

The horror had always been out there.

He has not looked out, until now, from within it.

Not truly, not like this, the black so dark around him it begins to take on dimension.

Begins to populate itself with pulses and colors and waves of anguish, all of them somehow embodied, living things, squeezing him from all sides.

He feels the weight of the earth around him, swelling ever so slightly, gripping him, constricting him.

The air grows hot.

He begins to smell his own stale breath as he inhales anew what he's just exhaled.

For a moment he is paralyzed in a way that he cannot remember being.

He has always been about action, movement, the next.

This, then, is what it is to have the life crushed out of you.

This is what it is to die.

But in the worst sort of way.

The dead at least die topside.

And do not know what it is to be buried.

Deprived of the most important goodbye of all.

To be on this precipice over the void, with no one to whisper it's all right, you've done good, that it will only be a moment, and afterward there will be the perfect, soft sunshine of youth rediscovered, inhabited, certain and forever.

Easy to say these things. You say them yourself, and you know they are lies.

The same lies from another's mouth—solace.

Another.

The whole of him for another.

For Ivy.

He cries.

There is no place one can be truer than in the earth.

He does not want to die.

Does not want to feel his breath abandoning him for the last time.

No one should die like this, shut off from the world, in silent blackness.

They should all have someone beside them, whispering.

It doesn't matter what the words are.

He begins to dig.

Blind like a mole.

Struggling against the earth, defying it.

Willing his way up to the surface.

Toward air.

Toward the light of radiant night.

Toward the men and their guns.

Toward a different death, but one that will have words.

The words that he wants are Ivy's.

Words that will tell him she can speak again, that she is recovering rather than worsening.

But he will take any words, even those of the men as they gun him down.

That way he will die in the land of the living, a solace all should be allowed, criminal or king.

THIRTY-ONE
CAGER

THE MEN HAVE beaten Cager mercilessly.

They've pulled him up to the watchhouse, shouted him down, demanded to know who he's working with, who he's working for.

Cager has played the fool, insisted he works only for himself, despite the fact that the ringleader of these men—who the others call Master Beddoe—has indicated that he knows for a fact the attempt is on behalf of the anatomist Percival Quinn.

"Don't be sammy with me, boy," Beddoe says. "You're just a wee rabbit sucker. Quinn wouldn't've entrusted you with this."

Confusion washes through Cager. It all happened so rapidly—they'd surprised him in the crypt, assaulted him almost immediately thereafter with kicks, punches—that it was all he could do to survive, keep himself together. And yet now, in these few moments of respite, he is able to mull over what he could not then: If Job is still down in that hole, that hole these men have unknowingly sealed up behind him—is he alive? Should Cager tell Beddoe and his men that Job is still in there, if only to potentially save his life, given that he's just been effectively buried alive? Is that what Job would want?

They hit him again. Demand that he talk again.

And again, in response, he plays the fool. Because he

knows he is the fool. He hasn't a clue what the right choice is. Does he snitch on Job to save him? To save himself? He doubts very much that either he or Job will be spared if he puts them at the mercy of these ruffians.

Bloody hell, it hurts to be hit like this. Again and again. Your skull rattling. Sharp constellations of pain exploding through you with each and every strike.

But what's the alternative? There isn't one. Not really.

THIRTY-TWO

FIFE

THE IRISHMAN LIES in the back of his gig, pillows his arm behind his head, tries to tease a star or two out of the fog above. Every once in a while, he lets loose a plume of cheap tobacco smoke, his own small contribution to the infernal layer of pollution above.

Oh, the world, he thinks. Pigs rolling in our own shit. Each of us doing our part.

Sounds assemble themselves unseen off to his left. At first he thinks it's the return of Job and the boy, though that would seem way too fast, too easy. Moreover, there is the sound of horses. And he is the horses of this operation.

Before he can sit up, a growler wheels past, comes to a halt a bit closer to the graveyard. Fife rises, makes sure to keep his profile low, tucked back behind the rail of his gig.

Two men are visible there, tying off the growler, arguing by the light of a small lantern.

Fife recognizes one of them. From where? In short order, he remembers where he's seen the blackened teeth and failing gums before. Outside Quinn's estate all those nights ago. The killer. He'd been with the woman with the crewed hair. Only now he is with a dumplin of a man, all waddle and overdress. He can hear them arguing. Really, it's the dumplin that's arguing, calling after the killer, who's dismounted the gig in silence and is looking over the unseen contents in the back of the growler.

"You wait on me, understand? They know me. You don't go in there first."

The dumplin's talking to a wall, Fife thinks. That killer, he doesn't hear him at all. He's got his back to him, he's looking into the bed of that growler, and it's like the dumplin doesn't even exist.

We're in bad loaf, Fife thinks. Men like these here, at this hour.

The dumplin seizes the killer's arm. The killer wheels on him, and Fife realizes the latter man's got a pistol in his hand. Fife tightens, half expecting the killer to gun the dumplin down right there.

Instead, the killer gives the little man an impenetrable look, pulls free, snuffs the lantern, and with that gun, strides resolutely toward the graveyard.

The dumplin, flummoxed, follows.

Fife sits back, head aswim with the unrelenting developments of the evening.

Blast my top lights, he thinks, all I wanted was to smoke some mundungus and maybe be away from the missus for a bit. Instead, this.

THIRTY-THREE
BEDDOE

THERE IS ANOTHER one here. I know it. More than one, likely. Love, they come for you. They would dig you from the earth like the animals they are.

But I will keep you safe. Our secret safe.

We beat this boy on the floor of the watchhouse. His blood is sweet on our fists. I would kill him now for thinking to dishonor you. But a thought comes to me. Maybe it is you who gives it to me. If there is another, and he cares at all for this boy, I can use the boy.

Follow. Come with me. Witness me—for you—an angel most furious. The pistol in my belt handcrafted by Joseph Manton himself up on Davies Street. The finest of weapons. Well balanced, light, fast handling. Woe to them that befoul this graveyard with their presence.

Yes. Back into the church. Back down into the crypt.

Do you rot for me, as I asked?

Do you putrefy, a thing to turn away from, with no hint of that mistake we made together?

There. See. The place in the wall from whence the boy was pulled. We checked it. Sealed it. But what if...

I clear the hole away with little doing. Yes, the muddy little burrow is once again visible there. They are animals!

Is there another in there, love? Tell me. They would be in your world, and you would know.

I shout into the darkness, and of course, there is only

silence in response. Such a cretin as one who would dig up the dead under cover of night would be too cowardly to face the world head-on anyhow. I would crawl in there and shoot him. But another thought occurs to me. Maybe you gave it to me.

There is a better way to ferret out vermin. The lanterns in the crypt. Resplendent with oil.

I need only empty that oil into the muddy gash in the earth, let it assert itself ever deeper into the passage.

Then a flick from my striker, and all shall be resolved.

You are wise beyond measure, love.

THIRTY-FOUR

ST. MARY'S CHURCHYARD

WHAT HAS UNTIL now been the earth, silent, abiding, indifferent bearer to the dead, finds itself witness to this:

The one called Cager, torn by the fists and boots of the three furious men looming above him, pulls himself back into fetal form, readying himself for death, welcoming it, if only for the respite.

Those three men, swollen with the intoxicating fire of domination, of being judge and jury to another, unchallenged, supreme.

But the fortunes of men are not fixed, if only for the very fact that they are fortune, luck. And luck is, as the earth knows, a passing thing at best, if a real thing at all.

For the door to the watchhouse swings wide behind these three self-appointed jurymen, and a new justice greets them.

It is the justice of chaos. The promise that those on high can never hold their primacy, for the world of men always intervenes in all its madness, its randomness, its heartbreak.

The one that enters is known as Beauchamp. He does not know these men; in any other circumstance, were they to pass each other on the street, they would not even notice.

But his head is filled with an elixir of the things that have gotten him to this moment, just as their heads are, and so a pistol flashes in his hand, and one of the men cries out and dies.

And see what radiates outward from that spasm of violence—the noise, the movement, the extinguishment of the first life—all of it conducted in less than a second.

The shock wave of that report echoes out through the stone walls of the watchhouse, splits the silence of the graveyard, punctures the very earth, the stolid refuge of the church itself.

In the shallow earth, that curious soul named Job, who would burrow like the rodents toward the windfall of a decaying body, hears it, that unmistakable sound of a weapon, a thing he has heard a thousand times before on battlefields, a clarion of death.

In the church, an impeccable blackguard has his conversation with the unhearing dead interrupted by the gunshot.

And outside the walls, there is an Irishman who cannot quite believe what he's hearing.

"God in heaven," he says to himself. "It's gone completely to shite, hasn't it?"

Mind you, this tour I have taken you on has all happened within a moment. We are just beginning.

Even as the first light is lit in the nearest house, the occupants roused from sleep, both curious about and fearful of what they've heard, the madman in the watchhouse is rotating the barrel of that latest piece of technology in his hand, ready to kill again.

Those three jurymen, which are two now, scramble to react.

The squatty fellow who is ostensibly Beauchamp's ally in all this looks on from behind, mortified, as his partner squeezes the trigger, emptying the second barrel, making no attempt to mute the sound of the report. It fills the watchhouse with that deafening, pulsing echo of death. The second juryman, scant seconds before puffed up with his unchecked power, dies, simpering ignobly for a few seconds before he does so.

Now what is in Beauchamp's head? It is this, apparently—inasmuch as you can apply rationality to a man well out beyond its borders—these men are in his way. There is bounty to be made tonight and no time for nuance. His woman, whose brain is dead, though her body yet breathes, lies alone out in the dark streets in the back of an untended growler. He has visited this twilight state upon her, and in doing so, something broke within him. The pain is too wide, too deep, and not something he will allow himself to inhabit. Instead, he will do what he always does: fight back against that pain, smash through it with a fury so great that in his wordless understanding of things, it will be obliterated. A thing vanquished, never to be dealt with again. It does not work that way. A man can only double his wager so many times in an attempt to recoup his losses before he loses everything, including himself.

He thinks, in that fractured perspective of his, that if he does this, and quickly enough, the prize he captures tonight can be spent upon the finest surgeon in London, who will somehow tease the life back into the eyes of that woman out in the street and bring her dead head back to life.

One man's madness: a shock wave.

Do not trust your position in the world. For these shock waves are happening in all places, at all times. Invisible. There is no such thing as lasting fortune. The only promise is chaos. I know its result. I bury its result every day.

The third and last juryman makes a spirited attempt to reach his own gun, but Beauchamp puts a bullet first in his leg, which fells him, then a moment later, rotating to the final barrel, delivers the coup de grâce to the fallen man's neck.

Scarcely five seconds have passed.

With it comes an interlude, as if we are at the theater. A momentary response of silence to the previous call of violence.

The players left standing in the watchhouse have very different responses to the three dead men that lie before them.

The small man—Wheeler—looks aghast and can scarcely breathe.

The gunman turns to next steps. The way has been cleared; it is time to dig up that particular grave they find so appealing. He shoves the little man out into the darkness and says to get on with things.

What's left is the boy, Cager. Whether Beauchamp mistook the bloody and unmoving boy for dead, or whether the pistol was spent and killing the boy by other means would be too involved, or whether—most likely—the boy had no bearing on Beauchamp's plan going forward and as such didn't matter to the madman, I cannot say, for he is a madman and I am the earth, subscribed to simpler and truer amplitudes. But what can be said is this: in all the time Beauchamp was in the watchhouse, he never laid eyes directly on the boy.

The boy, incredulous at the respite he's been given—and as briefly mad as the madman himself, though mad with life rather than death—bolts off into the night.

Again, remember, the great wheel of time has tightened on its axle during all of this. It screeches, squeals, labors to move forward. Has it been only fifteen seconds? Twenty?

Beneath the earth, the dying mole man carves his way to the surface.

THIRTY-FIVE

JOB

WITH A FINAL jab of his shovel, the surface above gives way, and the cool evening air spills in.

He stays ensconced in the hole, out of sight, drinking in fresh breaths of the world, the rapturous midnight-blue sky above.

It takes everything he has to suppress his gasps, which come hungry and desperate.

For they are out there.

Busily throwing wide the gates.

Bringing in a horse team.

He has not yet ventured above the surface, but he can hear them.

They make no effort to suppress their voices.

They are reckless, desperate.

Job peers out.

He sees Beauchamp and another man—one of Beddoe's men.

How such a pairing has come to pass, he doesn't know.

They drive the horse and gig across the churchyard, the wheels unceremoniously churning up grave sites, until they reach the mortsafe and slab beneath which Ella Beddoe awaits.

Even now it is surrounded by four lanterns, which bring the two men into sharp focus as they dismount the gig, consider the impossibility of the apparatus before them.

The rest of the graveyard is a forgotten thing to them, Job knows.

He slowly climbs out of his hole, slides on his side to a nearby headstone, presses himself into it.

No doubt he leaves a telltale trail of mud and blood, but it strikes him that the men before him are no longer vigilant.

They are frenzied, men that know they don't have much time.

Someone out there has surely heard the gunshots and now sends for the constable.

The whole endeavor is doomed.

The sweet, if still weak, cerulean blue of day bleeds up from the horizon, inexorably feathering its way up into the blackness above.

It's time to leave this place, Job thinks as the men squabble in the distance.

As they desperately affix ropes to the mortsafe and slab and their horses.

Though there are shovels in the gig, they ignore them.

There is no longer time to dig.

They are going to try to yank the whole of the mortsafe from the earth!

And with it, Job's great and final scheme will be for naught.

Butchered by madness.

His brain settles for a second, perhaps two, in which there is nothing but silence and clarity.

It is all right.

All of it.

Without money, the ship will go without him.

He will die, most likely this day or the next.

Ivy will have to endure without him, and of course she will.

She will not die.

She will recover.

She will speak again.

He only hopes it will be today, so that he might hear the sweetness of that voice one more time, the crispness, the paradoxical nature of its youth—that it is at once certain and uncertain of everything.

The world has irised down to that.

May she whisper to him as he dies.

The men whip the horses.

The horses whinny and strain.

The slab and mortsafe hardly move.

The bars seated in the earth complain but do not yield.

Job can use this moment to leave.

He summons all of his strength, begins moving between headstones, staying out of view.

The only way out is through the open gates, which lie just beyond the two men.

He will need to slip past them somehow.

Again they whip the horses.

Again the horses strain.

The mortsafe unseats slightly from the earth, the slab slides a little, but the apparatus holds.

Job deftly circles them, moving from stone to stone.

He is perhaps thirty feet from the gate; it will only take a final effort from him, and he will be gone into the night.

And yet another echoing crack splits the night.

At first he thinks it's another gun blast.

It is the mortsafe.

The bars give way under all the pressure, two of them snapping, causing an entire side of the cage to collapse under the weight of the slab.

The slab, in turn, slides down the angled top of the cage, wedges itself in the grass.

Despite himself, Job stops, watches as the two men, realizing their great progress, quickly refasten the errant ropes to the mortsafe.

"That's it," cries Beauchamp, "faster, you ass. It'll all come now."

Disburdened for the most part of the heavy slab, the cage wobbles in the soil as the horses are again driven forward.

The slab, half atop the cage, rotates as the mortsafe starts to unseat itself from the earth.

A moment later, it happens.

The mortsafe comes free.

The slab drops to the side in the grass.

The horses surge forward to a stop.

The men look on.

The soil of the grave, only recently turned during the burial and not yet fully hardened, has been churned anew by this tumult.

It is loamy, irresolute, scattered within the harder lines of the original excavation.

The bars of the mortsafe, planted as they were all the way to the bottom of the grave, have acted as a sort of sieve as they have rotated their way out of the hole.

Like a child's fingers through sand, dredging up the unseen.

Emerging from the soil before the men is the corner of a coffin, its black lacquered exterior catching the light of the lanterns around it, still spit-shined and not yet corrupted by the earth.

THIRTY-SIX

BEDDOE

I SEE THEM through the warped panes. I hear them. They've done something to you, haven't they? They've pulled you from the earth!

How they look now from this vantage, the truth of them made clear by this stained glass. They are hellish, dark, molten things that circle you, prepare to further defile you in your resting place. Unearthly carrion.

How they linger over you. What do they see?

Have you rotted as I have asked? As we have agreed?

I move now to a door. I open it, peer out. They are too absorbed in their Cimmerian act to know I am here. Yes, the two of them, they that dig away the dirt, pry open your casket ever so slightly at first chance, though it is still half buried, so craven is their greed! How could a soul do such a thing? Open what should be forevermore sealed?

Oh, how they linger! They seem, for a moment, paralyzed by what they see.

Sweet love, tell me you have become horrific. That you are black and bloated and your very visage is a punishment to these eyes that would contravene the civility of the world and look upon you.

But they are not deterred, are they? They continue to dig. They will unseat the whole of the casket from the earth before long. Then the lid will be properly thrown open and the entirety of you will be revealed to the world.

Have you not bloated? Why do they continue?

I ask for so little. You are dead and do not need to hold on to your beauty.

I live. Think of me. Let loose your vanity, let that beauty slough from you, sink away into the earth. Become so horrid the world retches at the sight.

But they continue to dig! Obviously that small peek they got of you did not deter them. Bitch. Bitch! You will give my crime away!

Well, then. As always, I must look out for myself.

No, it is too late. You have always hated violence, and that is half the reason I do this.

See how fast I move, out through the door and through the shadows. How fast I close upon them, that sweet masterpiece of pistol in my hand.

Even out here, they remain hellish and molten things. It was not the window that warped them. They are, in fact, beasts. Look at them! They are not silhouetted by the light but are verily made of blackness. Devils. They come for you, love.

And I come for them.

THIRTY-SEVEN
JOB

JOB IS WEAK and knows he should run, knows he's been given a brief window to escape this place, return to Ivy for a few final, sweet moments, if they are to be had at all.

But he must know.

He squats there behind the headstone, watching as Beauchamp and his accomplice lift the lid to Ella Beddoe's casket.

She is there, pristine in death.

Perhaps still a day or two away from bloat, experience tells him.

The anatomist could have used her.

Could use her.

Within that realization comes a temptation he knows he should not indulge.

Could there be a way he might yet salvage things?

Run, Job, run from this place!

Even now, Beauchamp sees you!

See how his eyes lock upon you, start to tease you from the shadows.

You have problems now.

They are between you and the gate.

This mad killer and his compatriot.

Both of them at full strength, their veins thick with fight, while yours, minus all that blood, carry virtually none.

The night flashes. Tiny and sudden, a nova—yes, Ivy, I

have listened to you—a sun being born, right behind Beauchamp's head.

It is there for a moment, then gone, accompanied by a gunshot.

Beauchamp pitches forward into the grave, dead.

His compatriot turns, sees the gunman, whom Job recognizes.

Marcus Beddoe.

The second barrel of Beddoe's fine pistol flashes, the night roars again, and the second man falls.

The report caroms around the headstones, echoes off the high walls of the church, and finally escapes into the night.

Then there is silence and Beddoe standing over his handiwork.

Job does not move, does not breathe, instead watches as Beddoe looks on the face of his dead wife, slowly begins loading his pistol again.

"Your beauty is too stubborn, isn't it?" he asks the lifeless woman before him.

All the while he packs the pistol.

Finally, without looking up, he says calmly, "Come out of there, man."

He is talking to Job, knows he's there.

Job thinks to run but doesn't want to die that way, a panicked thing.

He stands, comes into the light of the lanterns. The two men regard each other across the grave.

"I've one load yet," Beddoe says unceremoniously as he finishes packing one of the barrels of his pistol.

Job says nothing.

Instead looks at Ella Beddoe.

"I married the most beautiful woman in London," Beddoe

says. "But that's a thing for the living, isn't it? The dead should know their place. Should have the humility to sink away into the earth and become a memory. But this one," he says, nodding ruefully to the woman before him.

Job finally speaks.

"She can still be of use."

He knows Beddoe will shoot him for this, but Beddoe is going to shoot him anyhow.

Beddoe eyes him as if considering this.

He hefts a lantern, brings it close to consider his wife's still-pearly skin.

As if searching for rot beneath the perfect veneer.

Then, ever so slowly, he separates the tank from the wick of the lantern, begins pouring the oil contained therein atop his wife's finery.

Atop the silk, the gold, the gems.

"She can still be used," Job impresses again.

Beddoe takes a second lantern.

"She is a millstone. I have life in me yet, and she is a millstone—one that would drag me into the earth with her."

He slams the second lantern down on his wife.

The glass around the wick shatters, the flame catches on the dead woman's oil-soaked clothes, and both men must retreat before the small but earnest conflagration that ensues.

Job watches as the body burns, too spent to do anything.

In those flames, loss doubled in service of vanity.

In those flames, the selfishness of tight fists.

The dead do not care, only the living do, and for it we bring on more death.

Beddoe levels his now-packed pistol at Job.

He says nothing, thank God.

Job would rather die with a head full of his own sovereign thoughts than this man's words.

More words come, however.

They are not from Beddoe.

They come from Fife, who has materialized, somewhat cautiously, behind him.

The boy, beaten but alive, is with him.

"Walk on out of here," Fife says to Beddoe.

You brazen bastard! Job thinks.

You will get yourself shot, but you have made me smile!

You are unarmed but indomitable, as always!

Beddoe sizes up the situation, puffs himself up, makes the gun known if it was not before.

"You have no say," he says.

"Two ways this goes," Fife says. "You walk or there's a fight. You choose to fight, you may kill one of us, you may not. But either way what's left of us kills you. So make a decision, friend—die or disappear."

Beddoe eyes the strapping Irishman, the bloodied visage of the university student, the muddy, horrid mole man behind him.

He loves himself too much, Job knows, to ever yield to oblivion.

What matters most to him, it seems, is that his wife burns, that her skin is blackened and unrecognizable now.

Beddoe swears something furious, though the specifics of it are lost to the snap and hiss of the flames as they unseat and buckle the lacquer on his wife's coffin beneath them.

A moment later he is away, running for the gates.

Job can do nothing but sit back on a headstone, feel the heat of the flames on his face.

Pleasant feeling, that, it must be said.

A bit of heat, a bit of light, after being in the earth.
Even if all is lost.

THIRTY-EIGHT

JOB

YES, HE IS dying.

He has ignored it as best he can until now, subordinated it to the primacy of the mission at hand, but now that the mission is done, the whole unspiraling of life has reasserted itself with a determination Job knows cannot any longer be undone.

His thoughts dull.

They are hazy, echoes of what they once were.

As if they are being thought in a room adjacent to him.

The peripheries of his vision start to abandon him.

The world, constricting.

The boy and Fife have gotten him to his feet, move him across the churchyard, try to buoy him.

It is all bollocks, he knows, end-of-life sweetness, but he welcomes it.

Voices.

Company.

Fife is saying that it can all still work, that the ship can still be reached.

Job wonders how this is so, given that first light has already come.

Fife is saying something about tides, and for a long time, Job cannot make sense of his logic, the train of sentences the Irishman strings together in explanation.

Finally Job's mind assembles what Fife is saying.

It is low tide, low cycle for the month.

The Thames is mud for the next three or four hours.

No matter how impatient a captain is, no one's leaving those docks unless it's in a mud schooner.

And last Fife has heard, there's no such thing as a mud schooner.

There will be no departures until midmorning at the earliest. Job can still make it.

Can still make Quinn's, collect Ivy, and make the docks.

Job assembles some words of his own, tells them that all of that is dead.

That he only wants to see Ivy.

There is no money, there is no body, and most of all, there is no time.

"I can't speak to time," the Irishman says, "because I don't own it. But you may or may not be wrong about the other two."

They guide him to the gig with which Beauchamp's pulled away the mortsafe.

The horses are uneasy.

The gunshots have done nothing to put them at ease.

They look sidelong at the three men that approach, stamp their feet, but do not move from their position.

The boy, a study in blood, gasps with an enthusiasm that does not befit his appearance.

He recounts how, upon fleeing the watchhouse, he encountered Fife in the street, and Fife told him of something he'd beheld while waiting out in the darkness.

Something that had drawn his attention in the back of this

gig once Beauchamp and his colleague had left the vehicle unattended as they snuck into the churchyard.

Job steadies himself against the gig, peers in the bed.

Gray is there.

Tragic scritch of the slums.

Dead, as so many are tonight.

And yet, unlike the rest, she is yet rich with life.

THIRTY-NINE

QUINN

NEVA SLEEPS. THAT is good. She is numb to the pain, if only for this brief period that she has finally, mercifully, drifted off. Percival has been up with her all night, has sat in vigil beside her, has watched as she's fallen in and out of sleep. He has thought to nap as she naps so he will have strength when she needs it, but something in him has resisted. Better to see her like this. In peace. To witness her.

She sleeps, and he watches, and that's enough. The universe is, for once, yielding, though he knows it is a peace to be savored but not trusted. That it holds the seeds of greater silences, the vast and permanent kind. That it is but a false dawn before the final wrenching severance of death.

Leicester Square goes on outside the window in the first light of day, indifferent.

There is a knock on the door downstairs.

Brewer comes up a moment later, tells him he has visitors. That she's invited them into the foyer, if only to get them out of sight of passersby, for the presence of these men outside No. 21 Leicester Square, in her opinion, is welcoming public spectacle. And not the kind one would want, if there is any such thing.

Percival descends the steps to see three bleary-eyed men before him. One is a study in mud, another in blood, the last rendered hazy by the indecorous plumes of tobacco smoke with which he fills Percival's foyer.

"Looks like you've had something of an evening," Percival says, pleased to see Job, Cager, the Irish coachman. Yes, they are in a deplorable state, a couple of them by appearances in need of medical help, but their very presence suggests that Beddoe hasn't won. That they have survived, that Percival, despite himself, hasn't sent them to their deaths at the hands of a madman. No more deaths. Let him handle that process properly, in this house, alone. As all people do, with dignity if not heartbreak. But do not let it spread because of your need, your panic.

"He destroyed the body," Job says. He can scarcely stand.

"Even so. Let's clean you off, man. Brewer, bring a basin. Bring one for each of them."

Brewer nods, disappears.

"I can't stay," Job says. The words are halting, involve great effort. He opens the door slightly, nods out to the square. "We have something for you."

Percival peers out. Sees that the men have pulled their growler as close as they can to his door. The bed is covered with canvas. Passersby look at it with knitted brows.

"Kept it covered up," the Irishman says. "Don't think the cits would be too pleased. But you might be."

The foursome step out into the light of day. Job lifts the canvas just enough so that Percival can get a clear look at the dead woman within.

He has seen her before. One of the questionable purveyors of bodies he's crossed in the past. The one that ran with Beauchamp. Gray, was it? Her thick clothing has been pulled aside, and where before he'd thought the woman was merely plump, he now sees the shape of her, the distribution of her weight, differently. The telling protuberance of her belly.

Percival turns, looks to Job. "She's with child."

Job nods to the boy. "Your student thinks so."

Cager steps forward. "You tell me, sir. But that was my surmise."

Percival lifts the canvas a little higher, probes the woman's belly. Yes. Pregnant. But then a thrill, most horrifying, washes through him.

"The baby is still alive," he says.

The men's gazes meet. Percival nods to Cager. "Wash up, boy. We're going to do this right here." He gathers the canvas around the corpse, looks to the Irishman. "Help me get her upstairs."

They lay the corpse out in the drawing room.

Percival looks to Brewer. "Your mistress is not to know what is happening in here, understand?"

Brewer nods, as she must.

Percival removes his coat and folds his cuffs back, all the while thinking of the two gravid women lying in tandem in his house, separated only by a few walls. Each with child. Each, he hopes, with different fates.

He looks to Job. "There's a small box on the mantel over there. Your fifty sovereigns are in it."

Job finds it, takes it. The two men stand before each other. "I trust I will not see you again," Percival says.

"You will not."

"England loses a noble man the moment you leave her shores," Percival says.

"You still have the boy," Job says. "He will dig for you."

The boy shakes his head. "My next time in a graveyard will be as a corpse."

"You've learned something from this, then," Job says with a wan smile. He separates out a handful of gold, puts it on the table before the boy. The boy tries to fashion a protest, but Job shakes his head in a way that suggests there will be no negotiation.

Percival readies his scalpels. "Let's get on with it, Micajah. The oxygen in the blood will soon be gone—and the baby with it."

As they prepare the woman's belly for incision, Job meets Percival's eyes one last time. The men share tired smiles. Partners in the madness of it all.

Then Job is down the steps to the Irishman, who is busy shooing away the ogling crowd that has formed around his growler.

Percival hears the door close behind them and the din of the square dying out.

He puts blade to flesh a moment later, and there is blood.

FORTY

JOB

MORE OF HIS vision calves away.

The sun has risen above the buildings, but it feels as if it's filtered through trees.

Towering trees with dense foliage.

Though there are none in the Holy Land.

He lies slumped on an elbow in the front of Fife's growler.

Fife and his family bring Ivy out from their cellar.

They have washed her and given her clean clothes, but she is still swollen.

Still half aware of the world.

"There you go," Fife says as he and his eldest son lift her into the bed of the growler.

Another son climbs in beside her, steadies her until Job can come back and she can lean against him.

There is life in her, but she is tired.

She is in pain.

"I'm here," Job says.

She does not respond.

Fife's growler reaches the chaos of the docks.

Job's twilight brain wonders if it has always been this noisy in the world.

It thrums far off, in that adjacent room with his thoughts, but it is busy, isn't it?

A thousand voices crying out about one thing or another.

Job feels the strong hands of Fife and his boys on him.

They assist him out of the growler, guide him toward the nearby well-rounded brig.

But what of Ivy?

She is suddenly not with them.

She is nowhere in his cloistered vision.

Fife and his boys guide him up onto the deck, though he protests with words even he himself does not hear.

Somewhere there should be joy, that they've made it, that the ship is still here, but there is only absence.

Where is Ivy?

Then he is belowdecks—the sunlit world once again abandoning him—and into a cabin with the aid of a mate.

They lay him in a bunk.

There is no porthole.

And they are gone.

There is only the smell of the sea.

There is only shadow and his narrowing vision.

Where have they gone?

They've left him.

And in the way that the edges of his sight have abandoned him, so, too, does it seem that a great, irrevocable silence encroaches, alongside that grayness that has slowly, irrevocably stolen the light from his eyes.

The far-off cedes its place in his life.

There is only the immediacy of his body, the things he can see and hear right before him.

That silence growing in his brain, slowly sealing off his ears.

Then there is movement.

Fife and his boys have returned with Ivy.

She walks, their hands supporting her.

They move to lay her down in the bunk opposite Job, but she opts to sit.

She is lucid enough to have a point of view about things, and she wants to sit.

This is good, Job thinks.

If she is obstinate, then some of her is back.

Be obstinate, girl.

Do not quit the world or yourself, and for the moment, don't quit me.

Fife sits on the bunk beside Job.

"You sure you want to do this?"

The whole of Fife's face fills Job's vision, a continent jagged and noble, vast with love beneath its surface.

This is the way to die, Job thinks.

In these lands.

"She'll complete the voyage, but you will not," Fife warns.

Job smiles inwardly. Isn't that the sum of things, anyhow?

Fife reads Job's response in his face, grips his hand.

Presses the side of his face tight against the side of Job's.

Job can feel tears there.

He is sure they are the Irishman's, but perhaps they are his.

Either way.

His boys, too, come by, smile Fife-to-be smiles at Job.

Go, boys, conquer the world, Job thinks.

You bear title to continents with that love, do you know that?

Continents.

Then they are gone.

And once again there is silence.

He shifts his head slightly so he can see Ivy.

She swings her legs up from her sitting position, slowly straightening them as if stretching.

She studies the top of her feet as if waking up, as if the fog in her head is simply the residue of a restless night of sleep.

She is not all the way back, but she is present.

The bottom of her shoes face him.

He sees they are dirty from the Holy Land.

Dirty with her past, he thinks with satisfaction.

Those shoes won't know that cess again.

She meets his gaze.

With some effort, she gets up, crosses to him, sits beside him.

She puts her hand to his forehead.

He can feel the dried mud on him crumble slightly beneath her soft fingertips, that hand that Fife and his family so diligently cleaned.

He must look something pathetic to her.

A mud man.

As insignificant as the soil the world treads upon.

But from me may something good come of you.

"I am here," she says.

The whole of him wells when he hears this.

Yes, Ivy, you are here.

In this moment, you are everywhere.

And that is where I want you to be.

I am done trafficking in the future, for I have no future.

That is your job now.

Let us just be here now, in this shrinking little bit of light and sound that is life.

Be the thing I see until I see no more.

The ship shifts beneath them.

"We are weighing anchor," she says.
He can feel it.
The lightness of the vessel given over to the current.
The gentle rock and surrender.
"We are away," she says.
Yes.
We are away.
We are away.
We are away.

January 21, 1821
Bologna, Italy

Dear Professor Quinn,
I feel compelled to write you, though we have never met. Some months ago, I sailed aboard the brig Galvin *from London to Genoa, and it was during those long days at sea that I learned of your name and, more importantly, your largesse. My father, as you can probably guess from my surname below, was a colleague of yours. He spoke very highly of you. Of your generosity. Your unfailing embrace of people of all classes, including the poorest of the poor, of which I have long been a member.*

The reason I've taken so long to compose this letter is because I wanted to have something to say first—something worth saying. Experiences. Results. Fruits of both your and my father's efforts. You both have gone so far beyond what I have known people capable of: my father with his toils, you with your gold (you paid my father too much for that final job, but I think this was by design, wasn't it?), but even more so with your books. He may have built me with his will, his love, his morals, but just as truly, you built me with those books. You built my mind.

Do you know about the spectrum of light? I am entering my second term at the university here, and I am learning the foundations of astronomy. I am not the best student because my grasp of Italian is still limited, but I have recently been learning about Sir Frederick William Herschel's experiments with light. How one can channel it through a prism, dividing it into a rainbow of colors. Hidden inside everything is a rainbow. It's a wonderful notion, isn't it? That the light of the world is so much more radiant than we can ever know. Herschel measured the temperatures of the various hues of light in that rainbow, and as one would expect, the blue was the coolest, the red the warmest. But did you know that the thermometers ran even warmer when moved out to the far end of the spectrum, beyond red? Where to all appearances there is nothing? The warmest light of all is invisible. It is known as infrared light. It cannot be seen by the naked eye.

You have been that to me, sir. A warmth in the universe I have not seen but which has nevertheless sustained me. I am humbled beyond measure by what you have given me.

My father did not survive the passage to Genoa. I was with him at the end. In the final hours, I made a concerted effort to bathe him, to make him clean and at ease. A funny thing happened, though, as I washed his hands. Seeing that there were thick deposits of earth beneath his fingernails, I attempted to clear it away, but he stopped me. He preferred to die as he lived, he said: with dirty hands. He wanted no affect in death. As above, so below, he said. That has religious meaning, doesn't it? I was not raised to the Light (not the kind in churches, at any rate), but it rings a bell. What do you suppose he meant? The best interpretation I have been able to come up with is that it has to do with how memories are forged at the time of death, the nostalgias and legacies that ensue.

I think he toiled in an unsightly business, one of mud and decay, and he did not want that to be lost to generations going forward. I think he wanted to say that sacrifice was the noblest virtue, even if it was conducted in muck. That in the end, he was not ashamed of his station. For station is not the mark of a man, is it? It is what he gives away. And in my estimate, he gave away everything so that I might live and grow into a world of opportunity he would never know or witness. May I live up to it. May I be worthy of it. My father was the earth, perpetually composing and decomposing, fecund, complex, from which I grew and continue to grow. You are the light that I have never seen but which has nourished me all through that process.

May that same unseen light shine on you forever, sir.

Gratefully,
Ivy Mowatt

22 April 1821
Earl's Court

My Dear Miss Mowatt,
I was humbled reading your letter. Your gratitude is unnecessary. I agree that generosity and sacrifice are the highest forms of virtue, but I would add that for one with any means at all, they are a requirement. So while you characterize my act as largesse, I would demur. It was duty. To do less invites an echoing emptiness within, a sense of guilt, of failure. And I, for one, do not like those feelings!

Your father's work yielded more fruit than you know. He was colloquially known as a resurrectionist, a term I find amusing for it always evoked something Christlike, divine, even though the men that wear the mantle are usually the furthest thing from saints. As macabre as their work seems, though, from it comes life. We are generally too squeamish to see this.

And life, indeed, came from your father's work. Not just as embodied in your own story, which heartens me, although candidly, reading your letter, I'm fairly certain you would have found a way to flourish in any circumstances.

The last time I saw your father, he brought me a corpse at my behest. A woman with child. The circumstances are complicated, but I will try to simplify them here. While by trade I am an anatomist, in this case I was trying to solve a most pressing personal issue, in that my wife was near death with complications associated with the bearing of her own child. I had commissioned your father to disinter a rich woman who had died with a child still in womb so that I might study her, find a way to save my wife, but it was not to be. Nevertheless, your father managed to bring me another specimen, a woman from the slums who had died that night. Incredibly, the child was still alive in the womb.

I performed a Caesarean section, which involves cutting directly into the skin of the subject, removing the baby through that opening rather than the birth canal. (I hope this is not too unsettling for you, but you seem a person of science, and moreover, being of Job's blood, I suspect you carry some of his admirable imperturbability.) In this procedure, historically, the baby survives, but the mother does not. Given that the mother was already deceased, I did not have this problem.

The baby survived and lives today.

The mother's body afforded me a road map thereafter, one that illustrated the intense vascularity of the womb and how I might go about cauterizing and clamping the various larger vessels so that blood loss on the mother's part might be minimized in future operations.

That future operation came scarcely a few hours later. How terrible it is to operate on your own wife, your own unborn child, Miss Mowatt! Lord, how my hand trembled. I took the child, Oliver, from her first. Then I went about cauterizing and clamping all the major vessels in the womb. It's near impossible to get all of them—the womb is simply too vascular, a life-bestowing web of capillaries and veins for its occupant—and because of this, predictably, my wife lost considerable blood despite my efforts. In the end, she nearly died.

But "nearly" is a wonderful word in this context, isn't it?

It took her some time to recover, and we had to take on a wet nurse for the two children (the girl's name is Elizabeth), but in the subsequent months, Mrs. Quinn was able to leave her bed, and today we live with the chaos of two infants. They are irrational creatures, averse to sleeping, that cry all the time, that seem perpetually flummoxed. But how sweet that chaos!

Without that body, I would be alone in this house as I write this. Instead we are four.

Without that body, I would not have performed a second successful Caesarean procedure at St. Bart's just this past week.

The world advances. Those invisible currents of light you talk about, the warm, unseen efforts of others, radiate everywhere. You are right: they do not come from trappings of station, from the aesthetics of action or vocation, but instead from intent. It does not matter if you are a king or a body snatcher. It is what you add, whether you come from sludge or on high.

Your father gave life to three people, in my opinion. And more each day. In that sense, I should be thanking you.

I must go now, for Elizabeth is once again complaining in her cot. How marvelous that she will be raised with opportunity. How different it could have been. It is the same with you.

May you be well, Miss Mowatt. Reach as high as you can. Through the stars and all the way to heaven, if there is indeed such a place. But all the while, do not forget the earth beneath your feet, the soil. It is where you come from.

Yours,
Percival Quinn